After Love

Praise for Subhash Jaireth

For *Yashodhara: Six Seasons Without You*

'A book that will charm you with its lucid and pungent distillation of desire, longing and loss.' Judith Beveridge

For *To Silence: Three Autobiographies*

'A unique insight into the lives of two fascinating people, whose experiences illuminate a shared humanity that bridges language, culture, time and eternal truths that cannot be silenced.' Peter Wilkins, *Canberra Times*

'A must read for anyone interested in the long march of history and the frailty of the human condition itself.' Mridula Nath Chakraborty, *Mascara Literary Review*

'A finely crafted book that reads like poetry.' Claudia Hyles, *Australian Book Review*

'Ultimately about the mystery of creation itself, the silence from which all things come and to which they inevitably return.' John Hughes

After Love

Subhash Jaireth

MELBOURNE, AUSTRALIA

www.transitlounge.com.au

Copyright © 2012 Subhash Jaireth
Published by Transit Lounge Publishing

Cover and book design: Peter Lo

Printed in China by Everbest

This project has been assisted by the Australian government through the Australia Coucil for the Arts , its arts funding and advisory body.

ISBN: 978-1-921924-25-5

A cataloguing in publication entry is available from

the National Library of Australia: http://catalogue.nla.gov.au

For HJ, KJ and MJ & for Moscow

Part One

Footfalls echo in the memory
Down the passage which we did not take
Towards the door we never opened ...

T.S. Eliot, *Burnt Norton*

No story is ever told just once.

Michael Ondaatje, *Running in the Family*

I Don't Believe in Fate

Vasu

I wish it hadn't happened, I could have said. But I didn't because I don't like to look for excuses. It happened because we both wanted it.

That day in the café of the library there was simply a brief exchange of words. All hers. I just smiled.

'You smile too much,' she would often complain afterwards. 'It's a mask, isn't it? An excuse not to speak.'

'Is this chair taken?' she asked that day and, when I shook my head, asked if she could join me.

I simply nodded again.

She sat looking out at the roof-tops covered in snow, pigeons pecking in the bright sunshine of the square and the steady stream of people entering and leaving the library. She opened her bag, took out a diary, pulled out a piece of paper and copied a number. She closed the diary with the pen still inside. Then she suddenly raised her right arm and waved to someone outside. The man responded, paused for a minute, then walked away.

She pushed her chair back and got up, and the pen in the diary fell to the floor and rolled in my direction. I leant to pick it up.

'*Sposibo* (thank you),' she said, as I handed it to her.

I could have replied *Pozhaluista* (You're welcome). But I just smiled.

My Jijee-ma in India asked me to send her some photos of the snow in Moscow. She didn't like the picture postcards I had mailed her a few months before, although there was lots of snow in them. She wanted real photos of me in the snow. I asked Kobe, my friend from Uganda, to help. He knew how to take good photos and had his own camera. We walked up to the pine grove near the lake not far from our hostel and hired a pair of skis. He photographed me on skis with mounds of snow in the background.

'I want to make heaps of money, man,' Kobe often told me. He was crazy. At first he tried to pimp his girlfriends but soon realised that his camera provided a much better opportunity. In no time at all he gathered together a group of sexy girls who needed no excuse to take their clothes off. He was thrilled. 'Here's a number for you to ring,' he told me one day. 'Five roubles and a few packets of chewing gum for a whole night's fun. Do whatever you like.'

His photo albums were hot and sold well on the black market. Soon there was money everywhere, not only roubles but real American dollars. But good things never last and after a year or so a disgruntled militiaman dobbed him in and he was expelled from the country.

Jijee-ma liked the photos I sent her. In return I received a woollen jumper and a jar of mango *muraba*. The jam was delicious. 'I have followed Amma's recipe,' she wrote in the letter that came with the packet.

I remember nothing at all about Amma, our mother. My Jijee-ma, my older sister is, in a way, my real mother. Amma died five days after I was born. I was the eighth and the youngest child in the family. Amma endured twelve pregnancies in eighteen years of marriage, including four terrible miscarriages. 'Don't blame yourself,' Jijee-ma would often tell me later. 'Amma was exhausted. She couldn't take any more.'

I used to carry my mother's photo in my wallet. It is half the size of a postcard and although it is black and white, the smile on Amma's face is so bright that it is hard to look away. The wrap covering her head has slipped, revealing dark hair and a large silver earring hanging from the tip of her left ear. It glitters as do the little stars stitched across the wrap, her *dupatta*.

A few days before I left for Moscow, Jijee-ma showed me the earrings again. 'I have kept them safe for your bride,' she said, and laughed.

The day Amma died, Jijee-ma gave birth to a girl, Mithu. Jijee-ma suckled us both: me always from the left breast. Mithu preferred the right. 'Father didn't like me feeding you,' Jijee-ma would tell me later, 'and my husband hated it. He made me put you on the formula, but whenever I got a chance I gave you my breast. You are my son, my first-born.'

Anna and I met again one late Wednesday evening. I remember the day because I had not been able to sleep the night before because of a small fire in the hostel. On Wednesdays I used to work late in the library. That day it was hot and stuffy in the reading room and feeling sleepy I decided to go out for a stroll. I had reached the steps when she appeared out of the dark.

'Do you have a light?' she asked, holding a cigarette in her hand.

I took out a lighter from my pocket, although I didn't smoke. When she turned to walk away, I don't know why I decided to follow her. She noticed and stopped and waited for me. Together we descended the steps and turned towards the statue of Dostoevsky standing like a doorkeeper to the library. We said nothing about the freezing weather or the snow or the flu epidemic then running wild in Moscow. We just listened to one another's footsteps. With each puff on her cigarette Anna's face lit up for a few seconds. We strolled for as long as it took for her to finish smoking. Before I could ask her name or introduce myself, she stopped and said, 'I'm cold.' I just gazed at her, doing my best not to smile. 'I'm going back in,' she told me. Just before opening the door she turned and waved, then vanished.

'Is there anything wrong, Fyodor Mikhailovich?' I asked the tall dark shadow of the famous writer. Of course there was no reply.

I thought I would finish for the night at the library, pack up and go. But then I put on my glasses, turned on the table lamp and continued to work.

After an hour or two I looked up and saw that Anna was still working too.

It took me a while to learn to use a camera properly. I found it hard to look at the world like a photographer. My ineptitude frustrated me but I kept trying. To click non-stop and wait for the moment to trap itself wasn't an option. I wanted to create the moment itself and that required patience and perseverance.

That's why I decided to take up sketching. I would get up early each day and go into the city to catch it more or less empty. The silence helped me remain focused. I would find a suitable position to sketch a building and begin picking out its dominant shape. Once I had established that I would make a quick drawing. Only then would I set the camera on its tripod for a lengthy exposure. I would take just three or four photos each day, and while the camera was doing its job, I would make more sketches.

This is how I learnt to use the camera to fill in the details the sketches often missed. My pencil outlined the bones; the camera added the flesh.

In the library, Anna and I were often at our favourite tables. On Wednesdays I worked late but on Mondays and Fridays I arrived and left early, around three or four in the afternoon.

At first we didn't take much notice of one another, but soon we started exchanging harmless smiles. There were no expectations, no promises – just an acknowledgment of the other's presence.

One week I changed my library day from Friday to Thursday and after a few weeks noticed that Anna too had started coming in then. It didn't take us long to observe that we had started doing other things together too. If one of us decided to pack up and leave, the other followed. The smiles we exchanged weren't innocent any more, and we both knew that soon we would stop and chat.

'So you're an architect?' she asked.

It was our third meeting and the second in the library's café. She had seen me immediately, nodded and smiled.

'You have a new scarf,' I observed.

'My father's present from Budapest.'

'It's a beautiful city. The Paris of the East.'

'So you've been there?'

'Only for three days. I was stranded there.'

'How come?'

'It's a long story. But I love old cities with cobbled streets and arched bridges.'

'So you're an architect?'

I had been waiting for such a question. It opened a door for me. But perhaps the door had always been open, waiting for someone to walk in. It was mere chance that I accepted the invitation. I don't believe in fate. I am a scientist, trained to be rational, and yet every now and then I find myself wishing for a bird to fly out of my dreams and drop a bright new feather on the windowsill.

'Not really,' I answered. 'I design cities.'

'That must be interesting.'

'Not as interesting as what you do. You dig up ancient cities, don't you? You're an archaeologist. I can tell from the books on your table.'

'That's why you slow down when you walk past me. Why don't you stop and invite me to go for a walk? An architect walking with an archaeologist. Sounds romantic.'

'We did walk once. Don't you remember?'

'Yes – in the company of Dostoevsky.'

'He was an archaeologist too.'

'To me he seems more like a pathologist.'

We talked for a while, until I noticed that my coffee was cold, and went to get a fresh cup. The queue was long and I had to wait and wait. Anna kept on reading, every now and then looking in my direction and smiling. But when I took her glass of orange juice back to the table, I found she had left. There was a note on the table with a phone number: '*Prosti* (Sorry), I have to go. Call 322-83-68. Anna.'

I didn't call. Exams kept me busy.

And then I fell ill.

Anna

I was surprised that Aunty Olga hadn't said anything. To hide something from her is next to impossible since she knows me inside out. I can't imagine life without her. I was four when she took me to live with her in Kiev since my busy father didn't have time for me. She taught music in a school and from her I learnt to play the cello. It wasn't her favourite instrument; she wanted me to choose the piano. But as soon as she saw me with it, she realised that I was made for the cello and the cello for me.

Now Papa must have mentioned something to her. He answered the phone and turned to me. 'A foreigner is asking for you,' he said, smiling. But whoever it was had hung up before I picked up the phone.

Surely it was the young Indian I had met in the library? 'I don't even know his name,' I thought. Had I been too arrogant merely leaving my number on that piece of paper? Was I testing his patience, his persistence, his resolve?

He must have fallen ill. The flu this year is terrible and foreigners always go down first. I wondered if he had friends who could take care of him in this big alien city.

He was very friendly towards me. Shy but friendly.

'Who is this foreigner?' Aunty Olga soon asked. 'They aren't like us,' she added. 'Too different to live with.' Aunty Olga says she isn't a racist but just believes that we Russians are special, not superior or inferior – just different. I don't even bother any more to say that I don't agree with her. I know she doesn't want me to rush into a new relationship so soon after the messy break-up with Sergei.

'Sort out the mess with him first,' she said. There is no mess. That relationship is truly dead and buried. Seven years of life together. What a terrible waste! Didn't I work hard to make us happy? In the first few years it was great fun. But we were young, inexperienced and made mistakes.

Then Sergei asked me to come with him on his ship. I agreed. What a trip! I decided there and then that I wouldn't make that mistake again. Like all voyages the life onboard was monotonous, tiresome and boring, especially when we sailed from one site where they collected samples to another.

We tried hard to make the trip bearable by inventing

new ways of entertaining ourselves, often at one another's expense. An atmosphere of lecherous indulgence prevailed and only sudden violent conflicts provided some relief. I was amazed that people who were otherwise so respectable and correct, so polite and considerate, would suddenly turn into such monsters. These middle-aged scientists, overweight and alcoholic, tried to outdo one another in seducing the young lab assistants. The girls were bored as well, of course, and some were more predatory than usual. They knew that confined to the ship they had a rare opportunity to catch a *big fish*. They themselves changed hands like batons between the scientists. What disgusted me most was that the men who ravished them so casually didn't refrain from spreading sordid stories of their exploits.

'How can you live like this?' I asked Sergei. 'It's my job,' was all he said.

After my return from that awful voyage I asked him to give it up. He flatly refused. I asked him to stop going on expeditions. He refused again. He was a marine biologist and the expeditions were a part of his job.

I know I shouldn't even have asked. I too would have refused if he had asked me to give up my archaeological trips. It wasn't as if they were nice and clean either.

Then after one of his trips to Chukotka, he left me. I had been expecting it to happen because we had a huge row just before the trip. While he was away there had been no phone calls nor letters. Absolute silence.

A week after his return I found him waiting for me one evening at our place, his suitcase packed and ready to move out.

'Go, if that's what you want,' I told him. 'Go and never come back. And don't tell me that you're sorry, because you aren't. Nor am I.'

'Do you want to know why?' he asked.

'You mean your excuse.'

'I want children and you don't,' he said, ruthlessly.

What could I say? He was right.

'Galya wants to have babies,' he slyly continued. 'As many as we like.'

I finally lost my temper when he told me that he still loved me. I was the first love of his life, he said.

I picked up the vase from the table and threw it at him. He moved his head quickly to one side and the vase hit the wall and fell to the floor. It didn't even break.

He left at once.

Sergei Shumakov was *my* first love. Like all first loves, I suppose, it had to end. *Slava Bogu* (Thank God) we didn't have children.

Vasu

The hospital ward to which I was taken was full so the nurses found a bed for me in the corridor. There were already three others lying there. At around midnight a Czech tourist was brought in. He looked bad and three doctors and two nurses crowded round him. He died the next morning.

I spent that night between sleep and wakefulness. 'Sister,' I called to the nurse, Valya, 'tell me if that's the moon outside. Why is it stuck in a corner like something made of papier-mâché?'

'It's the street light, silly,' she replied, giggling and feeling my forehead for fever. Her hand was cold as the winter moon.

Next day Maria Fyodorovna, the doctor, showed me my X-rays. She pointed at several white splotches on the images and explained that I had flu-related acute pneumonia, and that both my lungs were infected. I was prescribed a heavy dose of antibiotics supplemented by vitamins. She knew that I suffered from bronchial asthma and said she would keep a close watch on me. 'In three or so weeks you'll be ready to go home.'

Soon I was moved into a ward with six other patients. It was much quieter and yet it took me a few days to get used to the snoring, the farting, the coughing, the sound of piss trickling into a urinal, the creaking beds, the flip-flop of slippers and occasionally someone swearing loudly. Most unsettling of all was the groaning from the bed closest to the window. Factory Director Vasili was dying, his body collapsing bit by bit. His legs were swollen, his lungs infected and his kidneys rapidly failing. Sensing that I was often awake, he would call on me for help. I would pass him the urinal and watch him struggle to release a few drops of urine.

Lonely and unable to sleep, I would pace the corridor most nights. If Valya was on night shift and not busy I would talk to her or sit silently nearby. She found my behaviour touching and started calling me 'my lonely little mouse'.

'I don't know what to do with you,' she said. 'You won't eat anything – which I understand because of the awful food – and you refuse the pills I bring. Plus no one ever comes to see you. Do I have to sing you lullabies?'

I smiled. Finally I said: 'Just a few stories will do.'

'What kind of stories?'

'Any kind. And I'll draw you a picture. A portrait, if you like.'

Most of Valya's stories were about the coalminers of Donetsk, her home town, where her father was a geologist and her mother a surveyor. One night I came across her and one of the other patients having sex in the injection room. I should just have walked away, but for some reason I stood and watched. Valya saw me looking.

Our night-time conversations came to an end.

Sundays were the most tiresome days in the hospital. I wanted them to disappear off the calendar. On weekdays the hustle and bustle of the ward kept everyone occupied. On Sundays everything, including the nurses, went into slow motion. No visits from the doctors, no tests, no examinations. Just the monotony of getting up and after long hours of pointless waiting, going back to bed.

On Sundays, more than ever, I waited for someone to phone or visit me. I envied Vladimir, the patient in the bed next to me. He had a continual stream of visitors. They came in throngs loaded with flowers, supposedly forbidden because of the asthma most of us suffered. His visitors brought packets of chocolates, cakes and biscuits and bottles of wine and vodka. Most of these goodies were given to the nurses, the orderlies and the cleaners, ensuring that Vladimir was treated like a king.

He was an actor at the Lenkom, the Komsomol Theatre, in Moscow. He had pneumonia too, but not as severe, and after a week he was parading up and down the ward cheering everyone up. Like most good actors he wasn't particularly handsome but he had charisma.

One evening he offered to paste mustard-strips on my back. I agreed only because I didn't want to offend him. But he didn't know the right way to do it. Within ten minutes there were burns all over my back.

Maria Fyodorovna was very annoyed. 'Don't let that idiot come near you again,' she warned me.

But Vladimir was quite likeable. Everyone in the ward loved his funny performances, especially the poems about Catherine the Great and her lover, Prince Grigori Potyomkin. 'Call me Volodya,' he told me, rejecting the formal Vladimir Vladimirovich.

'How about V V?' I asked.

'That sounds good. Very American.'

I found out later that he was a third-grade actor in the Lenkom. The grade wasn't a measure of his talent; it just reflected his current position in the theatre hierarchy. 'Little roles in big plays and slightly bigger in smaller ones,' he would complain. He had considered giving up acting but the fear of turning into a petty bureaucrat or an alcoholic stopped him. 'There is magic in your voice,' his friends often told him. 'Don't waste it.' Fortunately he didn't and had turned himself into a compelling reader and performer.

'You don't have a girlfriend, do you?' he used to pester me. 'I can find you one.'

Luckily Natasha saved me from further harassment. Her appearance one Sunday convinced him that I wasn't so lonely after all.

I had met Natasha in the drawing class at the University. She was a good painter but preferred sketching and watercolours to oils. She had noticed how unsure I was with my own drawing and started coaching me.

I was grateful for her help and enjoyed our weekend trips in the countryside around Moscow.

'You have a visitor,' I heard Vladimir saying at the door. 'He's missing you,' he told Natasha.

'I know,' she said as she approached my bed carrying armfuls of folders and plastic bags. I wondered why she looked so happy as she took off her blue coat and removed her *schapka,* her fur hat. She shook her head to release her long brown hair and kissed me, full on the lips. Her nose was cold and her breath sweet as morning dew. Her eyes had a warm glint that made me want to snuggle up to her.

'I hear you've been very sick. Didn't I tell you that this country isn't good for you? It's too bloody cold. Go home, you idiot.' She paused and regarded me again. 'And take me with you.'

She kissed me once more. 'Look at you,' she laughed. 'Haven't you been kissed by a girl before? I always wanted to do that, you know, but I wasn't sure how you'd react. But let me warn you: this won't happen again. That was your last kiss. Don't be scared; I won't come with you. I may hate the cold but I couldn't live without snow.'

'Show me your lungs,' she then demanded. As she examined the X-rays she whispered: '*Bozhe moi!* (My God!) How beautiful they are. Tell me, why are they sick?' I pointed to the white splotches. 'You mean these tiny buggers. Aren't they horrible?'

She abandoned the X-rays, opened her bag and pulled out presents: a big sketchbook, a few old issues of *The Times of India* and *The New York Times* which she must have got from Emma, my Scottish neighbour at the hostel, and a bag of red apples. 'The apples are from *Beryozka*.' This is the shop used by tourists and rich Soviet apparatchiks, that only takes dollars. 'I went with Emma and got myself a pair of stockings and a nice little bra. Here, you can feel it.' She pulled my head close and let me have a quick peek at the black bra under her white silky blouse.

She opened her bag again and took out a box of watercolours and brushes. 'You know I like watercolours and I want you to like them as well. Don't be afraid. Once you've learnt how to use them you'll never look at oils again.'

She paused and looked round the ward. 'Am I talking too much? Tell me honestly. Should I shut up?' I was speechless. I was still recovering from the shock of her sudden visit. 'Oh, I almost forgot,' she continued. 'I have something to show you. My real love is Saint-Exupéry. You know that, don't you?' She undid the strap of a large folder and spread before me illustrations she had drawn for *The Little Prince*. 'They're for you,' she said. 'My special present. I'm sure they'll gladden your heart.'

I examined the drawings but before she could get in another word, I told her about Anna. 'Is she pretty?' she asked, quite unfazed. 'I bet she is.' I said that I didn't know much more about her than that she was an archaeologist, that she wore glasses, and that the last time I had seen her she was carrying a beautiful Hungarian scarf her father had brought her from Budapest.

'Shall I ring her for you?' asked Natasha.

'No, please don't,' I hastily replied. 'I can wait.'

'But I can't. I'll go to the library and have a look at your

Annushka from Leninka.'

Natasha wrote down the details: where the reading room was, the location of the table, the time Anna arrived and left, the number of coffee breaks she took, and the type of perfume she wore.

'She sounds rich and bourgeois,' she announced. She noted Anna's phone number and added: 'And she lives in Medvedkova. My sister's dreadful boyfriend lives there too.'

I was confined to the hospital for six weeks, twice as long as Vladimir. The day before he was discharged, he asked about the newspapers Natasha had brought in for me. He wanted to see them regularly.

'I can't promise,' I told him, 'but I'll try and get them for you.'

He gave me his address and phone number. Then he shook my hand and said: *Dogovarilis?* (Agreed)

'Dogovarilis,' I replied.

Anna

Vasu had mentioned to me once that he liked second-hand books, and this shop on Kuznetsky Most was one of the best. I had come to look for something on Bach for Aunty Olga. He was standing outside examining the books spread across the pavement. Just as I left the shop, he looked up, saw me and smiled.

I liked the way he smiled, closing his eyes a little. His smile lit up his face. There was a scar on his chin which quivered as his lips parted, a blemish I found endearing. His smile didn't last long. It quickly faded and he became serious again, as if not sure he should have smiled at all. I was intrigued by his reticence. Why was he so unsure of himself, so insecure? But he seemed intelligent, honest and sincere and his shyness suited him.

Perhaps he didn't think that women found him attractive. He was wrong. He was attractive enough to invite more than casual glances, and then you felt you wanted to talk to him, draw him out. At least that's what I had felt when I first saw him in the library.

'I need a cup of coffee,' I told him and we found a café on Gorky Street. It had started snowing, those light powdery flakes that melt as soon as they fall.

That walk was special, he would later confess. So special that he used to relive it over and over in his dreams, in slow motion. He would remember the smallest details: my ponytail sticking out of my reddish cap; my opal earring; the tiny hole in my leather glove; the little flowers on my umbrella; snow sliding over my black boots. And the scarf, of course.

As the dream unrolled, he told me, he would be overcome with the desire to put his hand in the pocket of my coat. 'I was happy then,' he would say.

'Haven't seen you around,' I said. 'You must have finished your work in the library?'

As usual, he hesitated.

'You look so pale.' I prompted.

'I was ill. Pneumonia. But I'm feeling better now.'

'*Bednyashka* (Poor lonely man),' I thought. I raised my hand to touch his face, but stopped halfway. 'Why didn't you phone?'

'I did. Three times.'

'And … ?'

'No one picked up the phone.'

'I don't believe you,' I said and stared at him to let him know that I knew he was lying.

The café was crowded with people in wet overcoats, caps and boots. The air inside was hot, humid and stuffy. We found a table near the window and I offered to get the coffee. I brought it back, then left again for the bathroom. I was there a long time.

When I finally rejoined him, he looked subdued. 'You didn't have to wait for me,' I said. 'You thought I'd gone, didn't you?'

'But you left your cello.'

'I could have gone without it. Then you would have had to phone me.'

Again he was silent.

'Did you miss me when you were in hospital?' I asked.

He didn't answer but the tentative smile and the quiver of the scar on his chin told me that he had.

'You should have phoned and asked me to come and see you,' I said. 'I would have.'

Again he was silent and I realised that if I wanted to get to know him I would have to learn to endure his non-replies.

I fiddled with my scarf and gazed out the window. He followed my glance and we both saw a fountain, its round stony basin full of snow and a couple of pigeons having a snow-bath. Suddenly I felt a slight movement from his hand. *Come on, don't be afraid,* I wanted to tell him, but his hand remained where it was.

'Do you love playing the cello?' he asked abruptly.

'Of course,' I answered, still watching the pigeons. 'You know, I think I knew you were ill. Something strange happened to me one night when I couldn't sleep. I got up, picked up my cello and started playing. I sat near the window, looking out. And I felt I saw you. You were lying in a hospital bed. Your face was pale and resting on a raised pillow, illuminated by a cold white moon.'

He didn't say anything. I looked at my watch. I was late for the rehearsal. 'I have to go,' I said, and got up.

We left the café and walked to the Metro station. On the escalator I asked if he would like to come to the concert. 'I'd love to,' he replied and I quickly scribbled down the address. I told him that the concert was free and that I would wait for him in the main entrance hall.

My train arrived first and I rushed on. Didn't look back, didn't wave.

Vasu

I stood near the cloakroom watching the audience leave. Slowly the lights were turned off and the cleaners arrived with brooms, pans and brushes. Anna had told me to wait for her.

The concert had been wonderful. At least that's what I would have told Natasha, but the music I had enjoyed wasn't the most important part. As soon as it started and I saw Anna onstage I not only lost track of what I was hearing but failed to take in a single note.

I had read the programme beforehand and been ready to enjoy it all, especially the second piece, Shostakovich's String Quartet No. 12, because in it the cello took the lead. But my desire to keep watching Anna, every tiny movement she made, was so strong that I was forced to look away. I searched for something else on the stage to distract myself, but failed. Anna, beautiful and intense, was all I wanted to watch.

As I waited for her near the cloakroom I knew I had to calm down before she reappeared. Otherwise I wouldn't be able to talk to her properly and my stupid smile would make her angry and spoil the evening.

Perhaps I should just walk away? I even turned towards the door. Then I heard her call: 'Wait for me.' She was rushing down the stairs, her cello bobbing up and down. 'Sorry!' she said. 'I had to say goodbye to my friends. They've gone to the café. Would you like to meet them?' 'I really don't know,' I said and Anna quickly saw my hesitation and changed her mind. She said she would phone them later.

It was already late on a cold and windy night. There was not a sniff of snow in the air nor a speck of star in the sky. She let me carry her cello, put her arm through mine and spoke very softly. 'Let's walk together. I know you walk slowly. You do everything slowly; but I like your slow ways. I should slow down as well. "Don't rush", my Aunty Olga is always scolding me. She's my father's sister. Strict, but deep down very kind. She loves me very much and I love her too. She taught me the cello, you know.'

She peered at me closely. 'I hope she likes you. I know Papa will.' She paused and glanced in my direction.

'I liked your playing,' I said

'Why?'

I didn't know how to explain it.

'Come on – you should know. Give me at least one reason.'

'Maybe because of the way you were holding it, tucked between your knees and thighs, embracing it, and—'

'And?'

'The way you stretched your neck, then bent it to one side, smiled and—'

'And?'

'Breathed in. I could feel the breath go in and out and—'

'And?'

'Oh – I almost forgot.'

I suddenly remembered the bouquet I had put into my coat pocket. I pulled it out. The cellophane wrapper had slipped and one of the flowers was hanging precariously from its stem.

'I'm sorry.'

'Don't be silly.' Anna stopped, snapped the broken flower off and ate it. Then she started to laugh and cough.

'Do you need a drink?' I asked.

'No. No,' she laughed. 'But I want to know who told you to bring me carnations?'

'No one,' I lied.

An old woman who sold flowers at a kiosk at the University had recommended them. 'Take these, boyfriend,' she had told me. 'They're beautiful. I'm sure she'll like them. Don't be shy; give her the bouquet and kiss her hand.' When she saw my reluctance, she repeated it: 'Yes, kiss her hand. Do you understand?'

The woman warned me not to be out too late that night. I knew why: a maniacal killer was roaming the streets, attacking women and their companions. Eleven women, mostly young and wearing wedding rings, had been raped, killed or mutilated. As usual, nothing had been reported in the newspapers, leaving people free to spread wild rumours about the victims and the killer. Some thought he was an escapee from a mental hospital, while others suspected a runaway from a convict train passing through Moscow. Others believed there were two or even three killers, trying to outdo one another. The most bizarre theory was that the killer was a transvestite who dressed and behaved like a woman during the day but at night turned into a man.

When an official from the militia reported the arrest of a suspect, no one in the city believed they had got the right man. Women were still refusing to walk alone at night. Many carried bottles of vinegar or packets of hot peppers or chillies in their bags, if they had to be out.

By the time Anna and I left the Metro station it was nearly midnight. But nothing happened to us that night. We waited together for a bus which arrived right on time and took us safely to the last stop, a short walk from the apartments where she lived. We climbed the dark stairs to the second floor and before unlocking the door she showed me the doorbell. 'To call me you have to ring the bell twice,' she instructed. She entered first to check if there was anyone up, then whispered for me to come in.

Her room had a big window facing north, looking out over a little park with two swings, a fountain and a large oak tree.

We were both tired and slightly embarrassed. I know she would have let me into her bed if I had asked. But I didn't. I didn't want to make the first move.

I was glad that she didn't draw the curtains across the window. Lying on my mattress I could see the enormous oak nodding its long branch like an elephant taking a stroll.

Neither of us could sleep. Soon Anna began to sing, even though she knew that the retired nurse who slept in the adjoining room would complain in the morning. I turned on my side to look at her, then got up to sit with my back against the wall. She continued to sing her song. When she had finished I asked for more. She sang four songs, five. I came up close to her and sat down beside her. 'I'm tired,' she finally said. 'Thank you,' I said and kissed her hand.

Then I returned to my mattress and fell asleep at once. The next I knew I was awake and she was standing beside me holding a blanket. 'I knew you wouldn't ask,' she said and pushed me over to make room for herself on the mattress. She turned her body away from me and I put my arm around her. I slept again, inhaling her with every breath.

'I'm filled to the brim with you,' I wanted to tell her first thing in the morning. But as usual it was she who broke the silence. 'I saw you curled up on that mattress with the blanket lying on the floor and the pillow between your legs. "He must be cold," I said to myself, and came to you.'

'I love you,' I said.

'I know,' she replied.

Tonya, My Agitprop Mama

Anna

Vasu told me that he knew very little about his mother. Just like me.

There is a drawing in one of the scrapbooks I kept as a child. In the right-hand corner is my name and underneath the name of my school and the date. I called the drawing *My Mama*. The woman stands near a window looking out; her face is turned, strangely, away from the viewer. Outside is a small round hill covered in snow, bright in the sunlight. The drawing is in just four colours.

I was five when I drew it. Papa was surprised by my view but for Aunty Olga the reason was obvious. 'You were too young to know her face,' she said. She was right. Our family album did contain a few photos of my mother but they didn't mean much to me. Her presence in them was largely formal, as was her absence in my real life. I had been told that she died in an accident. This was thought enough for me to know.

One night in August, a few months before my sixteenth

birthday, I took three large family albums to my room and spent hours looking at them. I wasn't sure why. *Just curious,* I would have told anyone who asked, but it wasn't as straightforward as that.

I was disappointed that the albums contained only a handful of pictures of my mother. A few days later Aunty Olga showed me an old suitcase packed with bundles of loose photos. I pulled them out but most of them were so yellow with age it was impossible to see anything clearly in them.

I did, however, find photos that I liked. I put them aside to look at again. Papa knew a professional photographer who worked with the newspaper *Izvestia*. He made me some large prints. The process, Papa explained to me, wasn't simple: the photographer had first obtained a contact negative of the photos on an emulsion plate and then used this to print the enlargements, carefully controlling the exposure time.

One evening after dinner I asked Papa and Aunty Olga to tell me more about these four. Aunty Olga couldn't tell me much. Papa, on the other hand, seemed to remember everything about them.

Photo 1: Winter, 1948, Kuntsevo. My mother, Tonya, was then twenty-seven. This photo was taken a day after her birthday and I can't see her face clearly. That day she wore a dark olive-green coat and matching hat. It had snowed for two days, Papa told me. One of his friends had a *dacha* and had invited them to spend a few days skiing. The photo was taken late in the afternoon when the snow had stopped falling and the sky was clear, revealing a sun weak as the light of a torch. My mother is standing shadowed, a dark figure silhouetted against the endless white of the snow.

Photo 2: Autumn, 1949, Tsvetnoi Boulevard. My mother is sitting on a bench, smiling and wearing a pale blouse and a long striped skirt under a light autumn coat, unbuttoned. She holds an ice-cream in her right hand. Papa says that everyone then was suffering from the severe shortage of food. What they received on the ration card was meagre, although his wartime injury meant that he got a bit more than others. But even then one could go to Gorky Street and get cones and cups of delicious ice-cream. In the photo the light is bright, with leaves, mostly maple, scattered across the bench, the grass and the gravel path. My mother's hair is gathered into a ponytail and tied with a ribbon. I still can't see her face clearly.

Photo 3: Summer, 1950, Soboleva. My mother was born in this village, about fifty kilometres south of Leningrad, near a stream that froze in winter. She stands near the gate of a small wooden cottage, her right arm resting on it, her left touching her stomach. She is wearing a spotted summer dress with thin straps. Her hair has grown and is straight and smooth. She seems to have put on weight, but her arms are thin, and her skin appears silky soft. She doesn't look like a village girl. Was she? 'No,' Papa says, 'she was an actor working in agitprop.' Under her left hand I spot a bulge. So is she pregnant? 'Is she?' I ask Papa. When he nods, I say: 'So that's me in her belly?' 'Yes, you silly girl,' he replies.

Photo 4: Winter, 1949, A Studio on Kuznetsky Most, Moscow. At last I can see her face clearly. She is so beautiful.

Her face is small and a perfect oval. Her hair is cut short and curled. She is wearing lipstick and I see that her lower lip is sensuously fleshy. Her nose turns up slightly. But Papa's face lights up when he talks about her eyes. They were large and brown below neatly-curved eyebrows, he says. She is wearing a blouse with a frilled collar, short sleeves and a square neckline. Aunty Olga remarks that she looked very like Tatiana Samoilova, the actress who not only played the lead of a sexy, faithless woman in *The Cranes are Flying* but also won the prized role of Anna Karenina in the 1967 film. Aunty Olga is right. So why I am so plain and ugly? The only feature we share is our nose. 'Is she really my mother?' I ask. 'Of course,' Papa laughs.

I don't believe him.

One evening after I returned home from my cello lesson, Aunty Olga called me into her room to show me what she had found. From an old suitcase she took a light cotton dress. I knew at once what it was: the summer dress my pregnant mother had worn in the photo. Instinctively I tried to find out if it still smelt of her. Of course it didn't because it had been washed and dried and ironed since she had worn it.

I went into my room, put on the dress and looked into the mirror. 'A bit big for me, don't you think?' I asked, turning to Aunty Olga. She agreed. The dress was loose not only because I was fifteen but also because Tonya had worn it during her pregnancy.

It took me a few months to ask Aunty Olga if it were true that my mother had been killed in an accident. I surprised myself. Until then I had been content to believe what I had been told. But in the previous few months a feeling of desolation mixed with a faint heartache, strangely more soothing than painful, had begun to grow inside me. Perhaps the photos of my mother were now starting to speak to me. My longing to touch and hug the woman in the photo had become incredibly real and urgent. I suppose it wasn't a good idea to sleep the whole night in the dress. I should have put it straight back in the suitcase.

Early one morning Aunty Olga asked me to go into the city with her. We took the red Sokolniki Metro, then walked along Teatralny Lane for a few minutes, passing on the way the Malai Theatre. At Dzherzhinsky Square we turned right and crossed the street to reach the imposing Polytechnical Museum building. On the street near the bus stop, Aunty Olga stopped to indicate a spot near a lamppost. 'Right here Anna, my darling, Tonya was hit by a truck.'

There was hardly any traffic on the street and the bus stop was deserted except for an old woman who sat with a white cat on her lap, patiently waiting.

'I don't feel well,' Aunty Olga said. She asked me to run to the café across the street and get her a glass of water. When I returned I found her sitting on the kerb leaning against the lamppost. I gave her the water, patted her arm and sat down with her. The old woman's white cat looked at us and purred. 'Shush,' her mistress said, slapping her cat.

After a while we got up, went across to the museum and found a bench to sit on. Gradually the traffic on the streets increased, as did the people around us. Buses came, stopped and drove away as if nothing extraordinary had ever happened here. A short plump women wearing a white apron arrived with her vending machine and a small group formed around her. She was selling *pirozhki,* talking loudly the whole time. Another woman, almost a copy of the first, came to sell sweet white coffee in small paper cups.

I asked Aunty Olga if she wanted some refreshing coffee. She suggested we wait for the ice-cream woman, who appeared on cue, as if she had been waiting for Aunty Olga's command. We bought two cones of chocolate ice-cream and sat down again on the bench. A young man with a tired face spread a tarpaulin on the ground a few metres away and began laying out books. 'It's going to be a wonderful day,' he muttered.

It was indeed turning into a beautiful summer day, with not a scrap of cloud in the sky and the light so bright it would soon hurt our eyes. Suddenly an image flashed before me: my mother standing at the gate in the dress, her hand resting on her swollen belly, caressing it.

Aunty Olga began to whisper as if talking to herself. 'One late afternoon in November, Tonya came out of the Malai Theatre after watching a rehearsal of a play in which one of her friends had a small part. She walked along the lane, the same one we came along, turned right and stepped into the street to cross to the Polytechnical Museum. She was going to a talk by one of our leading scientists on the origins of life. She was already in the middle of the road when she saw the bus speeding towards her. She ran to avoid it but failed to see an army truck coming from the other direction. It was snowing, the road was slippery and it was hard to see. The young truck driver slammed on the brakes and his vehicle slid, lifted Tonya off the ground and hurled her against the lamppost near the bus stop. She died at once, said the young militiaman who came to tell us what had happened.'

'Where was I?' I asked

'With me at home,' replied Aunty Olga.

'And Papa?'

'In Siberia.'

'You didn't tell him?'

'Of course I wanted to, but I couldn't. I didn't know where he was. It took time. Everything took time then. You had to wait, be patient and hope against all hope. Hope was the reason, the only consolation to live, to survive—'

At home that afternoon, we made a pot of tea and sat in the kitchen sipping it, still talking in low voices. Even at home it seemed inappropriate to talk loudly, as if mere words would shatter the memory, scattering slivers and shards everywhere.

After a while, Aunty Olga went and got a small leather bag from which she took a piece of paper, Tonya's death certificate, and a short clipping from the *Trud* newspaper, 28 November 1952. I read the certificate and the cutting carefully and noted the date in my diary.

My mother had been cremated the following day and her ashes scattered in the stream near the cottage in Soboleva.

'*Vot i vsyo* (That's all). What else is there to say?' Aunty Olga got up and went to her room. She didn't come out until the following morning.

The following week when Papa returned from his field trip, he gave me two suitcases full of my mother's things. I put them under my bed, after I took out a few keepsakes: a necklace, an Uzbek scarf, the remains of a lipstick, a hand-mirror and a songbook.

In autumn the year after Aunty Olga had shown me the place where Tonya, my mama, had died in an accident, Papa and I went to Saratov to visit the village where he and Aunty Olga had been born. She didn't come with us. 'Bad timing,' she explained, 'I'm going to do the Pushkin walks around Leningrad. But don't forget to visit Grandfather Karl, and remember to bring me a pot of blackberry jam and some honey.'

We boarded the boat in Moscow and sailed down the River Volga to Astrakhan, the Caspian port town where the river flows into the sea. It took us seven days to reach Volgagrad, where we ended the journey. We would return to Moscow by train. Papa had wanted us to go to Astrakhan 'to taste the juicy melons' but in Volgagrad I came down with nasty flu.

Our days were spent visiting towns and villages, while the boat moved on at night. Papa had brought his Zenith camera with a whole set of different lenses, and he showed me how to take perfect photos. At first I enjoyed taking them but soon became bored. 'Don't you like the camera?' he asked. 'I prefer my own eyes,' I replied. When he pressed me I explained that my disenchantment was related to the photos in the family albums. At first they had seemed so real and my need so urgent that I couldn't stop looking at them. But slowly they had lost their magic, as if an Ali Baba had cast a spell and a door to them had swung shut.

I enjoyed being close to Papa and talking to him. We discussed how much he loved jazz, and he told me all about the book he had been working on for many years but which he was certain he would never finish. He asked about my school, my teachers and what I wanted to do with my life. I was most interested in history, I told him, especially the history of ancient nomads.

He told me about our Volga and how it would be hard to imagine Russia without the great river. The name Volga had been given by the Finno-Ugric people who had settled the areas upstream. The word Volga had several meanings: white, light, wet, humid, long, big and calm. The ancient Greeks who used to trade along the river called it *Ra*. For the Maris the river was *Yul*, for the Chuvash *Atal*, and for the Tatars and the Bashkirs *Idel*.

'Do you miss Mama?' I remember asking him. Once this question had been posed we both knew that the rest of the conversation would focus on avoiding the subject.

'Yes of course,' he said. 'Quite a lot then,' he added after a pause, 'but not so much now.'

'Did you love her?'

'What sort of question is that? Naturally. What do you think? I do even now, in a strange sort of way.'

'What do you mean?'

'We spent only a few years together, remember – just three or four. Then you were born and I was whisked away and—'

'And?'

'When I returned she was already dead.'

'Did you write to her?'

'I did, but most of the letters never reached her. They were confiscated, I think, and destroyed.'

'Were you angry? Are you still angry?' I realised that I had never seen him angry.

'Angry,' he mused. 'Perhaps I was. But anger cripples, you know. It just makes life more difficult to endure. You know that Tonya was a Communist, an agitprop comrade. She was driven. She wanted to change the world, make it better for the poor and the downtrodden.' He gave me a little smile. 'You know, the usual words, so commonly used and so meaningless.'

'It's nice to see you angry, even just a little,' I said. 'Was it very hard in the camp?' When he didn't reply, I quickly added: 'Of course it must have been.'

'It wasn't exactly a camp. In a way I was free, though not free enough to travel across the Urals. I was ordered to keep quiet and do whatever I was told, so that's what I did.'

Papa and I spent two days in Saratov. On the first we caught a bus and travelled to Komarovka, a *kolkhoz* village less than forty kilometres north. It didn't take long to find the grave of Grandfather Karl who, like his son, had worked as a foreman in a ceramics factory manufacturing tiles and pottery.

The untidy state of the cemetery didn't upset Papa. He had expected it. The cottage in which he and Aunty Olga were born had been destroyed in the War, like most others in the street. In their place stood a large farmyard and a workshop with trucks, tractors and bulldozers parked outside.

Papa knew the place where the cottage must have stood and guided me to it. It had stood near the present fence, looking down over a stream and fields of grassy tussocks. A power line now ran past the farmyard, across the stream and through the fields, four sagging wires stretched between wooden poles. Ravens sat on the wires, swinging slowly and steadily in the wind, as if silently contemplating their next short clumsy flight.

A tractor was driven out of the yard by a young woman in a red scarf who waved to us. All the ravens flew off except one tiny leftover, who kept on swinging.

Papa drew for me a sketch of the street and the cottage as it had been: a wooden house with a sloping tiled roof, a chimney and small windows, with a well out the back.

'There used to be two apple trees not far from the well,' he said. 'One of them would flower every year but never bore any fruit, while the other was always heavy with apples. My grandmother looked after a row of beehives and taught Olga and me to collect honey. Our honey smelt of apples.'

'Some of those grassy mounds,' he said, pointing across the stream, 'are the kurgans, the ancient burial mounds. Ploughing the fields we often used to uncover ancient coins and pottery shards, which I would collect. I've still got some of them at home in Moscow.'

'So is it true that our family are Germans—I mean, Germans from the Volga?' I abruptly asked.

I knew that we were: Eisner, our family name; our love of classical music; the old German editions of Goethe, Hölderlin and Rilke on the bookshelves; the ancient maps of German cities like Hamburg, Berlin and Stuttgart; the German hymn-books; and the etchings and the engravings of castles and churches.

So why had I asked? I suppose it was because I wanted to hear it from Papa himself.

We were in the bus travelling to the village. The sun was

descending, splashing the sky with colours. The jovial driver chatted loudly with an old lady in the seat next to him. Apart from her there were only two other passengers: a young woman with a red Pioneer leader's tie and an old man with a ghastly tennis-ball-sized lump on the side of his head.

'Do I feel German?' he mused after a few minutes of silence. 'I don't know. You should ask Aunty Olga. She's more worried about these things, although it's true that I once tried to change our name to Eisnerov. There were many who went right ahead and gave themselves new names. I didn't, but not because I didn't consider myself Russian. I think it was the War that finally forced me to think about myself more seriously. The day I went to enlist I discovered the entry in my passport. I was shocked – no, not at the entry, but at my failure to notice it earlier. The entry had been there all the time. Now I don't mind that there's a bit of German in me, but somehow it hasn't made me improve my German or go to Hamburg in search of my forebears. My parents' grandparents are buried in that cemetery we saw. My journey begins and ends here. Is there any point in going beyond that, searching for the sake of searching? I suppose some people like to and want to, and I'm sure they have their compelling reasons—'

'And what about Tonya, my mother?'

He didn't reply straight away. I guess he didn't know how to react to the way I used to say Mama's name: 'Tonya' followed by 'my mother', the two separated by a punctuation mark: the first to open a gap and the second to throw a bridge across it.

'Your mother,' he replied, 'was more Russian than any Russian I've ever met – which is strange, because her father was a Hungarian Jew from a village near Budapest. Her mother came from a prosperous family of Ukrainian Cossacks. They lived in a village near Rostov-on-Don.' He gave me a big grin. 'Now there's a reason for you to travel and see the world.'

He looked away. The silence that followed extinguished any hope I might have had of continuing our conversation. When a moment or two later he turned again to look at me and smile, I noticed that he was really ready to cry. He took his glasses off and tried to clean them with his handkerchief.

Then he put them on again and looked around, as if searching for Aunty Olga, his angel of a sister, to console him. *He needs a hug*, I thought and that made me both sad and angry.

A year after the trip to Saratov I moved back to Moscow to finish high school. Now it was Aunty Olga's turn to shuttle between Kiev and Moscow. Initially she was apprehensive about my decision, because she wasn't sure how easily Papa, her dear Leynya, would adjust to my presence. But when I told her more about our trip together, she relaxed.

It didn't take Papa and me long to get used to one another. We both loved music and, whenever we could, we played together, he on the piano or saxophone and I on my cello, improvising jazz tunes or classical compositions.

I didn't enjoy my final year at school. My history teacher started picking on me, mercilessly criticising my reading and writing. She didn't like my project work and never missed a chance to laugh at my serious devotion to my music.

I didn't say anything to Aunty Olga, scared that she would

confront the teacher and make life even more difficult for me.

One Friday evening in the winter of 1966, I felt the urge to rummage again through Mama's suitcases. The night before, I had been woken by a strange dream. During the lunch break at school next day, I found a desk in a secluded corner and sat down to record the dream in my diary. However, as I began to write I realised that the dream had lost the vivid details which had besieged my imagination.

Fortunately my friend Vera saw me in the library and asked if I wanted to go to her place. Her parents lived in a large well-furnished and comfortable apartment, because her father, an Armenian from Yerevan, held an important position in the Party branch of the Hammer and Sickle Factory. Vera loved chess and her coach, a celebrated Grandmaster, was convinced that he could make a world champion out of her. Vera, however, had other ideas. She was beautiful, with soft tanned skin, beautiful deep-set brown eyes and thick dark hair. She wanted to be a model.

We sat for a while in her room turning the pages of East German and Finnish fashion magazines, and then Vera opened her mother's wardrobe, pulled out some fabulous dresses, turned on some music and staged an impromptu show.

There was a mauve summer dress of Chinese silk, light and soft, that made my heart jump. Vera noticed my reaction. 'You like it, don't you?' she said and handed me the dress to try on. I refused. Vera insisted but I again said no. 'Take it with you, silly, and try it on at home.' She flicked the dress over to me. 'And don't worry about Mama. She won't notice. She's into diamonds these days.'

I took the dress home. Aunty Olga had gone to spend the

night with an old friend who was ill. I read her note on the kitchen table, heated up the dinner she had left me and sat eating and thinking about the two dresses, the one Vera had given me and my mother's. I had put both of them on my bed, side by side.

They looked so different. Was it because of the material, cotton against opulent Chinese silk, or the dots? The silk dress had tiny embroidered flowers all over it. I first put on my mother's dress and then slipped into Vera's. It felt so smooth and sensuous. I loved the way it caressed my body but I also wanted to get rid of it, as if its touch were contagious, as if by being in the dress I was about to betray Tonya.

But I was sure that Mama would have liked it, and that she would have looked wonderful in it. I took it off and put on her spotted dress again. Aunty Olga had been right; the dress now fitted me well, as if it had been waiting for me to grow up a bit, and as if the sole purpose of my growing up was to be able to fit into it.

I wore it for a while, and hung the silk dress in the wardrobe, where I avoided looking at it.

The suitcase from which I had taken Mama's dress remained open. The two leather straps which held the top together had broken, causing it to fall open and reveal a small pocket with a half-open zip. I noticed that something was stopping it closing. I stuck my hand in to remove the object and found a piece of glossy paper. I pulled it out. It was a passport-sized black-and-white photo, the upper left corner ripped from being stuck in the zip.

I took the photo to the table, switched on the lamp and studied it. I turned it over and read the words neatly written on the back: 'To dearest Tonya', and underneath, 'Paolo Prezzolini, March 1949'.

Quickly I returned to the bundles of old photos in the suitcase. Suddenly the face in the passport photo, the face of Paolo Prezzolini, was everywhere. In one photo he was impersonating Il Duce, standing beside a pathetic-looking Fuhrer. The 'partisan' woman, tucked between the two and holding a gun, was Tonya. This must be one of Tonya's agitprop shows, I thought. Paolo must have been an actor.

There he was in another photo holding skis and smiling at my mother. She had her skis on, and was ready to move. In another photo I found the two dancing in a club, surrounded by other couples. Paolo held her close, his left hand on her waist and the right a little lower. Her head was pressed against his chest.

I liked the next photo: in it Tonya is wearing the spotted dress, lying on her side, her head resting on her right arm. Through the v-shaped window formed by her elbow and her body peeps a bouquet of wildflowers. My mother's legs are bent and her dress has slid up to expose her lacy petticoat. But it's her feet, small, delicate and spotless, that catch my eye. I wanted to touch them, the feet of my dead mother.

In the picture Paolo is sitting with his right hand resting on her hip. His left leg is bent and the right stretched against Tonya's back. He is looking straight at the camera. It must have been a glorious summer day.

'Who took this photo?' I wondered. 'Who else was there with them?' And suddenly the world outside the photo came alive. The question broke the spell that the presence of Tonya and Paolo together in the pictures had created.

I felt angry. Why were they together, Tonya and this Paolo, who looked so excruciatingly charming? Why didn't I notice him before?

Who was he?

Questions rushed into my head. I went back to look at his picture more carefully. And that's when I began to notice the similarities. I had always known that I looked different from Papa and Tonya, although if I tried hard I could detect a bit of Tonya's nose in mine. Paolo's face was so familiar: the forehead, the eyebrows and, strangely, the ears.

'And guess what,' I whispered to myself, 'I smile the way the devil smiles. Is he my father then?' I wasn't really surprised. Now it all seemed so obvious.

I opened my notebook and jotted down a few dates: my birth, Papa's exile, Tonya's death in the accident, Papa's return. Of course I wasn't absolutely certain. My hunch needed corroboration. Corroboration, from whom? From Papa and Aunty Olga? Why should they tell me the truth now? In fact why should I believe anything they told me? Hadn't their silence implicated them? Implicated them in what? Perhaps they didn't tell me anything about Paolo because there wasn't anything to tell.

Perhaps Papa was indeed my real birth father. But what if he wasn't and I was the daughter of this devilish Italian?

At that point the phone rang.

It was Papa calling from Sverdlovsk. I didn't tell him what I'd found that evening. To all his questions my answers were short: *yes, no, I don't know, that's good, OK, right.* He noticed my monosyllabic responses and asked if I was all right. 'Sort of,' was my brief reply. He asked me to go to his favourite second-hand bookshop and get some books for a friend who was working on the history of mining in the Urals. He asked if Aunty Olga had gone to stay with her sick friend. He soon hung up.

I slept badly that night. The following morning I packed a bag and boarded an early morning suburban train to our *dacha* in Prudkino. Before I went I left two notes on the kitchen table, one each for Papa and Aunty Olga. I also left some photos of Paolo and Tonya.

With me I took my cello, my one and only soul mate.

I spent the whole of December and most of January 1967 at the *dacha*. Initially I did very little but gradually I willed myself to establish a daily routine. I played my cello, went for walks, wrote my diary, visited a woman in the neighbourhood who wove cotton and woollen wall-hangings, and spent time with Sergei who lived across the street. We had known each other for many years but had until then never really talked.

Papa came to see me two days after I arrived. I was pleased to see him but couldn't bring myself to discuss our situation. He understood why and didn't torment me with questions or explanations. Instead he helped me chop wood for the stove and the fire. Before he left he gave me money for groceries. When I went to the station to say goodbye I felt sorry for him as I watched him go. He looked old and fragile and his limp was accentuated, as if from the weight of the sadness that had suddenly confronted us. He was frightened, he confessed later, that he would lose me forever.

Before boarding the train he hugged me. I surrendered myself to the hug, his sloppy kiss and his 'Please look after yourself.'

Aunty Olga came to see me three days later. She was upset and didn't say much for several hours. Her red eyes and puffy wrinkled face showed that she had been crying. When I asked her about her sick friend, she snapped that it was none of my business. Then she added that her friend had died three days ago and that she had come straight from the funeral. I hugged her. She didn't resist and we hugged and cried, and cried and hugged.

Soon some of the missing parts of my mother's story followed. Aunty Olga stressed that she had never really discussed 'these unfortunate events' in any detail with Papa, and that she was telling me her own version of 'the tragedy'.

Did she hate Tonya for 'getting into trouble'? My mother had starting going out with Paolo a few months before Papa's arrest and exile. Paolo, the son of a locksmith from a village near Turin, had arrived in Moscow to attend the Party school. During the War he had been active in the Underground, and after the fall of Mussolini been sent to Moscow to train as an agitprop artist. He was handsome, lively and, most of all, made Tonya laugh. He was so different from the serious, always cautious, strangely burdened and irrevocably scarred Leynya.

Tonya was smitten. There were few who could have resisted Paolo's charm, said Aunty Olga, and perhaps that's why the affair didn't last. 'I knew he wouldn't be faithful. He didn't know how to be loyal.'

So did she try to discourage the relationship?

'He returned to Italy a month before you were born,' she continued. He had begged Tonya to go with him, but she wouldn't.

'Stupid Italian!' Aunty Olga was angry. 'Flew in like a whirlwind and ruined everything.'

I wondered if Paolo knew about me. Why not? He certainly should have. He made my mother pregnant, didn't he? And she must have told him. But perhaps she didn't. She was proud, wasn't she? She would have done her best to pretend that he wasn't my father. She had her reliable Leynya in whom to take refuge, to hide behind.

I felt so sad for Papa and Tonya. For Paolo Prezzolini I didn't feel anything but indignation and contempt.

How could my mother let this happen to her? Was it because the love she had for Papa was flawed from the beginning, doomed? Is it true that the seeds of our failures are planted in us at our birth; that the potential for disaster exists in all of us; that we live our lives fighting our demons; and that happiness is nothing but a temporary deferment of the final calamity? During that long cold winter of 1967, I remained alone at the *dacha*, slowly finding a way through my turmoil. Papa visited me every weekend, and Aunty Olga tried to spend as much time there as possible.

By the time I returned to my room in Moscow, I had found a kind of balance. Still, the thought that my appearance in this troubled world had come about through some sort of a betrayal often distressed me. Of course I knew, and Aunty Olga repeated several times, that only time and my capacity to believe in the basic goodness of people would eventually help me live through this ordeal.

I waited for Papa to tell me his side of the story. I knew he would eventually and didn't want to rush him. The questions I needed him to answer were simple: Did he ever meet Paolo, and if so, why didn't he protect Tonya from him? Why didn't he fight for her? Why didn't he fight for himself?

Then one day after we had been playing together Papa, still at the piano, told me that he had never doubted I was his daughter.

'But look at me,' I said. 'I look like him.' He ignored this with a dismissive *meaningless*. What mattered most, according to him, was the voice inside him which told him that I *was* his daughter.

He smiled and although I sensed that he wasn't telling the truth, I believed him because that's what I always did.

Uncle Triple K

Vasu

Anna came to my room to help me translate a Russian article on Roman architecture and, seeing a photo of Uncle Triple K on my table, asked who he was. My father's younger brother, I said. Both friends and foes called him Uncle Triple K. For his friends he was Kamrade Krishan Kakkar and his enemies used the insulting Kamrade Kana Kakkar. Kakkar was his surname and Krishan Lal his given name, often shortened to Kishnu, KL, Kisna or even Lalu.

Kana in Hindi means one-eyed.

Uncle Triple K was a Communist. I don't know if he ever actually joined the Party but everyone in the family knew that he was close to its members. This was odd, because my father hated Communists with a vengeance. He hated them because they didn't believe in gods or religion and he hated them even more because they wanted to make rich people like him poor and (he claimed) the poor even poorer.

My grandmother used to call my uncle Kishnu and he was

her favourite. Perhaps that's why my father and grandfather let him stay on in the large family home.

My uncle was the third child in the family of four children, small by Indian standards. My father was the first-born, the chosen one. My proud grandfather used to call him *ghar ka chirag* (the shining light of the family). Next in line was my Aunty Shanti, the invisible one. She was as quiet as a little mouse and did whatever was asked of her without fussing or fighting back. Her younger sister Radha was fiery and appropriately known as Phuljhari, the sparkler. She knew her value and didn't hide from anyone that she was the Queen Bee of the family. Together she and my father ruled the household. To disobey them was not only unwise but dangerous.

Uncle Triple K and Aunty Shanti were treated as outcasts. My aunt was given away in marriage as soon as she finished high school, and moved to live in Chandigarh. There she gave birth to four children in quick succession, which won praise from her in-laws because all four turned out to be strong and healthy boys. Her father-in-law pre-planned everything. Now he would have a doctor, a lawyer, a railway engineer and a businessman in the family. In his view this was the essential combination for success in any Indian family.

Once Uncle Triple K realised that my father was going to be the sole inheritor of the family business, he began to concentrate on his studies. He did well at high school, won a scholarship to a good college in Delhi, and completed a PhD in French Literature and Philosophy.

While at university he rented a small apartment in Kamala Nagar, a crowded suburb not far from the campus. It was on the second floor of a block next to a big shopping centre, and had two small rooms and a kitchen. One room contained a wooden bed, a chair and desk on which sat an old Remington typewriter. This was my uncle's study where I used to spend most time with him. The other smaller room was occupied by Mala Didi, my uncle's friend and secretary. To accommodate the visitors who frequently arrived, most without prior notice, the wooden bed was removed to the hallway to make room for mattresses and *dharis*.

These visitors came from all over India. An old fisherman arrived once or twice every year from a village at the southern tip of the country, after travelling thousands of kilometres on foot, and in buses and trains. He was spare and short and had pitch-black skin, but what used to fascinate me was his white-as-snow beard. We used to call him 'the *sadhujee* from Kanayakumari'. He would tell me stories of the sea: the storms and the sacrifices the fishermen made on nights of the full moon to appease the angry monsters living in the dark depths.

Another frequent visitor was a young doctor from the coalmining town of Dhandbad. He brought patients with him and sought Uncle Triple K's help with finding doctors and hospital beds. I still remember a three-year-old girl, who came with him one day. Her face was swollen from a ghastly tumour in her right eye. The doctors were able to remove the tumour but made a mistake with the blood group for her transfusion. She died an hour after the operation.

Visitors came to the apartment even when my uncle was away. They stayed for a few days, did whatever business they had in Delhi, then went home, soon replaced by new arrivals. Mala Didi looked after them. She was tall and thin and always kept herself busy doing something that seemed important. I liked being with her and often helped her with chores.

She loved listening to music and songs on the radio, but I never heard her sing or hum anything herself. Although she looked after my uncle's visitors well, most found her dull and severe. This was a misreading of her character because I knew she was kind and often forgiving. What made people withdraw in her presence was the sadness which used to cloud her lovely face.

The secret of her eternal sadness was accidentally revealed to me by Jijee-ma, my older sister. Mala Didi, she told me, was born in Peshawar, seven years before the 1947 Partition of India, into a rich family of drapers and tailors who were forced to leave Pakistan as refugees. One night at the border of newly-independent India, the train was stopped and attacked by an angry mob. Mala Didi's whole family was butchered in the train.

One day just after my fourteenth birthday, Uncle Triple K took me to the tiny village of Rampur, a hundred or so kilometres north of Delhi. He wanted to show me the brick kilns and let me meet the workers, some of whom he said were even younger than I was.

We were running late and had to board a bus which was unusually full. Uncle Triple K didn't get a seat and had to travel standing. A young man, maybe one of his students, offered him his seat, but my uncle declined. We travelled for an hour and then the front tyre of the bus exploded. There was a loud noise and the bus skidded, shuddered and stopped.

Luckily the shoulder of the road was sandy and the driver, clearly used to such mishaps, halted the bus without tipping it over. We were ordered to get out and wait for his young assistant to change the tyre. Uncle Triple K didn't want to wait. He spotted a camel cart and asked the old man on it for a ride. He knew the brick kiln and dropped us near the village, where a young man, Yadav, had brought bicycles to meet us.

Yadav worked for the local trade union and had invited my uncle to meet the labourers. We rode for half an hour along a dusty track, avoiding potholes and the sharp spikes of *kikar* trees.

At the kiln we found three children playing with a bicycle wheel. They ignored us. One of them was using a stick to steer the wheel as he pushed it with his left hand and ran along with it. The other two, a boy and a girl, completely naked, ran with him, whooping and shouting. The girl, the youngest, would stop every now and then to cough and catch her breath.

Uncle Triple K was not pleased. He hadn't expected the kiln to be shut and deserted. Yadav, however, didn't seem at all surprised. He told us he had been expecting something like this. The bonded labourers who worked the kilns were illegal and banned by the government. Occasionally the police raided and freed anyone they found there. But the contractors had their informants among the police who gave them advance warning of the raids. They would round up the labourers in advance and drive them off into neighbouring villages.

Yadav checked the kiln and as we were about to leave we heard someone scream from a hut near the large furnace. The boy stopped running with the wheel. We all froze. Then again we heard the desperate howl. We rushed in the direction of the hut, following the three children.

When we entered the tiny dark space, the older boy was already inside. 'Amma is ill,' he said. She was leaning against the wall clutching her large belly and breathing heavily.

'She's in labour,' my uncle said. 'Quick,' he continued, 'we need a doctor – urgently.' Yadav ran outside and cycled off to get the doctor from the neighbouring village.

Meanwhile Uncle Triple K asked me to find a bucket and fetch some clean water. The boy showed me the well, the rope and the bucket, and together we pulled up a load of water and took it to the hut. My uncle had already found a lantern and settled the woman on a mat on the floor. He told us to light a fire and heat up the water. Outside the hut the boy and I put together some of the bricks that were lying around, gathered some dry wood, leaves and scraps of paper, found some kerosene and managed to get the fire started.

Meanwhile the woman in the hut had stopped screaming, but by the way she groaned we knew that she would soon start wailing. My uncle asked the boy if there was a clean sheet in the hut. He pulled out a worn but clean Bengali sari from a basket in the corner. The woman glanced at the sari, nodded, smiled and then began to scream again.

All I remember are her screams, which seemed to go on and on. Then all at once she stopped and looked at Uncle Triple K, raised her hand and pointed at something in between her legs.

'Look, the head,' he whispered. 'The baby is coming out.'

I couldn't see much in the darkness of the hut. Uncle Triple K raised the lantern. I watched the woman take a long breath and gather all her strength to push. That's when the baby slid out. My uncle quickly dropped to his knees and caught the child in hands that were trembling slightly. Then he cut the cord, cleared the baby's mouth and the first cry of the newborn girl echoed round the hut. He washed the baby, wrapped her in the sari and my woollen jumper and gave her to the mother for her first feed.

It was more than an hour before Yadav returned with the doctor. He examined the mother and the baby and said they were both fine.

The three children who had witnessed the birth of their new sister had not said a word. They still looked stunned. Then the little girl got up and went up to the baby, to touch her face. When the baby gave a cry she quickly withdrew her hand.

The doctor invited my uncle and me to stay overnight at his house. Uncle Triple K gave Yadav some money and asked him to buy food and milk for the family. The doctor's wife found two blankets, a sari and some clothes for the children. She also packed a small box of sweets, to mark the happy occasion of the birth.

On our way back to Delhi, my uncle explained why the woman in the hut had been so pleased that her baby was a girl. Boys born at the kiln inherited the bondage of their fathers and were trapped there, whereas girls, when they grew up, were given away in marriage to husbands in neighbouring villages. They had a chance to be free.

Later when I was in Moscow there was a postscript to one of Uncle Triple K's letters to me. 'Do you remember the baby who was wrapped in your woollen jumper? She died before she was two. But don't be sad (although I know you will be), because in a way it's better that the poor child is dead. She escaped the suffering of that wretched life.' He added: 'It breaks my heart to know how little hope there is for these people. I feel despair knowing that, like so many others, I am unable to help them.'

❊ ❊ ❊

It was eighteen months after our visit to the brick kiln before Uncle Triple K and Yadav persuaded the police to organise a proper raid to free the labourers. The contractor was arrested and charged.

My uncle returned to Delhi and wrote an article about the kiln-owners and the ruthless way they exploited their labourers, who included little children. 'That evening in the village I helped a mother give birth to a baby girl,' the concluding paragraph of his article reads, 'but I am not sure how happy I am about that. Look around you: there are children everywhere, cleaning shoes, selling newspapers, serving tea, washing dishes, scavenging rubbish, collecting waste. I have seen them in stone quarries, carpet shops, on railway stations, in spinning mills, and in illegal *bidi* and fireworks factories. I ask you to pause and think. Do you see any future for them? And if not, is there any future for us?'

Uncle Triple K was a good writer, simple but persuasive. He wrote columns for newspapers, plays for street theatre groups, and songs, slogans and jingles for protest marches. What I liked most was his ability to explain complex ideas simply and gracefully. Perhaps that's why the Sunday edition of a national newspaper began publishing his column, *Notebook of a Dilettante*. I used to collect these columns and read them, hoping to learn to write like him.

My collection of Uncle Triple K's columns contains a brief news report which appeared on the fourth page of the Delhi edition of *The Times of India*. The report is short, very much like the incident it describes. For the reporter it was a minor assault. But it changed my uncle's life.

One evening my uncle and Mala Didi were walking home after attending the editorial meeting of a literary magazine he had started with some friends. He had got off the bus and walked through the bazaar, paused for a few minutes to look at a cinema billboard, stopped at the *paan*-shop to say hello to one of his friends, declined his offer of tea, and gone into a grocery store. When he came out he had turned into the narrow lane behind the shopping complex just a few metres from his home.

Suddenly two men armed with *lathis* rushed at him from behind. They knocked over Mala Didi. One of them hit my uncle's legs hard and he fell down. The other rained down blows on his back and his head.

Shaken and shocked by the attack, Mala Didi took some minutes to get up. Then she saw Uncle Triple K lying face down, bleeding and moaning. She ran across the lane and called for help. Someone rushed to get a doctor from a surgery across the street, the *paan*-wallah scurried to ring an ambulance, and an old man who had seen everything that had happened hurried to call the police.

The doctor found my uncle unconscious and badly hurt. A couple of ribs were broken, there was a small crack on the back of his skull and part of his jaw was shattered. Worst of all, his left eye was damaged.

Jijee-ma didn't let me visit my uncle in the hospital. 'Not

yet,' she said firmly. 'Maybe in a week, when he's better.' I saw him first after ten days. By that time, to use his own words, he was 'nicely patched up and re-assembled'. Most of the upper part of his body, including his head and neck, was bandaged and there was a black patch over his left eye. His face was still scarred and puffy but he smiled as soon as he saw me.

'Where is your camera?' he asked. 'Don't you want to take my photo in this spacesuit?' I said nothing. I was trying hard to hold back tears. He asked me to come closer but instead I ran from the room.

Mala Didi came to get me. 'He'll be fine,' she tried to reassure me. 'The scars will be there, but he'll come out stronger and more determined. I know him well. He isn't someone who will give in easily to those who want to hurt him.'

'But what about his eye?' I asked her. She didn't say anything then but after a few days told me the whole story.

As Uncle Triple K fell, his glasses slipped off and when he hit the ground his face smashed into them. Each blow from the *lathis* pushed his face into the broken metal frames. Their sharp edges pierced his left eye, dislodging the eye-ball from its socket.

His eye couldn't be saved. It was removed, leaving an empty hole in his face.

For a few years afterwards he wore awkward-looking glasses. An eye transplant was suggested but quickly dropped because of the irreparable damage to the optic nerve.

He had a glass ball placed in the hole. Uncle Triple K soon learnt not only to live with one eye but also to joke about it.

'What a shame,' he would often say. 'A Leftist forced to

look at the world with his right eye.'

'For proper balance, Kamrade Kakkar,' his friends would say, and laugh.

Stalin's Heart

Anna

That Vasu adored his Uncle Triple K terrified me. I wasn't sure if I should tell him that in our family we didn't feel comfortable with people like him, that we were highly suspicious of them and even feared them.

'Stop seeing your Indian,' Aunty Olga had told me. 'He isn't one of us.'

'But that's the very reason I like him,' I replied.

'Don't be stupid,' she said and warned me that nothing good would ever come from this relationship. I was glad when she returned to Kiev because if Vasu had phoned she would have told him to leave me alone.

I hadn't talked to him for a while. Too busy planning the expedition, and then the message arrived from Poltava and I had to leave.

I didn't want to leave Moscow so soon because of the fires and smoke. Most of the forests around Moscow were on fire and almost the whole of the south-west was covered in smoke.

Papa had told me that the fires would continue for months, because once peat starts to burn it is very hard to control.

I was worried. Papa suffered from high blood pressure and often forgot to take his pills.

'Don't worry about me,' he repeated and laughed. 'Just concentrate on your work.'

He was right. That field-season in particular was extremely important for me and the expedition. I needed to focus on my work.

Maybe I should have phoned Vasu to find out how he was coping with his asthma in the smoke. Maybe he would want to join me in Poltava and work on the dig with me. I knew he loved old cities and what could have been older than Gelon? 'Come, my friend,' I imagined myself telling him, 'and walk with me in the streets of a town so old it was described by Herodotus. We'll map its shape and size and argue about the site where the Scythians chose to build it.'

If he came I could show him the remains of the Scythian boat which we had dug up the previous season. It had been buried in three layers of sand and clay and had taken us a week to get out.

Had I fallen in love again? Had I started to miss him? Of course, Vasu was in love, desperately. He would have dropped whatever he was doing and come to me.

There were five of us in my team, two men and three women. I would have preferred more men. It was easy to work with them, especially when you knew, as I certainly did, how to deal with their hungry looks and unwelcome advances. Boris Ivanovich Gryzlov, a linguist, was our leader. Vasu would surely enjoy discussing Sanskrit hymns and Hindu gods with him. Nikolai Nikolaivich Kravchenko, the second in command, supervised the diggings. The women in the team called him 'Boris Godunov, the Usurper'. He and Maria Shulskaya, the surveyor, ruled jointly over us. Maria, from Leningrad, was so enormous it was hard to imagine that she had flown fighter planes during the War.

My special friend was Tetya Shura, born in a Cossack village not far from Rostov-on-Don. Her grandmother had died of hunger in Stalin's famine and so her father had been brought up in an orphanage. Her grandfather joined the Red Cavalry of Budenov and was killed in a battle near Kiev, but not before he named his son *Revolyutsiya* (Revolution).

Tetya Shura was an expert on ancient pottery and knew the provenance of most of what was found in the region. She could date it merely by looking at its colour, glaze and ornamentation.

Each morning Kravchenko chaired a meeting to discuss the tasks for the day and plan the work schedule. Often a group of volunteers from the *kolkhoz* school or the technical college in Poltava joined our party.

Our work had so far revealed remnants of a town spread across the valley lying between the River Vorskla in the east and a dry creek which ran to the west before merging with the Vorskla a few kilometres south-east of Bel'sk.

The remains of three fortifications and a system of walls and moats had been exposed and mapped. The eastern fortification, we had concluded, had stood on a river terrace rising a hundred metres above the river valley. The northern fortification guarded the port. Boats from the eighth-century Greek colony of Olbia, in the delta of the River Bug on the northern coast of the Black Sea, would have sailed along this river. The Greeks would have traded wine, textiles and fresh olive oil for grain, cattle, hides, furs, timber, wax and honey. The rivers beyond Gelon weren't big enough to carry large boats, so barges would have been used to carry goods and people to the north and east.

I was asked to join the team because they needed someone who knew how to describe and map both ancient and present-day landforms. My job was almost done. I had finished a map which I would have loved to show to Vasu because he understood patterns of ancient settlements better than I did. On it I had plotted the locations of the ancient Scythian settlements along the banks of streams criss-crossing the steppes between the River Dneiper in the west and the River Don in the east. Gelon was one of the biggest centres where the otherwise nomadic Scythians had decided to settle down. A complicated system of moats and walls was still visible in aerial photos although the fertile *chernozem* fields with their black topsoil rich in humus had been ploughed and planted for centuries. I used pairs of aerial photos to give me a three-dimensional view of the ancient kurgans we planned to dig. Unfortunately a large number seemed to have been disturbed, opened and robbed.

Three weeks after my arrival at the site Papa called to tell me that Vasu had been trying to contact me. He was surprised that I hadn't let him know about going to Poltava. I told Papa that Vasu should come round and be available when I called the following week. He sounded terrible on the phone, wheezing and coughing. But he was following my advice, going swimming and taking saunas, which meant he felt much better. I didn't even ask if he wanted to come to the dig. He already knew how much I wanted to see him.

Three days later he arrived, I met him at Poltava Station. I was delighted to see him; he looked and sounded much happier.

'I am blessed,' he wouldn't stop whispering, which I found embarrassing. He is in love with being in love, I often thought. I knew that I was his first love, the very first woman in his life. This both pleased and alarmed me.

He began to accompany me on my mapping traverses, helping me understand the design of the ancient settlement. He had come prepared, carrying his own copy of Herodotus' *Histories* pasted with stickers. I would often take him to the highest point in the area and spread my maps before him and he would pick the best sites for settlement, imagining he was one of the ancient architects. The words poured out of him and although his speech was slow and measured, the intensity with which he spoke amazed me. He would pull out his notebook and begin to draw, explaining to me how villages grew organically into cities. I was impressed by the delight he showed in being with me at the site.

'He is in love,' Tetya Shura would say to me and laugh. I was glad that she came to like him. He in turn appeared captivated by her warm husky voice and her melancholy ballads of Cossack horsemen, their lovely women and loyal horses.

One night he witnessed her in all her glory. The anger and

anguish in her voice must have surprised him as he watched the drama unfold in front of his eyes.

We were sitting around the campfire after dinner, discussing the funerary ceremonies of the Scythians so vividly described by Herodotus. Tetya Shura seemed very aggressive, as if she were trying to pick a fight. Maria Shulskaya said something trivial about the funerary ceremonies, to which Tetya Shura reacted sharply. Someone hastily changed the subject to Saqqara, the Egyptian city of the dead built around a stepped pyramid near the western bank of the Nile. That's when Gryzlov was able to show off. He knew more about gods and goddesses than anyone else on the team.

But Tetya Shura ruthlessly interrupted Gryzlov's exposition.

'My own favourite, you know, is Ma'at,' she said. 'She's the goddess of fairness, or what the Egyptians used to call "right order". Before committing a dead person to his grave, the Egyptians used to extract his heart, still warm and soft as a peeled mango. It was weighed in a balance against Ma'at. If the heart weighed more than the goddess, the person could look forward to a blissful life after death; otherwise he was condemned forever to live in horror and misery.'

She paused for a moment to take breath, gulped a mouthful of cognac and continued: 'Imagine for a moment that Stalin is dead and that our Soviet apparatchiks are ready to weigh his bloody heart. *What nonsense!* some of you may say – and I agree the proposition is quite absurd. There wasn't any heart in the body of that brute, just a black hole and nothing else.'

She took another drink. 'Yes, I hate him, even though I know that hate only demeans us. But can you imagine: my father, the idiot, never stopped reminding me that he went to

War for *Tovarish* Stalin, the same bloody Stalin who deported his wife, my poor mother, to die in the camps.'

She got off her chair, pushed it aside, asked Gryzlov for a cigarette, and walked off.

Soon it began to drizzle. The fire died. 'You'll catch cold, you fools,' we heard Tetya Shura yell from inside her tent. A prolonged bout of coughing followed.

'Go to bed,' she barked again, spat lumps of phlegm and swore.

The drizzle continued through the night. From inside our tent we could hear Tetya Shura pacing up and down, unable to sleep because of an asthma attack. I took her a hot water bottle but it didn't help. She asked Vasu if he would give her an injection. She had everything necessary: syringes, needles, rubber band and capsules. We tied the band round her arm and struggled to locate a vein by the dim light of our torch. Once the vein had been found it was easy to insert the needle. Within an hour, Tetya Shura had settled down to sleep.

But for a long time we couldn't. We lay awake listening to the rain.

'Why are you so quiet?' I asked Vasu.

'I'm sad for Tetya Shura,' he replied.

That's when I told him the whole of Tetya Shura's story so terribly punctuated with tragedies: famine, deportation, camps and executions.

It rained the next day and the day after that. The digs in some kurgans were flooded. A pump was brought from the *kolkhoz* and we began draining water from the site. The rain had ruined our season. We felt cheated.

If this was really where a large Scythian town had stood,

we should by now have found the remains of at least one, if not more, royal tombs. But we hadn't discovered anything remotely significant. Most kurgans had in fact been opened and robbed. Apart from a few minor trinkets, some coins and rings, nothing major, no gold nor silver, had been recovered. There were only a few ceramics, iron and bronze tools and weapons, mirrors, pots, vases and decorated bone jewellery, but not enough to establish beyond reasonable doubt that the site we were digging was indeed Gelon.

Fortunately, however, the rival team working at a site near the Don hadn't found anything either.

We decided to stop our fieldwork, wind up the camp and return next season.

On the way back to Moscow we met Aunty Olga at Kiev Station. She wanted us to break our journey and stay with her.

'The chestnuts are blooming,' she said. Vasu wasn't well, which Aunty Olga noticed. She made us stay the night. The next day she phoned a friend and got him a pocket inhaler.

'He looks fine now,' she whispered to me as she farewelled us the following day.

Tamrico's Apple

Vasu

It was three o' clock on a September morning, cold but not unpleasantly so.

I was sitting huddled round a tiny kitchen table celebrating the thirtieth birthday of Vladimir's girlfriend Katya. It was also a birthday party for Shurik, who had turned thirty-five on the same day.

I had met Shurik, a criminal lawyer, when he had come to see Vladimir in the hospital. He loved telling stories about the Moscow militia. Tales from *Slukhovaya Pravda* (The Pravda of Gossips) he used to call them.

His draftsman uncle had once worked with Konstantin Melnikov, the famous constructivist architect, and just a week earlier, Shurik had led me along the cobbled streets to Melnikov's cylindrical house. We even went inside to look at his large desk and examine some of his sketches of Gorky Park. A few streets away we found the block of apartments where, in a room on the third floor, Shurik had been born. On that walk he also showed me the building where his mother Vera had died in the summer of 1943, fighting fires started by Nazi bombs. After his mother's death four-year-old Shurik was sent to an orphanage in Tashkent.

His mother, a designer, had been a minor official in the Party at one of Moscow's textile factories. Her marriage to Isaac, a Polish Jew from Lvov, was brief, because Isaac was soon deported to a camp in Kazakhstan, where he died of cholera.

Shurik once showed me the manuscript of his book *The Private Life of Shurik Z*, in which he described his trip to Kazakhstan. The book had several photos of a lakeside resort and salt mines where his father had been forced to labour.

Shurik's wife Tamrico was an actress in the Moscow Youth Theatre. She came from Georgia and assured me that one day she would take me to her wonderful Tbilisi to drink wine and dance the *lezginka*. I liked her, and not only because she played guitar and sang beautiful Georgian songs. During this party she saw that I was tired and bored and told me to pick up my parka and leave. 'There is nothing as beautiful as Moscow in the early hours of the morning,' she told me. 'Go, you idiot, and don't worry about Katya. She won't be offended.' Then she took an apple from the table, kissed it and shoved it into my pocket. So here I was, a solitary flaneur, ready for the city to reveal itself to me. I was dead tired and wanted to sleep but a voice inside told me to keep walking.

It was still dark and the moon that would turn full later in the week moved along with me. Outside the Hotel Prague I saw a waiter sitting on the steps, smoking.

'Come and have a cigarette,' he invited. 'Talk to me.'

I ignored his invitation, turned right onto Gogol Boulevard, and stopped at the famous writer's statue. It stood with its back to one of the most beautiful boulevards in Moscow. On the granite plinth I spotted a dog trying to chew the plastic wrapper off a bouquet of flowers. On the other side an old woman slept under a filthy blanket.

The week before at this very spot I had witnessed a protest by four dissidents: three men and a young woman in a bright yellow sweater. They held a long red banner with white letters, the top line in Russian with an English translation underneath. The English words 'freedom' and 'travel' were misspelt.

A crowd of onlookers had gathered to the right of Gogol. Facing them stood three militiamen in uniforms and two men in caps and black leather jackets. Two vans were parked across the boulevard, with more militiamen inside. It was a silent protest and nothing much had happened. Then suddenly a man in the crowd pulled a camera out of his backpack and took some pictures. One of the leather-jackets rushed towards him and snatched the camera, opened it and ripped out the film. The three militiamen moved quickly towards the protestors to pull down the banner. Only the young woman resisted. A militiaman, who later revealed herself as a good-looking blonde, pulled hard at the banner and the woman in the yellow sweater slipped and fell. She scraped her nose, which bled, but she kept hold of the banner.

None of her friends moved to help her. The banner was ripped apart and lay on the ground between them. The militiawoman pulled it again and was finally able to grab it. But as she pulled it in she also ripped the sweater off the young woman who had nothing on underneath, not even a bra.

The crowd giggled at this spectacle and the militiawoman threw the sweater back at the protestor, who struggled to her feet and joined the other three.

All four stood silently for a while and then merely walked away. Amazingly, no one was arrested.

As I walked past Gogol, I tried to recall the name of the woman in the yellow sweater. 'Galya,' I told myself, 'yes, her name was Galya.' The older of the three men, I recalled, the one with a beard as thick as Marx's, had asked: 'Galya, are you OK?'

From the statue the boulevard sloped down, slowly curving then taking a sharp turn before culminating in the impressive arched pavilion of the Metro station. The eastern side, along which a stream used to run, is raised. The water was channelled into a huge pipe when Moscow was rebuilt after the fires started by Napoleon's army of occupation.

During the day the place would be crowded with many chess players, their boards spread across the tables in front of a small three-storey building standing humbly next to a palatial house with five Ionic columns. The small building housed the headquarters of the Russian Chess Federation.

As I reached the Metro station and stepped into the street to cross, I quickly retreated as two ambulances, followed by a militia-van and three Soviet ZiL limousines rushed past. They were no doubt carrying an important Party official to the special hospital near the Lenin Library.

I crossed the street as mist rose above the open-air swimming pool and a row of blinking neon lights. I walked down towards the bank of the river and noticed that two letters, the first and the last 'a', of the sign on the pharmacy had blown off, and the third 'm' was blinking on and off in a strange rhythmic fashion. 'I'll go and sit for a few minutes on the embankment, eat my apple and then walk along the bank,' I told myself.

I found a spot where the river divided into separate canals, the upper following the southern wall of the Kremlin. The stone bridge over the canals looked bare and ordinary compared with the light and delicate Krymsky Bridge in the distance.

I sat and rested but didn't eat the apple. I took it out, looked at it and put it back in my pocket, remembering the red stain of Tamrico's lips. I felt its warm roundness. As a child I used to carry a marble in my pocket. I would take it everywhere, even sleep with it. Jijee-ma used to laugh at me but she always made sure that the marble was with me.

I touched the apple again. It seemed to be helping keep me awake. Because it was there, so red and so real, I knew that the city divided by the waters of the meandering river wasn't an apparition, that I wasn't dreaming, that my walk was real.

I got up and walked towards the giant Ferris wheel hanging over the green treetops of Gorky Park. Suddenly I heard a splash and in the disturbed water the boats near the bank bobbed up and down in the river. After a brief moment I saw a head and arms illuminated by a bright searchlight. The person in the water was swimming towards the far bank. 'Masha!' I heard someone scream from the boat, '*Ne duri*' (Don't be stupid).

But Masha didn't stop, didn't turn back. Soon she reached the other bank, dragged herself out, lay flat on the ground for a few minutes, then got up and staggered out of sight.

I walked down some stone steps with the words '*Masha,*

ne duri' still sounding in my ears. At the railway I decided to cross the Metro Bridge, and as I approached I heard a goods train rattle across in the opposite direction.

I stood for a few minutes in the glimmer of early morning, watching the giraffe-like towers standing over the big bowl of Luzhniki Stadium. Soon the trucks arrived to sweep and wash the streets. On the opposite bank, I noticed the hill rising and falling like an enormous python. A ridge thickly lined with trees followed the river's curve and moved beyond it. It was slashed with steep narrow gullies full of rocks brought down by frequent landslides. Just a few weeks ago the slope had been brilliant with autumn colours. They had faded now. Only tinges of yellow and orange remained, pierced and poked by the green spikes of pines.

I suddenly felt hungry, pulled out the apple and took a bite. I finished it very quickly and chucked the core into the river. That's when I spotted the trampoline on the opposite slope, hidden under the arched span of the Metro Bridge. A few hours ago, as I began my walk, it had surely been the giant slalom trampoline that had flashed through my mind.

When I reached the trampoline I wondered whether I should climb up or just go back to the Metro. I was tired and didn't want to climb up the slippery steps. However, I knew that once I reached the platform I would be able to see the most wonderful panoramic view of the city.

The climb was hard and I was overcome by the dank, pungent smell of decaying leaves. I reached the lift tower used by skiers going up to the platform. But the lift was closed and the door to the stairs seemed to be locked. I pushed at it and to my great surprise it opened.

At the top of the platform there was a strong wind and it took me a few moments to stand up against it. I looked out in the direction of the Metro Bridge and saw the blue coaches of the trains rush through the station. The bridge trembled and I felt the platform beneath my feet shudder, as if disturbed by a mild tremor.

'Soon the sun will rise,' I thought, knowing that I would see the city as I had never seen it before. But then it started to drizzle and the sun hid behind the early morning clouds. Rain began to fall in thin sheets. It fell into the river, at first gently then in big gushes and splashes, as if someone had put water into a jar and shaken it.

A ferry appeared, blowing its horn and producing clouds of stinking smoke. Its engine's heavy *chug chug chug* and its delayed echo were shattered by the rough crowing of ravens which suddenly took off, circled the platform a few times and disappeared.

I waited for the rain to stop. Soon the sunlight broke in and the city opened out before me. But I felt cheated, realising that even this wide view showed just a slice of the vast city. Slowly I began to trace the route of my walk. From where I stood I couldn't see the Arbat and Gogol Boulevard but I could guess their position from the high-rise buildings lining Kalininsky Prospect. I saw the embankment and as I looked around I spotted the place where the girl had jumped into the river. I saw the streets curve and bend and intersect with others, all converging towards a central point. Suddenly the ring-like shape of the city I had often seen on maps revealed itself.

I lingered on the platform for a while. As soon as I came

down I felt terribly tired. All I wanted now was to reach my room on the fourteenth floor of the University building. It wasn't far, just half an hour's walk away.

Back in my room I quickly fell asleep and slept soundly until the early hours of the following morning. Then I got up to write a letter to Anna, even though I knew I would see her during the day. I told her about the shapes of old cities and how they grew like complex living organisms. I told her about *Vastushastra*, the ancient Hindu practice of architecture and town planning, and the relation between astrology, architecture and the human body, the body of Adipurusha, the first man-as-god or god-as-man.

'Although I see you every day,' I wrote, 'I still miss you all the time.' Suddenly I began to write about Shurik. I told her that in spite of all his jokes and funny stories he seemed to me to be deeply sad; that I had gleaned the shades of a similar sadness in Vladimir and in many others I had met during my four years in Moscow.

The Interview

Anna

I was surprised to find a rather long letter from Vasu. He hadn't told me anything about it when I had met him at the library. In the letter he described his early morning walk after Katya's birthday party. I liked the letter, although his habit of theorising about this or that seemed somewhat tedious. But I was intrigued by the sadness he had seen in the eyes of his Russian friends in Moscow. He called Shurik mysterious, his melancholy romantic and his story tragic. 'Wait until I tell him Papa's story,' I thought. 'It isn't so much sadness which permeates our hearts, but the fear that we are doomed.'

The following day I phoned Vasu to tell him that Papa wanted to meet him, and that he had also summoned Aunty Olga from Kiev.

'Is this the interview then?' he asked.

'It certainly is,' I said but assured him that he shouldn't worry. Papa would be delighted to see him and would readily bestow his approval and blessings.

'But what about Aunty Olga?'

'We'll soon find out,' I said, laughing. Vasu, unusually for him, arrived late. I heard him walk up to the door and ring. I didn't respond and let him ring again, then opened the door and helped him take off his *pal'to* and *schapka* and handed him a pair of slippers from the rack. 'It's quite windy outside,' he began nervously. I chose to ignore this and called Papa to come and meet him, at the same time handing Vasu a hairbrush. He noticed signs of irritation on my face and recoiled. I sighed. This would irritate Aunty Olga even more.

I had advised him on the phone to come suitably dressed, in a nice jacket with matching tie, but he had decided to please himself and although the woollen jumper made him look fresh and young I still felt let down.

After the introductions I ushered him into the library. He refused to sit on the sofa and moved to a chair next to Papa.

Papa reached for his tobacco pouch and began to roll a cigarette. He could hardly have missed the expression on the face of Aunty Olga, who hated his smoking.

We chatted. Papa said that our block, like many similar multi-storey apartments, had been constructed as a housing co-operative for scientists.

'It isn't big but it suits us perfectly,' he added. Aunty Olga complained how cold winds whistled between the towers and Papa explained that this was because of poor siting. If the blocks had been built a few hundred metres closer to the nearby pine forest, this would have provided a shield from the wind.

Vasu was meanwhile studying our packed bookshelves.

'Anna calls this mess disorderly order,' Papa said, looking slyly in my direction.

'Needs a massive cull,' Aunty Olga snapped.

'Perhaps after I retire,' said Papa, and both Aunty Olga and I laughed, because we knew this would never happen.

Vasu laughed as well. As yet he hadn't spoken a single word. To stir him up a little I reminded him of the bag he had brought with him, which was still sitting near the door. When he went to fetch it I followed him and whispered that he should cast off the dumbness he found so comfortable. But he just smiled and shrugged.

Back in the library he opened the bag and took out his two presents: an LP for Papa and a scarf for Aunty Olga.

He actually handed the woollen scarf to me. I pushed it away and pointed him in Aunty Olga's direction. Papa seemed both pleased and humbled with the LP. He excused himself, went off and returned with the *radiola* from my room. He carefully removed the record from its sleeve, placed it on the turntable and gently lowered the needle. As it began to play he adjusted the bass and treble and fiddled with the volume. 'This is such a rare recording,' Papa said. It was the celebrated 1956 Verve release of *Ella and Louis*, the two jazz greats, in its original jacket. 'You didn't have to bring me anything, you know.' But he was obviously pleased.

'Where did you find it?' I asked Vasu.

The smile on his face showed his own pleasure. It was only later that he told me how he had unearthed the record. Vladimir had given him a name and a phone number, and a meeting had taken place inside the Mayakovsky Metro station. A young hippie had handed him a bag and taken away two cartons of Marlboro cigarettes.

Soon Aunty Olga ordered us to move to the dining table. As

usual, she and not Papa took the seat at the head of the table. Papa and I sat on her right and Vasu sat facing us. Before she took her seat Aunty Olga turned the music down low and in the silence that followed I heard the muted humming of our old fridge. Outside the window the wind howled, occasionally penetrating the cracks. It had stopped snowing.

It was only when we started eating that I noticed Aunty Olga was wearing Vasu's violet woollen scarf.

'Isn't it pretty?' I said.

'And warm. Pure Cashmere, I think,' she said. She looked at Vasu and actually smiled.

The dinner was simple: borscht with onion, cabbage, potato, carrot and a small dollop of sour cream; chicken with walnuts and garlic; a potato and zucchini *zapekanka* with mushroom sauce (especially for Vasu); and for dessert, Aunty Olga's special, a fabulous cheesecake. Papa opened two bottles of Romanian wine, a present from a colleague who had recently returned from Bucharest.

During the dinner Aunty Olga asked Vasu about his family in India and he told us how he had been brought up by his older sister, his Jijee-ma, after his mother had died giving birth to him. Both Papa and Aunty Olga seemed shocked, and to get over this Aunty Olga told him about Tonya, my mother, who had also died before I knew her.

I sensed that at this moment Vasu would want to look at my face. But I turned away and suddenly the fluorescent light in the library exploded and we were plunged into darkness. I asked Vasu to help me carry in the lamp from my room.

Together we set it up next to the table and resumed eating as if nothing had happened.

'Why did you come to Moscow?' Papa asked Vasu.

'Because of Uncle Triple K,' he replied. 'He told me that Moscow would change my life forever. Although he teaches French literature and philosophy he also speaks good Russian.'

'Has it changed you?' Papa asked.

'I suppose so,' Vasu said. 'Before I came here someone gave me *Doctor Zhivago*. After I read it I couldn't stop thinking about Russia.'

We watched his face as he spoke. His Russian was good and his slight accent made the words – and him – even more attractive.

Aunty Olga sat back in her chair, impressed.

'What I liked most was the description of the changing seasons,' Vasu continued. 'In India they tend to come and go unnoticed. Here the change is so swift and intense.'

'But I love sun and heat,' I said, to tease him. 'Winter is depressing.'

'What a liar,' Aunty Olga interjected. 'You should read Prishvin and Paustovsky,' she said to Vasu in her typical teacher's voice.

But he turned to Papa and asked about the *taiga*, the Siberian forest. 'Yes, the *taiga* is breathtakingly beautiful, but treacherous,' Papa said. It was a subject dear to his heart. Then he began the tale Aunty Olga and I had heard many times before, about the time he had spent working in the *taiga* supervising exploration for gold, diamonds and gas. 'A young couple used to work for me,' he said. 'Their job was to find the diamonds trapped in ancient volcanoes. They were in love and did everything together. The girl told me they wanted to save money to get married and their youthful exuberance cheered everyone up. But one day out among the trees a hungry bear attacked and killed them. It was a tragedy! I was asked to identify the bodies and couldn't stop cursing myself. I shouldn't have let them go out so far on their own. I felt terribly guilty; I still do. They were so young. Look at me, old and useless and unscathed. But I shouldn't complain. It's good to be alive, even if I do feel such guilt and shame.'

He paused for a moment, took off his glasses, wiped them with his napkin and said: 'I've got some photos of them somewhere.' He got up and went into his room. We all noticed the slight limp in his walk.

'*Voina* (war),' Aunty Olga sighed. 'I'll bring you some fresh coffee,' she said and disappeared into the kitchen.

Papa returned with a box of colour slides. He set up his little projector on the table and arranged a white screen against the wall near the piano. Then he turned off the lights, ignoring Aunty Olga's 'It's getting late, Leynya.'

As he adjusted the focus on the first slide, he cleared his throat and started his story. Papa talked and talked and when he finally finished showing us slide after slide of his life on the sweeping *taiga* it was too late for Vasu to get back to his room in the hostel.

Midway through the show, Aunty Olga had left the room. She came back to say that she had made Vasu a bed in her room. Vasu started to object, but I told him to stop. Arguing with Aunty Olga would get him nowhere. 'She'll sleep in my room, on the camp bed,' I whispered. 'You should be pleased. She likes you.'

Vasu

Anna seemed to think that Aunty Olga liked me. I'm not sure. Actually she terrified me, especially that look which would come into her eyes.

'You're so much like Papa, her dear Leynya,' Anna would often remind me. 'Slow and steady, unsure but reliable.'

That night I couldn't sleep. Nor could Leonid Mikhailovich, Anna's father. I heard him playing *Ella and Louis* softly in the library, over and over again. He was recording some of the songs for a friend, he would explain later.

I lay listening to Aunty Olga and Anna talking quietly in the next room. Their whispers reminded me of water trickling from melting snow.

I felt out of place. 'You shouldn't still be here,' a voice inside me insisted.

Aunty Olga's room was hot and stuffy. I got up, opened the window and stood looking out. The wind was blowing strongly and in the courtyard a red ribbon swirled and whirled across uneven mounds of snow. I heard a glassy rattle and saw an empty vodka bottle roll and slide along a bench. I waited for it to fall off, but it continually rolled to the edge and then back. I waited and waited until I was so cold I shut the window and returned to the warm bed.

I stared at the roof and tried to focus on the treacherous beauty of the *taiga*, a thought that had started to form slowly in my mind. But my eyes led me to a corner of the ceiling where a small piece of wallpaper had peeled off. The thought disappeared. On the bookshelf a small icon of *Bogomateri* (Our Lady) glowed, its eyes reminding me of Jijee-ma.

Suddenly the door opened and Anna walked in. She took off her nightshirt, flung it on a chair and slipped into bed with me.

'I just want to lie beside you,' she whispered. 'We can't make love, not with Aunty Olga sleeping on the other side of that thin wall.'

She turned on her side and pulled me close so that her head rested on my left arm. My right stretched across her body.

'What are you thinking?' she asked.

'About silk,' I replied. 'And water.'

'Silk and water,' she whispered, 'milk and honey, and the sweet smell of freshly-baked bread.' She looked at me. 'Tell me about your mother who died giving birth to you.'

I told her about my mother in her sky-blue *dupatta*. I told her that my sister had a sky-blue wrap scattered with silver stars and that when she came to put me to bed she would cover me with the wrap and assure me that it would entice the starry sky to send me sweet dreams.

'Why would the sky be so benevolent?' Anna asked.

My sister and I had a favourite star, I told her, neither the brightest nor the biggest, but the one which shone with a steady light. That star, Jijee-ma told me, was where Amma, our mother, had gone to live. From there she watched over us.

'Is that why you call me "my sky-blue *dupatta*"?' Anna asked, and laughed.

'What about *your* mother?' I asked. 'Tonya: that's a beautiful name.'

'Her full name was Antonina,' she said. 'And she was even more beautiful than her name – not an ugly duckling like me.'

Then she kissed my hand and went to sleep.

In the morning she wasn't in my bed. I looked around the

room and found her nightshirt on the floor.

Strange Fruit

Anna

When I saw Papa and Vasu together that night, I was surprised how similar they were.

'Of course,' said Aunty Olga. 'It isn't easy to love them,' she added.

Vasu told me how much he liked our apartment. 'Because it overwhelms me with silence,' he explained. He's right. I'm glad he doesn't find the silence oppressive. Sergei hated it. 'You live inside a grave,' he used to complain.

We don't have a television and the radio is invariably turned off. When it's on, it plays only music. The apartment is our refuge from the outside world. We don't let it inside but leave it at the door with our coats and parkas. We aren't unusual. There are many like us who have decided to live a double life, one for the outside world and another only for us.

We love music. It lives in every nook and cranny of our

home. We cherish our trusted Estonia piano which fits snugly into the library. It is old, scratched and stained but, like Papa and Aunty Olga, has survived the War and all the other upheavals.

I know my mother used to play it. 'She played badly,' Aunty Olga often says, 'but had a decent voice.' She used to sing to Papa's piano accompaniment. Now he does the same for me on my cello. Sometimes I improvise, following his jazz tunes. We have never talked seriously about his love for jazz.

But Vasu is very curious about Papa's jazz. His insistence to know everything about us irritates me. Like Papa, he wants to get to the bottom of everything.

The other night I saw them talking in the library. It was hot and humid and I couldn't sleep, so I had gone to the kitchen to have a drink. As I returned with a bottle of water I saw Papa at the piano and Vasu sitting on the floor leaning against the wall. They saw me and grinned, the guilty smile of naughty kids.

'*Duschno* (It's stuffy),' Papa said and asked me for some water. He took a swig from the bottle and invited me to join them. Reluctantly I obliged.

'Vasu thinks it unusual for a Russian like me to enjoy jazz,' began Papa.

'But you aren't a typical Russian, are you?' I said, surprised at the irritation in my voice.

'I fell in love with jazz in America,' he continued, ignoring my prickly interjection. 'I was twenty-five then and had spent a year at the famous School of Mines where Stalin sent me to study. He hoped I would learn the secrets of the greedy capitalists. On the way back home I stopped in Kansas City for three days and it was there I heard Count Basie's orchestra at the Reno Club. What a place it was! A dingy sort of building with a whorehouse on the second floor. You bought your hamburger or hot dog, a glass of local or imported whisky, and watched the band in a room packed with people, noisy and musty with sweat and smoke. You had to pay extra for a seat close to the band. Listening to Count Basie's piano made me jumpy. I wanted to get up onto the stage and play myself. Of course I didn't.

'I still remember the saxophonist Lester Young and his beautiful sax. There's nothing as fine as a tenor sax. I don't know why people like trumpeters so much. Maybe because most of them sing as well? I can't imagine anything more exciting than Lester Young pouring his soul into the brassy body of his sax. I'll give up the piano, I used to tell myself, but Count Basie's whispering tones reassured me. He was short and round and bent close over the keyboard. He didn't beat it like a percussion instrument, trying to rip it apart or get inside it. Instead he seemed to glide across the surface, selecting a note here and there and letting it speak. People go crazy about his *One O' Clock Jump* but I loved his *How Long How Long Blues*: nothing but piano, guitar, bass and drums. Pure rhythm and mood.'

He paused briefly. 'I did try once or twice to play the sax – but soon found that it wouldn't work for me. I don't have the courage to stand up in front of an audience and play. The piano gives you space to hide. 'I met a young Negro girl in a club in Kansas City. Tall, thin with a smile as bright as the full moon, and when she spoke or hummed, her voice made your whole body ripple. Josephine Taylor was her name. "Josie, you can call me, Josie Taylor," she said after our first dance. Her grandfather was a sailor from Marseilles. She wanted to go to France and see it for herself, the best port-city in the world, so her mother had told her.

'She didn't believe me when I said that I came from Moscow. "Bolshevik?" she asked. "Not really," I replied. "Go to Chicago," she told me—and took me there. I didn't see many rich and greedy Americans in the cities. Most of them looked poor and unhappy. There were beggars, whores, tramps, burglars, thieves, bootleggers and, most pitiful of the lot, the homeless. The fear of suddenly becoming poor ruled the streets. The Great American Dream seemed built on this fear. When I returned to Moscow, our Union of the Soviets didn't look so bad in comparison, even though a more deadly form of fear had taken root in our country.

'While I was still in America I asked Josie to come with me to New York, and she agreed. We heard Jimmy Lunceford's band at the Cotton Club, but my heart had been captured by Basie's piano and everything else seemed just an imitation. Even Louis Armstrong's band at Connie's Inn didn't make a strong impression, although over time I have come to love his music.

'We bribed the doorman to let Josie in, on condition that she would keep out of sight, but soon people at the other tables noticed her and we were told in no uncertain terms to leave. But not before we'd heard the great *Gut Bucket Blues*.'

He took a sip of water. 'Blues – now there's an interesting English word for you. There's nothing like it in Russian. The critics say that a vocalist makes music with his or her head, throat and heart. The head determines the musicality of the sound, the throat works as an instrument, and from the heart come the emotions. Louis Armstrong got the balance right every time he sang.'

'What happened to Josie, Papa?' I asked, handing him a cup of coffee that Vasu had been making in the kitchen. After Vasu resumed his seat on the floor, Papa finally said, slowly and hesitantly, that he didn't know. When I asked if he had ever written to her, he ignored me, got up and removed a book from the shelf. He pulled out an old postcard from Josie showing the Brooklyn Bridge. Vasu tried to read it but found the writing illegible. Most of the words were either smudged or crossed out with thick red ink.

He would later find out that Josie had written several letters to him. He saw them for the first time in the Lubyanka interrogation room. They were brief and bare and yet they and his love for jazz would tip the balance against him. He was banished to Siberia without any hope of returning.

But as he sailed from New York in the winter of 1935 his heart, as he told us that night, had been full of hope. He had truly believed that he was one of the chosen ones, and that being sent to America to study meant that he was special. Now it was his duty to return to help his people realise their cherished dream of building a free, just and classless society.

During that fortnight on the ship he planned the outlines of three books: two of them scientific and the third about jazz. He had finished the two scientific books within a few years of his return and received several awards for them, only missing out on the Stalin Prize because he wasn't a member of the Party. The book on jazz, however, remained unfinished, although he continued to collect stacks and stacks of useful material.

That evening he showed Vasu and me some of the rare items in his collection of drawings, cartoons, posters and photos. There was a picture of Malyi Kislovsky Lane, where in October 1922 Valentin Parnakh gave the first jazz concert in Russia. The picture was pinned to a cartoon sketch of Parnakh with Meyerhold, sitting at a table in Meyerhold's drama theatre. There was a 1927 coloured picture of Sidney Bechet outside the Metropol Hotel, when the famous soprano saxophonist had performed in Moscow with Tony Ladnier's band. He showed us several photos of Utyosov, the most interesting of which was a picture of the State Jazz Band of the Russian Federation performing at Sverdlov Square on 9 May 1945. Utyosov is facing the band and behind his back, just at the level of his right-hand coat-pocket, the nose and the left eye of a face is visible, the right eye hidden behind the army cap of a man standing in front of him. 'That's me,' Papa told us, 'and Tonya was to my left, just behind Utyosov.'

I wanted to know from Papa if Aunty Olga was right: that it was really because of Josie Taylor's letters that he had been arrested and exiled. Papa didn't give a straight answer.

'The times were bad,' was all he would say, 'so frightfully bad that it was impossible to judge the difference between right and wrong. The War had been won and, for a year or so, most of us hoped that like a good father, Stalin would forgive our mistakes, take note of our courage and sacrifices and reward us. But we were wrong. He didn't have a morsel of love or compassion for us. He was cursed and so were we. Ridiculous as it may sound now, many of us believed that we deserved our punishment, for losing faith in him. We lived in fear and had no idea how to avoid the terror he had unleashed.

He told us what to do and we obeyed. We even spied for him and turned ourselves into informants, fabricating lies. We thronged the show trials, gave evidence and denounced our own kith and kin. Even educated people like me, who once cherished our basic common humanity, suddenly discovered the devil within and made a pact with him. For some it was the lure of the dream; for others it was just to make life a little more bearable. And then there were those who only wanted to avoid trouble.'

I had never seen him look so sad.

In the second week of September 1949, two men and a young woman had entered Papa's office at the Institute and taken him away. It would have been pointless to resist. His office was sealed and his secretary ordered to go home and keep quiet. She didn't, and paid heavily for her indiscretion. Tonya was away on a trip with her agitprop group and it was Aunty Olga who had to endure the raid. The apartment was sealed and she had to seek refuge with a friend.

By the time Tonya returned and was able to reach people with power and influence, it was already too late. Papa had been forced into signing a 'confession'.

They didn't torture him. But for two long nights they kept him awake in a cell under the strongest of lights. Then he was subjected to a lengthy interrogation led by two women. The younger seemed familiar. She had dark bobbed hair, a kind round face and wore attractive glasses.

Once the confession had been signed, she revealed that she had attended Papa's university classes and that he was her favourite teacher. She had written the 'confession' herself. It did not contain anything which Papa could have called a lie.

The inferences were sound and well-substantiated. He could have mounted a credible challenge against them, but then of course he would have had to ask friends and colleagues to support him, endangering them. That was out of the question. He wasn't going to put his friends' lives at risk.

The 'confession' was detailed. It was true that he, Leonid Mikhailovich Eisner, was a Russian of German descent; that he belonged to a respectable and well-to-do family of Volga Germans; that although he was an active member of the Komsomol he had never tried to join the Party; that he had spent a year in America and kept in touch through letters with a Negro woman called Josie Taylor, the granddaughter of a French sailor known to have been an active member of the Paris Commune; that he loved jazz and had produced a large amount of questionable material for a book about this decadent form of American music; that the proposed book contained a full account of the life of Valentin Parnakh, who had been sent to the camps for reformation and re-education; that Papa had contributed short articles and reviews to a little magazine about jazz; that he sympathised with Meyerhold, whose theatre and methods were denounced by the Party as formalist; that as chairman of the evaluation committee of the Ministry of Geology and Mining he had ruled against commissioning two tungsten mines in the Caucasus, a gold mine in Uzbekistan, one chromite and two lead and zinc prospects in the Urals, and that some of these were later found to be economically viable; that he had made serious and deliberate errors in judging the importance of exploring coal, oil and gas deposits in Siberia; that he was authoritarian in his dealings with his colleagues and often overlooked their recommendations; that the Party Committee at the Institute had given him several warnings about his behaviour; that he harboured scant respect for rules deemed essential for the proper functioning of a socialist collective; that because of his mistakes, the War effort against the Nazis suffered setbacks; that he and his wife had fraternised with foreigners who came to study at the Party School; and that he had invited them to parties at his home and been involved in the illegal exchange of records, tapes, books and other similarly objectionable material.

A week after the 'confession', Papa was allowed to meet Tonya in the presence of the second female interrogator. They sat on opposite sides of a small wooden table, one leg of which was shorter than the other three, so that each time one of them put an arm on its surface, it wobbled. For a long time he could only gaze at her face and, when the interrogator wasn't watching, touch her hand. Tonya whispered: 'Leynya, *Dorogoi Leynya* (Dear Leynya), *bednyi Moi Leynya* (My poor Leynya)' and kissed his hand. '*Ne plach, ne nado* (Don't cry; there's no need),' Papa replied. He could hardly bear to look at her.

Neither of them really knew what to say or do. Papa was overwhelmed by a desire to rise and reach out for Tonya and hug her. He wanted to hold her pale face in his hands and kiss her. He wanted to touch her and beg her to take care of herself and the baby. He wanted to do something he had never done before: put his head against her shoulder and sob. He wanted to turn into a four-year-old boy and run to her and hide his face in her lap, blocking out the rest of the world.

The meeting lasted fifteen minutes. Then the interrogator put away her book of Mayakovsky's poems and told them that their time was up. Tonya rose and took a few steps towards the door, then turned back, went right up to Papa and kissed him. The interrogator started towards them but she was too late. Tonya gave her a single look then ran out of the room.

Papa was overcome by a wave of nausea and felt for the chair. As he sat he saw that Tonya had dropped her mauve scarf. He tried to pick it up, but hit his forehead on the sharp metal edge of the table. As he held the scarf he felt the blood trickle from a cut above his right eyebrow. He used the scarf to stem it, but it kept flowing. The next thing he remembered was opening his eyes in some kind of clinic. His wound had been stitched up by a nervous male nurse who did a bad job for which he later apologised.

The stitches were removed the day before Papa was taken away. With time it healed, but the scar from the botched job remained forever.

Nothing else remained of the fifteen minutes he had shared with Tonya in the meeting room. The only world they shared now was in their dreams. Only in their imagination could they talk, hold hands or kiss one another; only in dreams did they tease, laugh and shout; only in dreams did they allow themselves to hope against every hope. In their everyday worlds there was neither hope nor the will to hope.

'I wasn't sent to a camp,' Papa said. 'Tonya and that ex-student of mine must have been able to pull strings. I never found what price they paid for extracting this concession. The River Lena marked the boundaries of my freedom and I was told not to go beyond the western bank. All towns and cities with more than a thousand people in them were out of bounds. There was a small village on the eastern bank, twenty or so kilometres downstream, called Tatyur. I spent most of my five-and-a-half years of exile there. 'It took me close to a year to get used to the utter loneliness of the long Siberian winters, but once the freezing cold became familiar, I found a way to endure the long dark nights and short sunless days. I had heard that everything froze in winter but I didn't know that little creeks, like the one beside my wooden cabin, and the tiny lakes that pock-marked the low-lying wetlands froze completely.

'A seven-year-old girl in the primary school where I was made to teach science and geography once showed me a slab of ice that her father had dug out of a lake. Two young taimens, similar to salmon, were trapped inside, like insects in amber. She was a curious little girl and wanted to know how amber was made. So I told her that when drops of resin released by conifers are buried with sand they turn into amber.

'The winters were mostly quiet and windless and the sky empty, without even a crumb of a cloud, and the stars were so enormous and seemed so close that I was scared they would fall and explode. I found the sounds alien at first, uncanny, intimidating, but slowly I got used to them as well. Trees twisted and thrashed and often split; the ice cracked during the day and froze again in the evenings; the wind whistled and wheezed through the cracks in our huts and rolled over the roofs or swished through the grainy snow. Cows munched, horses sniffed and snorted and dogs barked; the gate next door creaked and clanked; and throughout the night the wood in the stove hissed and spluttered.

'I lived through my first winter in complete silence, trying to make sense of finding myself banished to that strange, harsh land. An old man, Zakhar Dudkin, who lived on his own in the shack nearby, seemed older than anyone I had ever met. I would visit Ded (Grandpa) Zakhar, set up the samovar and boil water for the sweet tea we would drink together. Occasionally we unearthed a bottle of foul-smelling vodka but he preferred a good cigarette. One winter I was sent a parcel of books which also contained a packet of Cuban tobacco. Zakhar was in seventh heaven. "What should we do?" he asked. "Should we smoke the whole packet tonight or little by little, to spread the pleasure over a few more days?" We decided to go slow and let the tobacco last for as long as we could. Then maybe by some miracle another parcel would arrive.

'It didn't take Ded Zakhar long to discover that I wasn't much of a talker and that he would have to keep our conversations going. Most of the time he mumbled and nibbled at words, chewing and spitting them out with no apparent order. But once I got used to this I began to make sense of his stories, often the same ones told over and over with merely a few variations.

'Once a week his daughter Maria would come to see him, to check that there was food in the kitchen and wood in the yard for the stove. She worked in the dairy of the *kolkhoz*, where she and two other dairymaids were often forced to milk hundreds of cows a day. She was short, broad and incredibly strong, but the best thing about her was her laugh, loud and infectious, that remained to cheer us up for hours after she had left. She brought a few things for me and news of the outside world. She once saw me struggling with my washing and pushed me aside. "It doesn't suit you, dear professor", she said. "You write your books and leave such things to me."

Papa smiled, perhaps remembering her infectious laughter. 'Maria didn't want me to write a book on jazz. She loved her beautiful River Lena and asked me to write about that instead. I didn't tell her that writing about jazz was just a pretence to hide my longing for Tonya and our little girl who must by then have been walking and talking.'

'How did you know that the baby was a girl, Papa?' I asked him.

'I didn't. I just imagined it. No, that's not true. I *wished* our baby to be a girl.'

Then he went on: 'I was amazed that in that cabin, without all the research material I had collected, my imagination soared. I was free. It may sound strange but I was rescued by the capricious nature of our memory. To my surprise it erased many unnecessary details – the noisy background, as we say in geophysics – leaving with me the essence of songs, people and places. "Why do I remember this and not something else?" I would ask myself, and that's how I came to write *The Short Story of a Song*.'

The song was Billie Holiday's *Strange Fruit*. That night in America when Josie and Papa had been forced to leave Connie's Inn, Josie had taken him to a nightclub in the Bronx. It was there that they listened to Billie Holiday. At first he didn't know what to make of her, but gradually that distinctive smoky voice possessed him and when, after twelve days at sea, he landed in Leningrad, he discovered that her voice followed him everywhere. It leaked into his thoughts and spread into the crevices of his memory. Often it was so strong that he would drop whatever he was doing to listen.

In 1945 at the end of the War, a few months after the

Victory Day parade in Red Square, his friend Kolya Shturmov had come to see him and brought a record of Billie Holiday's songs. *Strange Fruit* was one of them. Kolya, an engineer in the army, had through luck, skill and good judgement survived the War and made his way to Berlin, where he had met a pilot from Liverpool who had played in a jazz band. The record came from him.

'I played the song many times so that I could fully understand the words,' Papa told us. 'I could pick out the tune on my piano but it took me a couple of months to translate the words into Russian. I tried to sing it in my own language, but it didn't work. Perhaps it can't. Perhaps it's the voice that makes it what it is. Billie Holiday is so simple: no shouts, no screams, not a hint of histrionics, and yet she shows us grief so raw, so bleak and so natural, that our hearts shrivel.

'Then I read a piece in a jazz magazine and came to understand the song's secret. Billie Holiday sings the song on a strangely unresolved note, the critic wrote, moving back and forth like the dead black men swinging on the poplar trees waiting for the crows to come and pluck the fruit.

'When I started to write about *Strange Fruit*, it wasn't only the lynched Negroes who were preoccupying me. News had begun to arrive of mass executions in the camps. The prisoners were trying to break out. Some even managed to escape, but the poor souls were inevitably found. The air force planes tracked them down and shot and bombed them like wild animals. Many of those who remained were executed and their corpses thrown outside.

'Ded Zakhar told me that for weeks peasants in the *kolkhozes* near the camps carried dead bodies in their carts. It was left to those poor terrorised peasants to bury them with some dignity.'

Papa paused, then his face lightened. 'The *taiga* summers are short but breathtaking. The days are long and warm and stars appear in cloudless skies for an hour or two, then disappear. The world comes to life in a flash, as if rushing to realise what is expected of it: flowers, fruit, everything flourishes. It doesn't matter that autumn is just a few weeks away. Summer even transforms the way people in the *taiga* speak. No one mumbles any more, or whispers. Words come out full, loud and resonant, wanting to be heard.

'One summer I took the boat from Yakutsk and sailed to the sprawling delta at the icy mouth of the Arctic Sea. To help a geophysical survey, was my excuse. Luckily no one bothered to check. The following summer I got the opportunity to make a short trip in search of where Maria's wonderful Lena begins its journey. A few kilometres north of Lake Baikal, hidden in the ranges, is a small lake, perfectly round. It's about sixteen hundred metres above sea level. There the Lena appears through a narrow crevice, a stream less than a metre wide and only a metre or so deep. I walked downstream for ten kilometres as it widened to five or six metres and flowed fast and noisily like a little girl who has just learnt to run, feet thumping on the ground – much like little Anna, I thought, a bit wobbly, unsure where and how to stop.

'I remember the trip to the delta that summer not simply because it was so incredibly beautiful, but also because on my return I found a small parcel waiting for me at the cabin. It didn't have a return address and I didn't recognise the writing. It contained a white bag tied with red ribbon, wrapped in three layers of brown paper. In the bag were a pair each of socks and gloves, which I instantly recognised, plus a sheet of folded paper ripped from a school notebook. I unfolded the sheet and a photo fell out.'

Papa got up from his chair and walked slowly out of the room, his lit cigarette in his hand. We heard him in his room, coughing then swearing.

'He must have bumped against the bed,' I whispered to Vasu. 'He often does that.'

Papa reappeared with a tiny black-and-white photo which he handed to me. In it, two women sat on a bench and, standing against its curved back, stood a little girl with a ponytail. She leant against the younger woman, her right hand clutching the collar of her coat. The other woman's hand touched the girl's shoulder. Only the girl smiled. 'I've seen this photo,' I suddenly remembered, went into my room and brought an album, opened it and pulled out a picture. The three of us looked at the two photos and discovered that they were slightly different: the same three figures but in different positions. The two women had swapped places in the second photo, and the little girl with the ponytail wasn't sitting but standing on the bench. The girl with the ponytail was of course me, and the woman next to Aunty Olga was Tonya. And there was one more difference between the two photos. In Papa's photo, the bench near the right leg of the little girl was stained.

'I used to carry it everywhere in my pocket,' he said. 'Once when I was making my way across a rope bridge, I slipped and fell. Something sharp, a rock or a twig, must have pierced my skin. I noticed the blood only when I returned home that night.'

10 July 1952, the back of the photo read.

'You must just have celebrated your second birthday,' he said. Then he went on with the story. 'I received three more parcels in the next two years. Later Aunty Olga explained to me the complicated route they travelled before reaching me. It took Tonya and Olga several years to find this safe way of sending the parcels. First they mailed them to Leningrad. A contact there repacked them and posted them to an address in Sverdlovsk, from where they were dispatched to Irkutsk to begin their short trip to me.

'The day I received the parcel with the photo I planted a young birch in the front garden, not far from the wooden gate. Maria and Ded Zakhar warned me that it wouldn't survive, but promised to help me look after it anyway. They were wrong. It began to grow, hesitantly at first. Once it rooted, it burst into leaf as if touched by the benevolent hand of a magician who wanted to spread hope and joy. *Be patient,* the little tree seemed to be telling me, *your time will come. Wait and hope, hope and dream, and let your dreams nurture new hope.*

On 6 March 1953, the day we were told about the death of the Great Leader, that day the radio never stopped playing Tchaikovsky's *Pathétique,* Maria and I, watched by a sceptical Ded Zakhar, erected a small wooden bench near the tree. "To sit one day in the blessed shade of the beautiful tree," Maria pronounced.'

'Paul Robeson had come to Moscow in December 1952, to receive the Stalin Peace Prize. That was on the seventy-third birthday of the Great Leader. "The standard-bearer of the oppressed", Robeson was called, "a fighter for the freedom of the Negroes, a beacon for honest Americans struggling against the might of imperialist reactionaries planning a treacherous war against Communists". His concert in Moscow was transmitted live on radio. I'll always remember his final song. It was the Song of the Warsaw Ghetto Uprising, in Yiddish. But you know what? In later broadcasts that song was left out. It wasn't very hard to guess why. I don't know what to make of Paul Robeson. I loved his voice, his songs and his kind face. But they say that in 1953 he wrote a touching tribute to our Beloved Comrade. We all have our blind spots. There were many like him who wrote such things after our Great Leader's departure.

'Freedom! I hate and love this word so much. It was returned to me as suddenly as it had been stolen on that cold winter evening in Moscow. When I think about it now, it seems I'd already begun to see its smiling face in my dreams, feel its touch, kiss its wonderful lips and hear it call me Papa. It was winter again, the last week of February 1955, when Nikolai, the young geologist heading the exploration party, knocked on my door. He pulled a bottle of vodka from his rucksack, asked for two glasses, opened a tin of salted cucumbers and called: "Let's drink to your freedom, Leonid Mikhailovich." We drank together and talked about everything: music, geology, surveys, and my book on the application of geophysical methods in the permafrost. He was a kind man who loved poetry and sang ballads to the music of his guitar.

'Maria too knocked on the door that evening. "Ded Zakhar is poorly and I have come to check on him," she told me. She noticed the vodka bottle and the opened tin of cucumbers on the table, and I showed her the official paper. "To be freed at once and rehabilitated," she read aloud and smiled.

'She hurried off and came back with all sorts of good things. In no time at all a bright yellow tablecloth was spread on the table, a bottle of wine opened, a big round loaf of rye bread sliced, a plate of salad arranged, and the party began. Nikolai played the guitar and Maria sang. After a drink or two, we all began to dance. Maria let down her hair and it shone as she swayed in the flickering light of the stove, as her scarf swung and her skirt swirled.

'I don't remember falling asleep but when I woke I found myself in bed. Through the half-open door I saw Maria and Nikolai on the floor sleeping together. The blanket over Maria had slipped, revealing her beautiful back. It glowed like a painting forcing me to look. I felt free and happy, and then, without making noise, I crept out.

The full moon was just slipping below the horizon. I sat for a few minutes on the bench near the birch tree that I had begun to call Annushka. Then I opened the gate and walked to the frozen lake where snow swirled. I heard from beneath the ice the trickle of water, soft but clear like a flicker of hope in a dream. If sunlight could make a sound, it would be that sound.'

Papa hadn't left Tatyur immediately. He had waited for winter to pass, for the ice to thaw and for spring to show its bare feet.

'I wanted to live through another winter there,' he said. 'Perhaps I wasn't sure that the words typed on the paper were real, although they were stamped and properly signed. Perhaps I had lost confidence in the goodness of people; perhaps the snake of doubt had entered my heart and left its poison there;

perhaps I was frightened to go back in case I discovered that in my absence everything had changed. Perhaps I had found the measure of my own insignificance in the great scheme of things.'

A few weeks after the first ice floes began to move, Papa decided to pack his bags and prepare for his departure. He went to Yakutsk to say goodbye to his friends, taking a wood-saw as a present for Maria's carpenter son. For the little girl who had been curious about the fish frozen in the ice, he found some amber he had received in one of the parcels from Leningrad. For Ded Zakhar, he managed to extract a packet of dry imported tobacco from his biologist friend. But he couldn't decide on anything to give Maria. Nothing felt right. But then in a window he saw a pair of beautiful bright red leather boots. Luckily they fitted her perfectly.

Before he boarded the truck to Yakutsk, they sat together for a while on the bench near the birch, holding hands.

'Don't worry, dear professor,' Maria told Papa, 'I'll look after your tree. Now just get up and go—and don't turn and look back. Do you hear? Go, my dear man. May God be with you.'

Vasu

I didn't have the courage to go to Anna's apartment after her father told us the story of his exile. She left messages with the secretary of my department and with the woman on duty at the hostel, but I didn't return her calls. I wanted to talk to her but I couldn't. Did I feel guilty about her father? I don't know. But I did write a long letter to Uncle Triple K soon after, telling him about the sad life of Leonid Mikhailovich. I wanted him to write back and explain why we humans fear each other so much. Is it because we know that like all machines we too will break down, that the tendency to fail is engrained in the very nature of things born or made, and that the potential for failure is always there?

We fear that our neighbour who knocked on our door to borrow a torch at night; who came and congratulated us on the birth of our children and grandchildren; who willingly shared with us his bread and salt, honey and water, milk and mangoes; who used to walk with us to the bus stop every day, will one day break into our home and attack us.

We fear that to save his own life our neighbour will agree to spy on us, to fabricate evidence, to spread rumours, to bear witness against us and incriminate us. Unfortunately the seeds of our failure to trust our own ability and the ability of those around us to remain true to our humanity are spread as soon as we become conscious of our presence in the world.

We fear others because we know that they, like us, are weak and prone to failure. We fear that we'll lose control and hurt or even kill people. We are our own worst enemies

I wrote to Uncle Triple K about my professor, Asiya, who taught a course on the history of cities. Her lectures were like stories, illustrated with wonderful images, and she rarely used notes. An overhead projector would beam an image on the screen and she would begin to weave her stories around it.

She once invited me to dinner. There I met her younger sister Rukhaiya. Asiya and Rukhaiya were both born in a Siberian village, lost their parents when they were little, and were brought up in an orphanage named after Feliks

Dzerzhinsky, the founder of the KGB. Asiya used to be the secretary of the Party branch at the university.

'Did you know about Stalin and the camps?' I had asked them.

'Yes,' they replied. 'Most of us knew. It was hard not to know, but harder still for us to do anything. Everyone was terrified. Now it's different.'

'Is it really different?' I asked.

'Of course,' Rukhaiya said. 'Now if you speak out, you don't lose you life. They just come and scare you a little. Those closed trials serve the same purpose.'

'After Khrushchev's famous speech,' Asiya insisted, 'things have definitely changed. People want to know more. And they *do* know more.'

I read my letter to Uncle Triple K a number of times and put it away, unable to decide if I should mail it to him. It sounded contrived, apologetic, hollow.

The following afternoon I spotted Leonid Mikhailovich in the university café. He had come to attend a meeting. He asked me to join him.

'Thanks for *Ella and Louis*,' he said. Then he told me that he needed my help to translate an English article into Russian. He asked me to come to the apartment one evening and work with him. He also wanted me to know that Anna was worried about me and that I should call her.

'You love her, don't you?' he said.

Then suddenly he began talking about his ex-student, the young female interrogator who had made him sign his 'confession'.

A year after his return from Yakutsk, this young woman had come to see him. He didn't know how she had found his address, but it wouldn't have been hard, since after all she worked for the KGB.

She introduced herself as Nadezhda Golubkina. Fortunately Aunty Olga wasn't home, because she would have definitely sent her packing.

His student asked him if she could come in, and Leonid Mikhailovich let her pass through the door. She walked into the study and waited to be asked to sit down. He took her things, placed them on a chair and remained standing.

She opened her bag and took out a record wrapped in cellophane. Since she knew how much he loved jazz, she said, she had brought him this old recording of Utyosov's songs. She said that she was going back to the university, not in Moscow but in Leningrad, and she would try and finish her degree in physics. She was three months pregnant, she confided, and because she was soon going to be a mother she had decided to come and see him.

Leonid Mikhailovich didn't say anything, fearing that he might embarrass or humiliate her in some way.

And then she uttered the words she had come to say: 'I'm sorry.'

'I know,' he replied. But he didn't want the meeting to continue, so he told her he was seeing a friend. 'But so nice of you to come. And thanks for the record.'

She rose, put on her coat and hat and left without another word. He stood at the window watching her walk away. She stopped and looked up and he thought she might come back, but then she started walking again, turned the corner and disappeared.

Of course he was meeting no one. He had lied, probably

because he didn't want her to tell more lies and further demean herself.

Leonid Mikhailovich finished the story, opened his bag and started looking for something. He pulled out a photocopy of an article from an English magazine, handed it to me and said he would be interested to hear what I thought of it.

It was a short article of just three pages, one with a photo of King Oliver's Creole Jazz Band in Chicago in 1923. Third from the left was Louis Armstrong, standing next to King Oliver.

Part Two

There never really was a 'we' or 'ours'
Derek Walcott, *White Egrets*

Letters from Kabani

Anna

A letter has arrived from Vasu, in India on a field trip. He had wanted me to go with him, but I couldn't drop my work just like that. He didn't understand how hard it was for us to get a passport to travel abroad.

'They won't let me leave the country so easily,' I explained. 'Yes, not even if we are married.' In fact getting married wasn't going to be simple either.

In his letter he wrote about the River Kabani. 'Just as your Papa has his Lena, I too have a river of my own. It starts as a trickle from a high mountain lake, gushes through narrow ravines, cascades over waterfalls, then slows to a more sedate flow as it reaches the foothills covered with lush forest.'

He enclosed a map and a postcard. The map showed three large rivers, and I guessed that the tiny blue curve joining the majestic Cauvery was Vasu's Kabani.

The postcard showed the Nilgiris, the Blue Mountains of the Western Ghats. 'Like all mountains, they appear blue from a distance because of the haze caused by moisture, dust and tiny globules of oil,' he wrote on the back. 'But the Nilgiris' blue comes also from a plant called *neelkurunji*, which flowers every twelve years and creates a blue carpet across the slopes. The elephants roaming the *shola* forests eat both the grass and the flowers, then turn into giant, harmless drunks. The ground shakes as they walk and when they mount the females, they must feel light and lost like autumn clouds.'

Sergei, drinking coffee with me, picked up the card, read it and began to laugh. I shouldn't have agreed to meet him, but he had been so insistent. I suspected that things weren't going well with Galya, she who had promised him babies. Sergei looked seedy and I took pity on him. I had picked up Vasu's letter from one of his Indian friends, who had collected it from the Indian High Commission. The students used the diplomatic bag to send and receive their letters, not because they were secret, but because the service was cheap and fast.

Sergei and I had run into one another on the escalator in the Metro. I tried to avoid him but as I left the station to catch my bus, he had called out and caught me up.

'You look terrible,' I greeted him. We sat in a café talking about his work, Aunty Olga and Papa. He said he had heard rumours that Papa might be getting a big prize and a medal. He told me he had read a review of one of our string quartet's concerts.

'Why don't you give up archaeology and concentrate on your music?' he asked.

I didn't reply, and let him talk. Galya was not even mentioned

He noticed my disinterest, which must have hurt him.

To hurt me back he said: 'I hear you are going out with a foreigner.'

'I'm living with him,' I wanted to say, but his sneer stopped me. That's when, to avoid his gaze, I opened my handbag and the postcard fell out. He grabbed it and began to read. And laugh.

'How interesting. An Indian. Do you love him?'

'That's none of your business,' I replied.

'Oh yes it is. You know I still care about you.'

'I don't want you to care about me. I can look after myself.'

'I know you can,' he said, and paused. 'But you want to escape, don't you? This is a dangerous game you're playing.'

'Stop it,' I whispered. 'Not one more word.'

'You'll get hurt. I know you will.' The mocking smile on his face enraged me. I picked up my coffee, wanting to throw the cup at him. Luckily I didn't. I just pushed back my chair and walked off.

I was glad he didn't follow me.

I decided to take a long walk, just to calm down, and soon found myself near a cinema. I bought a ticket and went in. The newsreel had just finished and when the main film began, I was astounded that it was none other than *The Cranes are Flying*. I sat through most of it in a kind of shock, unable to work out if this was just a coincidence. I left the cinema before it ended.

Aunty Olga was sitting on a bench outside the apartment, waiting for me. I had pleaded with her many times to stop doing this but she wouldn't listen. 'It's such a beautiful evening,' she said, and she was right. It was bright and unusually breezy. I sat with her for a few moments and told her about the film.

'Samoilova has put on weight,' she said, 'and doesn't look so pretty any more. Just a few weeks ago I saw her in a play. We all get old, don't we?'

I was pleased that she didn't take the opportunity of reminding me how beautiful Tonya had been.

'Let's go home,' she said. She put her arm in mine. Just as we were about to mount the stairs, a girl ran past, crying. Aunty Olga pulled her arm away, turned round to look, slipped and fell.

It wasn't until later that night that we found she had broken her right wrist.

Vasu

The day after I arrived back in Kalpetta it began to rain, and it rained on alternate days after that. But the rain didn't hinder my work. I went to meet Comrade KPS, the Chairman of the Board of the Co-operative, whose proper name was K.P.S. Nair. He told me that he had been working with the coffee farmers of the area for more than thirty years, and was one of five founding members of the Co-operative. He also held a position of some influence on the Executive Committee of the Communist Party, which ruled the state.

Comrade KPS wanted the design of the village to be attractive as well as functional, a model for other state-run co-operatives. Two young surveyors helped me prepare a good topographic map of the site, with details and contour lines. I had been assigned a field assistant, an old man called Kody. 'His job is to look after you,' Comrade KPS explained to me in his office. 'He'll show you the hills, the coffee and pepper gardens, and keep the elephants and monkeys and snakes away.'

I was expecting the village to be built on one of the terraces of the River Kabani, but the state government, I was told, didn't want to give up prime land close to the river and the main road, so the site had been moved a few kilometres upstream of a creek which joins the river near the town of Kakanakote. The stream flows from east to west and its northern bank is higher than the southern.

I had been here for three weeks and had missed Anna every minute of them. At times I missed her so much that it hurt. During the day I was busy and the feeling of her absence retreated into the background, but in the evenings sitting alone in my room I felt miserable.

The other night I woke up startled that I had clearly seen her sitting in the chair next to my bed. Of course, she wasn't there. It was a dream in which she sat gazing at me like Aunty Olga's *Bogomateri*.

Anna would have laughed at me, I'm sure, if I told her that I carried two watches. The one she gave me last year for my birthday still showed the time in Moscow so I could keep in tune with the rhythms of her life. The Budapest scarf, which she had lent me, was folded under my pillow. Perhaps that is why she was always part of my dreams, each leaving a trace of her presence for me to carry throughout the day.

One night when it was raining yet again, I lay in bed hoping to hear the sound of her cello. I waited, then frustrated by my failure to imagine it, I walked out to the balcony. For a brief moment the rain stopped and the clouds vanished, opening up a patch of starry night, moist, fragrant and mysteriously silent. Not a leaf stirred. The street was empty but for a monkey sitting under the dim light of a lamppost like a figure in an absurdist painting. At the other side a man squatted at his tea-stall, coughing insistently, his stove glowing bright red and yellow against the darkness.

I stood on the balcony waiting for something that seemed about to happen. When the silence became unbearable I turned to go inside. Suddenly there was a heavy downpour. I looked out again. The monkey hopped about then sat still, stuck in the painting. The tea-stall man turned his face up towards the balcony.

I went inside, made myself a cup of tea and drank it there, enjoying the silence that followed the downpour.

Anna

Aunty Olga's wrist and right arm were put in plaster. Although she wanted to return to Kiev, Papa convinced her that she should stay in Moscow. 'Annushka will look after you,' he promised. But he didn't know how hard it was to please his 'angel of a sister'.

Meanwhile letters from Vasu kept coming and coming. When did he find the time to write at such length? Clearly he was lonely. There was no question of my writing back as frequently as he expected or desired, let alone as charmingly as he did, as if trying to impress me.

He wrote that he missed my cello. Before he left for India I had been rehearsing French 'songs without words' which we wanted to include in one of our concerts. His favourite was Ravel's *Kaddish,* which he would make me play again and again. His take on music is rather naïve and all my attempts to make him appreciate Faure's *Tristesse* and Massenet's *Elégie* have failed.

Then suddenly one day Vasu's friend Vladimir phoned, wanting to know when he would be back. We started talking and out of the blue he invited me to accompany him to a live reading of Isaac Babel's story *The Widow*. I knew the story, and although I didn't particularly like it, I agreed. He said he would send us two tickets to the opening night of the play *Dialogues with Socrates* at the Mayakovsky Drama Theatre. He was playing one of his small roles.

Papa and I went to the play together. It dramatised the trial of Socrates and his execution. Vladimir played the leader of the chorus. The Armenian actor who played Socrates looked and sounded remarkably as I imagined he would. In the final scene Socrates ascended the stone steps of a Greek theatre, his head encircled with a halo like a god, and disappeared into the darkness.

This ending spoiled the play for me. There was no need to make an immortal hero out of him.

As usual after it finished the whole cast came out onstage. The director stood with them and they all bowed while the audience applauded. Then the director waved at someone in the wings and the playwright, a short man with a big smiling face, joined them. The applause began again. A young woman ran on, handed the author a bouquet of red roses, kissed him on the lips and disappeared.

As the actors began to move off the audience remained standing, as if waiting for something more to happen. The playwright raised his hand, waved the bouquet and a spotlight flashed through the hall, coming to rest on a man in the second row of the dress circle. He stood and bowed. He was tall and thin and stooped, with patches of grey hair around a bald head. He wore a grey suit which fit rather badly and a long thin red tie. Although he was smiling, he was clearly feeling awkward.

The playwright led the applause. 'Who's that?' I whispered. 'Sakharov,' Papa said. Someone in the audience shouted *Bravo!* More voices joined in and soon the hall was filled with loud applause.

Sakharov waved and began to clap back.

'Sakharov is our Socrates,' Papa said as we left the theatre.

Vasu

In the middle of July I suddenly came down with malaria. As a result I lost two whole weeks of work. I should have been more careful. How would I tell Anna I would have to extend my stay?

Two weeks after the illness I went out of my hotel room to take a short walk. It hurt to move, but Kody assured me that I wasn't looking too bad and that in a week or so I would recover fully. But the parasite, he warned me, would never leave my body but live in it like a stubborn tenant, feeding on my juices and announcing its presence with fevers when the seasons changed. Taking quinine each year would merely tame it, never destroy it completely.

Malaria is a strange illness. The cycles of sudden coldness followed by high fever and sweating, last for four to six hours. Fortunately they only occur every other day. On the days when the fever showed mercy and left me alone, I was able to do some work. I completed three different versions of a plan for the village and sketched huts for two-, four- and six-member families. The designs for the cultural centre and the administrative block were finished. Comrade KPS was going to hire an architect to work on the details and an engineer would choose 'Green' building material. I told Comrade KPS that I was interested in building a bio-gas plant running on organic waste because such plants had the capacity to generate close to seventy per cent of the power needed for the village.

In my plan the huts were located on either side of the stream, in rows angled towards the water. The banks sloped upstream and I was going to use the rising elevation to site the huts on terraces so one did not obstruct another's views. There would be space both front and back so that from a bird's-eye view, they would appear like black and white squares on a chessboard.

The number of huts in each row would decrease as you moved upstream, creating a pattern resembling a leaf of a coffee plant, with the stream forming its midrib. Anyone entering the village would clearly see its leaf-like shape.

The road connecting the place to the main highway would only reach as far as the administrative centre. I placed three small bridges over the stream, since I loved designing them. But because I didn't want them to stand out I asked that they be built of local wood. They were meant to appear simple, light and delicate.

Once the whole design of the village had been approved by the Board, then properly re-drawn and drafted, it would be shown to the members of the Co-operative. I wanted to know what the members really thought about my 'village' but had doubts that Comrade KPS would allow them to talk freely to me.

I had received very few and rather brief letters from Anna. I was hoping that more were waiting for me in Delhi with Uncle Triple K. I had asked him to mail them to me, but since not many had arrived, I assumed he had other more important things to worry about. Lately he hadn't been well and the arthritis in his knees and wrists following the attack had become unbearable. He could put up with bad knees, he told me, but the pain in his wrists often forced him to give up on writing or typing. That must have been a terrible blow for him. Mala Didi thought that his continual depression was caused by his difficulties with writing.

The day after the Board approved my design, Kody took me to meet his cousin, an expert coffee-maker, in a little village an hour's walk from Kalpetta. I had come to like Kody although he probably didn't feel the same about me. I enjoyed my long walks with him, tracking through the forest and learning how coffee, cashew nuts and spices were grown. He no doubt thought my ideas for the village utterly impractical, in contrast with his own understanding of the world, grounded in his experience. But he was a true guide and I was grateful to him. Without him it would have been impossible to complete the project.

Coffee, Kody's cousin told us, had been introduced into the area some two hundred years before, by a man named Baba Budan. Returning from the Haj to Mecca, he had fallen ill as he passed through Yemen. There a merchant had given him seven magical beans of *Coffea Arabica*. Back in India he had planted them in a small garden on the hillside near Chickmagalur. To his amazement the plants relished the sun, the moisture and the soil and began to flourish.

Kody's cousin wanted to impress me with more stories about Baba Budan but Kody rudely shut him up. The cousin was younger than Kody but looked much older and seemed sickly. 'Liquor, women and too much smoking,' Kody whispered to me. He told his cousin the main reason he had brought me to meet him.

'Will be done sir,' the man said, and pulled out a mat for us to sit on the floor. Jute bags were lined up against the wall of his hut. He opened one or two, considered them, and then settled on one tied up with thick red string. Out of it he took a handful of round beans with pointed heads, bluish-grey and leathery to touch. '*Robusta Kaapi Royale*,' he announced proudly, 'the best variety. They're strong and they're royal.'

He roasted the beans in a pan and then put them into a hand-grinder. He brewed the powder in a small pot on a kerosene stove, heating it for a few minutes without letting it boil, allowing it to settle and then pouring it into steel glasses with rimmed mouths. He added creamy milk followed by two spoons of sugar for each glass.

Kody showed me how to drink coffee out of the glass with the rimmed mouth. He raised it and tipped in half a mouthful, swirling the coffee around to enjoy its soft, smooth, mellow flavour before swallowing. He waited for me to follow him. I did, clumsily, spilling the coffee.

On the way back Kody told me stories of gruesome events that had happened in the area. I suspected he thought I harboured some affection for the Party. That he was suspicious of it and held it in contempt wasn't news to me. In fact, I had been surprised that he had agreed to work so closely with Comrade KPS.

These were the years when Prime Minister Indira Gandhi had declared a state of emergency in the country. 'To save India from anarchy,' she announced, but most people believed that she was really trying to save her own hold on power.

The main reason for her paranoia was her son. He and his cronies ruled India. He was a dictator, brutal and ruthless. He wanted the country to be rich and prosperous and he wanted it to happen fast. He was desperate to make the cities beautiful and wanted to clear the slums where the poor were forced to live. He wanted to control the growing population by forcibly sterilising the underprivileged and the ignorant. He hated the unions and wanted to get rid of them. They were either banned or bribed. The factories, he declared, should run without strikes and the trains should operate on time. 'All power to the government' was his motto.

His mother announced a ten-point programme to remove poverty in India, but his own plan was simpler. He wanted to get rid of the poor themselves. 'He's a very dangerous man,' said Kody. 'He is Ravana, the ten-headed monster.'

One of the stories he told me concerned Rajan, a student at an engineering college in Calicut. The police had arrested him along with some other students, and taken them away to be questioned. Rajan never returned home and his body had not been found. Everyone knew he had been tortured, Kody said, because the police accused him of being a member of the Naxalite Party that had attacked the Kayanna Police Station. The students were beaten and then tied to a wooden bench. A heavy wooden roller was run over them. *Roly-poly* it used to be called, *roly-poly with a lollipop*, because they would gag them with a foul-smelling rag.

Equally brutal was the 'pencilling' used on others. The interrogator would roll a sharp pencil in his hands, then suddenly stab it hard into the suspect's thigh, working it deeper and deeper into the flesh. The chief police interrogator, who often administered the punishment himself, was an educated man, thoroughly cultured, said Kody. He loved the devotional songs of Thyagaraja and often played the violin at home, accompanied by his daughter on the harmonium.

I hesitated to tell Anna such stories in my letters. She wouldn't be surprised, but Leonid Mikhailovich and Aunty Olga might be. They seemed to believe that in India, blessed with bright light and warm sun, people weren't aggressive and kindness came to them naturally. Of course this wasn't true. Brutality and barbarism know neither country nor passport.

Anna

When Aunty Olga said that she didn't want to talk about something, it invariably meant that she had an important revelation which she would deliver when she felt like it. Being hurried along didn't work with her.

It was obvious that she wanted to return to Kiev as soon as possible. Her wrist being in plaster didn't matter. 'I can look after myself perfectly well,' she kept muttering.

She phoned me at the Institute during my lunch break asking if I had picked up a parcel redirected to her from Kiev. I told her I was on my way to the post office. The woman there checked the note Aunty Olga had given me, examined my passport and handed me a packet ripped along the top. I carried it back to work and dropped it towards my desk. But somehow it slipped and fell on the floor.

There was a sharp crack. Quickly I opened it to check what I had broken. I found a thick book in German, *Travelling with Bach*, published in Munich and lushly illustrated with coloured photos, paintings and engravings. What had cracked was a framed black-and-white copy of an engraving showing the castle of Köthen where Bach had worked as *kapellmeister* in the court of Prince Leopold. I carefully removed the broken pieces of glass and found the engraving intact. Underneath it, however, were tucked two photos: one of Aunty Olga alone and the other showing her on a bench with a handsome man. *Dorogoi Olechke* (To dear Olechka) it said, on the back, and it was signed Grisha. No date. No place.

I put the frame and the photos back in the packet and gave it to Aunty Olga that evening. I lied to her about the breakage, saying that the woman at the post office had apologised for the damage. She didn't ask if I had looked inside, but I'm sure she knew that I had seen the photos.

'Aunty Olga has a secret admirer and his name is Grisha' is how I began my letter to Vasu. He would have loved to have seen the expression on the face of our dear Aunty Olga looking at the photos, an expression worthy of preservation in another photo.

Grisha's face seemed familiar. I remembered a man like him visiting Aunty Olga when I was a child. He never stayed overnight but each visit had been marked by an elaborate dinner.

He took me to the circus a few times. *Maya Dorogaya Lastochka* (My dear little bird), he used to call me as he hoisted me onto his shoulders. He taught me to skate and would glide along beside me. He was large and strong but moved like a well-trained dancer.

'Why don't you ask Aunty Olga to skate with you?' I said to him once. 'She's a very good skater.'

'I know,' he said, 'but I'm scared of what might happen.'

He told me that many years before, when the two were still young, he had tried to lift her above his head as skating couples often do, but that he had found he couldn't support her. He had slipped and fallen on the ice, injuring the back he had already hurt in the War.

Aunty Olga was all right but Grisha decided that it would be wise not to go skating with her again.

Grisha as I remembered him was a handsome man. He would dress very elegantly, his thick black hair neatly combed and his shoes or boots always polished. But my strongest memory was the way he smelled, of some distinctive cologne.

'It reminds me of Tbilisi,' he told me. So dear Grisha was a Georgian, like Shurik's Tamrico.

I had once asked him to bring a little bottle of the same cologne for Papa.

'Leynya doesn't like such things,' Aunty Olga had intervened.

After the parcel arrived there was a week of silence. Then Aunty Olga filled in the missing details of Grisha's story for me. She told me that he had courted her for more than thirty years. They had met in 1955 in Volgagrad, where she had gone to remember Misha Schubert, the first and real love of her life,

131

who had died defending Stalin's city. Grisha had been injured in the same battle and his war finished there. After that they met during her annual pilgrimage to the city. But she had told Grisha firmly that she would never marry him and that to live with a man as husband and wife was now impossible for her. She had her dear Leynya and his daughter to look after. Besides, she was moody, strict and very hard to live with. It would be better for him to find someone more suitable.

Grisha already had a wife in Tbilisi, a Georgian with dark eyes and a slender waist who, he told her, walked like a gazelle. That meant they had to wait.

'Wait for what?' I asked Aunty Olga.

'Wait for her to die,' she replied. His wife had terminal cancer.

After his wife died Grisha had proposed but Aunty Olga had refused him. Soon he found another woman to marry while still visiting Aunty Olga in Kiev and often staying with her. I doubt if their relationship ever became intimate, but Grisha was an attractive and charming man, and it's possible that Aunty Olga did consent to sleep with him.

When I talked to Papa about Grisha Guramshvili he said he had met him several times and that they were good friends. They wrote to one another and whenever Papa went to Tbilisi he stayed with him.

So why were the photos in the packet hidden?

'He's dying,' said Aunty Olga simply, 'and he wants me to visit him.'

'Go,' I said. 'Go, my dear stupid Aunty. I'll even come with you to say thank-you and goodbye to your Grisha.'

Two days later I went to the airport to see her off. Grisha

died a few minutes before her plane landed in Tbilisi. She was, however, able to attend the funeral and the wake.

'But we love you too'

Vasu

A week before I left Kalpetta, a large packet from Delhi arrived. It contained three letters from Anna, one of which brought bad news. Tamrico had been hurt. She had been waiting at a bus stop not far from her theatre when a truck swerved off the road and ploughed into the crowd. Three adults and two children were killed on the spot. Luckily her injuries were minor but she had been taken to hospital for a check-up and observation.

As for Aunty Olga, it was hard even to imagine her injured. To me, she seemed absolutely indestructible. Strangely, Anna's story about Grisha didn't surprise me. Grisha, I suspected, was a kind and sensitive man able to breach the wall of indifference that Aunty Olga had erected around herself. Silence and understatement were her trusted friends. To endure the upheavals of her life without them would have been impossible. She preferred the beauty of life's subtle gestures. It came from her music, I remember Anna telling me once.

In India that week I made a day trip to the port city of Calicut to buy a proper frame for an aquarelle I had painted for Kody as a reminder of our walk to the lake which feeds the Kabani.

The overcrowded bus took two hours negotiating the bends down the winding road through the Ghats. A student on the bus told me about an archaeological museum in the city and after my arrival I went looking for it. Since it was closed for maintenance I decided to visit an art gallery just across the street. Its paintings were simple, excessively naturalistic and too bright and loud. The sculptures were more attractive, reminding me of Henry Moore's reclining figures.

An old man at the gallery told me about a second-hand bookshop with a good collection of books and records. The young woman there was unusually friendly. I told her that I was looking for atlases of colonial and pre-colonial maps of the area. She produced a book containing four beautiful sixteenth-century Portuguese maps of Calicut, but it was too expensive for me.

I was putting it back on the shelf when I discovered that the book next to it was facing the wrong way. As I turned it round I suddenly heard the unmistakeable sound of Bach being played on the cello, one of the six cello suites Anna had been rehearsing last winter. I was stunned by the coincidence. Both books slipped from my hand, and as I tried to catch them, I lost my balance and bumped my head against the shelf.

The young woman rushed to help. 'Are you all right, sir? Would you like some water or Pepsi?'

I was embarrassed. She brought me a chair and I soon

regained my equilibrium. Meanwhile the record continued to play, and as I listened, stray images began to rush in: the starry night with Anna in Gelon, the melancholic voice of Tetya Shura, the red apple in Tamrico's outstretched hand, and the *Bogomateri* in Aunty Olga's bedroom

I walked out of the shop still wondering about how the music had affected me. 'My time here is over,' I thought. 'I should pack my bag and head straight home to Anna.'

While I waited for the bus I examined two records I had bought in the bookshop. One was a 1967 recording by Thelonious Monk, the great jazz pianist, intended for Leonid Mikhailovich. The jacket was slightly damaged, but there were no scratches on the vinyl. For Anna I had bought a German recording of Bach's St Matthew Passion.

On Thursday 16 November 1977, I wrote my last letter to Anna from Kalpetta, informing her that I was leaving the following morning. I told her that I would try to be as adventurous as she, and that is why instead of catching the express train from Bangalore to Delhi I would board an ordinary one in Calicut and travel north to Mangalore, then take a boat to Goa and another train to Delhi.

Why Goa? In that bookshop I had seen a seventeenth-century map of Goa drawn by a Portuguese cartographer. The turtle-like shape of the settlement on the peninsula fascinated me, and I wanted to confirm that the real city was even half as beautiful as the one on the map.

I told Anna that I would stay in Goa for two days, strolling the narrow winding streets while watching for the garbage that might land on my head from above; that I would admire old houses embellished with delicate balconies, enjoy the bright sun warming the red-tiled roofs and sketch the dazzling whitewashed churches; and in the evening when the sun was ready to dip into the sea I would go for a swim. During my two days there I wouldn't stop thinking about her for a minute, and like her Budapest scarf those joyous thoughts would keep my heart warm.

I wrote to her that in the race to reach her, it was likely that I might beat my letter home by a day or two.

As it turned out, I didn't win the race.

In Delhi I met my childhood friend Suresh, now teaching history in a college and working on a book on Mughal-era Delhi. He showed me the old Delhi he had discovered. For three days we walked the narrowest of streets, dark, damp and smelly, searching for the *havelis* of merchants, *begums*, courtesans and *nabobs*. We feasted on *samosas*, sherbets and *kulfi* and talked to a couple of kite-flyers. We found the dilapidated house of Mirza Ghalib, the nineteenth-century Urdu poet who had taught the last Mughal Emperor, exiled to Burma by the East India Company after the failed Mutiny of 1857. In the same street we climbed the dark narrow stairs to a little shop on the fourth floor, which sold posters of Bollywood films.

I was overwhelmed by the continuous onslaught of colours, smells and noises of the streets. I felt uneasy, out of place, confused. 'Don't worry,' said Suresh cheerfully. 'You'll get used to it again. You're an Indian, after all.' But it was as if my eight years in Moscow had entirely squeezed India out of my system.

And what about Anna? Would she ever feel at home in this India? Wouldn't she feel crowded, smothered? Wouldn't she think that it had been a mistake to come here with me?

'Of course she would,' Suresh said, 'and rightly so.' He wanted me to forget the idea of asking her to live here. 'Come back home on your own,' he said. 'Marry a nice Indian girl and live happily ever after.' What saddened me most was that he was quite serious. He was convinced that marrying Anna and bringing her to India would end in disaster.

'But I love her,' I insisted. 'Isn't that important?'

'I'm sure you do,' he said. 'But that's why you should let her go.'

When I returned to my father's house, Jijee-ma noticed at once that I was more than usually anxious, worried and irritable. She didn't deserve that. I wanted to tell her that her fears were groundless, that I had missed her and that I was happy to be back. But somehow none of this sounded convincing.

The big house was more crowded than ever and although Jijee-ma tried to shield me from all the bustling activity, we both knew we would only be able to spend some quiet time together late in the evening. She was kept busy all day managing the household. It was only at night, after all the many visitors had left, the servants had finished their work and family members, especially the children, had been put to bed, that she brought a glass of sweetened milk for me and we were able to sit down and talk.

She sat on my bed with a small bag of almonds and walnuts on her lap, reached for her nutcracker, and began: 'You *are* going to come back, aren't you?' I put away my pen and notebook, looked into her tired smiling face and prepared myself for the chit-chat.

The following night she entered without the bag of nuts, sat on the bed and asked me to pull my chair closer. 'I want to show you something,' she said, and pulled out a packet of photos which she spread in front of me. They were all of young women.

'This one is Meena. She's a gynaecologist at the All-India Institute of Medical Sciences. Her father is a diplomat and at present he's posted in Germany. This girl in the *salwar kameez* is Asha. She teaches history at Miranda House. Her father is a manager with Bata.'

Seeing my indifference, her voice became warmer. 'Do you remember this girl? She used to live nearby and she was at your school.'

'Chandani?' I said.

'So you *do* remember her.' Jijee-ma was pleased. 'You would hardly recognise her now. Such a pretty girl! They say even Bombay film directors are chasing her. She lives in a posh house in South Extension and runs a beauty clinic. I've heard that she wants to start a chain of shops all over India. She isn't one of our *mamul-shamul* (ordinary) Indian girls; she's very modern and outgoing. Nor will she just sit at home and look after her babies. I like her. She has guts. Like you, she calls me Jijee-ma.'

Still I said nothing. 'But this girl,' Jijee-ma continued, noting my silence, 'is the best of all. Her name is Bindiya. She isn't pretty but she's tall and slim. Her father Lala Chaman Lal owns the Dunlop factory in Baroda. Bindiya (can you imagine?) is the only child. She also has a green card, and I'm told she wants to go and live in New York. That would be nice, wouldn't it? I could come and visit you there.'

She left the photos on my table so that I could have a better look at my leisure and make a shortlist. Then I was supposed to give this to her and arrange times to meet the girls. I knew how the system worked, and that's perhaps why I felt anxious and humiliated. I simply listened to Jijee-ma's comments on each one and kept quiet, knowing that my silence would be misinterpreted.

But after my Jijee-ma left, I picked up the photo of Chandani. I was intrigued by her film-star looks. She used to sit next to me in primary school and often shared her tiffin with me. But her fiery temperament had been obvious even then. I hadn't forgotten the fight we had over a mere pencil sharpener. In a terrible rage she had thumped me over the head and bitten me hard on my right arm, leaving behind the deep marks of her savage teeth.

On the third night when Jijee-ma came in to talk I took from my wallet a small black-and-white photo and handed it to her.

'Who is she?' she asked.

'Anna.'

'And who is Anna?'

'My friend.'

'What sort of friend?'

'My girlfriend.'

'Like Chandani at school?'

'No – a real girlfriend.'

'I don't understand.'

'I mean that we live together.'

'Are you married?'

'No, not yet.'

'And what about her parents? Do they know? Have you told them?'

'Yes.'

'And—?'

'They don't mind. Why should they?'

'How long has this been going on, this living together?'

'Almost two years.'

'Two years! And you didn't tell me anything about it! At least you could have written to me. I am your Jijee-ma, aren't I? Not a word! And you used to tell me everything. Don't you remember? No secrets at all.' She turned away and caught her breath. 'You never kept secrets from me. You were so transparent, so simple. How could you do such a thing? What will our father think? He'll be so upset, so angry, so humiliated. Oh my God, what shame, what terrible shame!'

She put on her glasses to have a closer look at Anna's photo, shook her head and sighed. I knew that soon she would start crying, making it unbearable for me to face her. But Jijee-ma didn't cry, and it was then that I realised I was in for much harsher punishment. She would just walk out of the room and lock me out of her world. She would continue to look after me, but there would be no time for friendly chats. No affection would be offered and all possibilities of compromise shunned.

'How old is she, this Anna of yours?' she asked after a brief pause.

'My age. A few months older, I think.'

'And she isn't very tall.'

'No, not very tall.'

'And she isn't very big either, like all the other Russians I've seen and heard about.'

'No, she's …'

'And she has a small face. A kind face, I think.'

I didn't answer.

'And I'm sure she smokes and drinks and eats beef.'

'She wants to give up smoking.'

'And do you drink and smoke and eat beef?'

'No, not at all Jijee-ma. How can I?'

'But you live with someone who drinks and smokes and eats beef.'

I stayed silent. Jijee-ma looked at the photo again, put it aside, then picked it up and looked once more. After a long pause she uttered words I knew expressed her deepest fears. When I went to Moscow, she had always dreaded that something like this would happen and now, faced with the reality, she was more scared than ever. She had never feared accidents or other mishaps because she was confident that her Ganesha would keep me out of harm's way. What had terrified her was the lure of the foreign country and its way of life, but most of all its women, free and attractive.

'So you aren't going to come back?'

'I'll certainly come back. No doubt about it.'

'Really? And you'll bring your Anna too.'

'I hope so.'

I realised that Jijee-ma expected something more convincing, but I couldn't manage that. My future with Anna still remained mired in uncertainties.

'You hope so. I hope so, too,' Jijee-ma snapped. She got up.

143

'I know I've lost you forever. Yes, forever.'

She took off her glasses and tried to put them back in the case, but she dropped both because of her shaking hands. I leaned down to retrieve them but she pushed me away. She picked up the case, found her slippers and started to leave. At the door she turned and looked straight at me, still holding Anna's picture in her hand.

'She loves you, sure. But we love you too, you know.'

And she stalked out of the room.

It felt as though she had walked out of my whole life, leaving me cursed and abandoned.

The following day, after she went to the temple, I packed my bags, called a taxi and left my father's house without saying anything to anyone.

I moved in with Uncle Triple K and Mala Didi.

Of course both of them were pleased to see me. But news of my argument with Jijee-ma had already reached them. They left me alone and didn't trouble me with unnecessary questions. The best way to avoid the topic was to talk about my project. I showed them the design of the village, which they admired. They said they were pleased that I had been able to complete my work in good time.

Uncle Triple K seemed subdued. Mala Didi told me that a few months earlier he had finished his book on labour protest songs, but that his English publisher was taking his time with the contract.

'Your uncle isn't feeling well,' she said. 'His arthritis keeps him awake at night, and during the day he has so much to worry about. I think he's feeling old, tired and useless.' When she saw how worried I looked, she patted my arm. 'Don't fret.

His spark will return and that 200-watt smile will re-appear.'

I stayed on for a few days but it didn't. I had no idea what to do. Before I had gone to Moscow, everything between me and Uncle Triple K had seemed simple and natural. A few words from him were enough to clear any doubts and ease my concerns. Life had seemed easy and the world orderly and meaningful.

Now, looking at my uncle's state, I felt confused and lost.

Had the spark really gone? Not knowing the answer made me even more restless.

The row with Jijee-ma and the uncharacteristically cold response from Uncle Triple K convinced me that I wasn't ready to return to Moscow. Of course the thing that I desired most was to board the next plane and fly off to Anna. Only she could save me. But I didn't want to meet her again feeling wretched. I needed time to think, to understand the nature of my unease and regain control of my feelings.

Perhaps that's why, standing in front of the Air India office, I suddenly decided to go to Leipzig, the city of Bach. Before facing Anna I would immerse myself in music and architecture.

'I'll sit quietly in the churches and walk around them with my notebook and sketch. I'll marvel at the light glowing through the stained glass. I'll listen to the choirs and the organs and wonder at the sounds, dense and voluminous like water but also light as a feather. And then I'll return to Moscow, and Anna will gaze at me and smile and touch me. And all my worries and apprehensions will disappear in an instant,' I tried to convince myself.

'I've come home,' I would say to her and, warmed by

this thought and her presence, I would tell her about the connection between the oval-shaped Baroque spaces and the rhythmic structure of Bach's sonatas.

'Is that so?' she would laugh. She would kiss me and ask me to focus on buildings and spaces and leave music to the experts. Her laughter would cheer me up. With her hand on my arm I would walk through the cold forest, greedily breathing the chilly, moist, scented air.

I would forget that I had ever been unhappy in my life.

It wasn't meant to be so hard

Anna

Vasu and I got married in March. I'm glad that it's over. It was so hard to organise: papers and more papers. Luckily Shurik helped. He has contacts and knew how to pull strings and grease greedy palms. I was interviewed three times by the authorities, just to confirm that I wasn't doing it to get an exit visa.

I had been a *komsomol* my whole life. I became a member when I was young. Everyone had to. But like Papa I never joined the Party and this was what worried me most. The officials didn't trust non-members. Aunty Olga had been smart enough to join, making her life a little easier.

The wedding ceremony was brief and formal. Vasu and I had two witnesses. Vika, my friend from the music school, stood beside me and Vasu had asked Natasha to help out. Aunty Olga refused to come. 'I'll cry like a stupid cow and spoil it,' she said. Papa arrived at the registrar's office with all his medals and stars pinned to his coat. 'Just to convince them that you are the proud daughter of a distinguished man,' he said, 'and to show that the marriage isn't some kind of joke or pretence.' He looked ridiculous.

Yes, that's what irritated me most, the thought that Sergei and others like him would assume that I was marrying a foreigner simply because I wanted to leave the country. I would hardly have chosen Vasu if that had been my intention. There were other much more promising possibilities. Swedish Sasha Lundberg, half-Russian, handsome, kind and ready to fall in love, would have been a much better bet. He was a violinist who had come to learn music at the Conservatorium and we had played together with Vika. I was living with Sergei then and didn't want to risk it, but I had been tempted by Sasha once or twice.

Sasha's mother was Russian and yet he seemed to hate everything Russian. This scared me. With Vasu it was just the opposite; he loved Russians and our country. Sometimes I even felt that he loved me mainly *because* I was Russian.

The ceremony at the registrar's office was followed by an intimate party at Shurik's *dacha*. Vladimir sang and Tamrico played her guitar. Aunty Olga's present was a little gold necklace from which hung a Siberian sapphire. It had been my mother's, a wedding present from Papa. We had invited Tetya Shura but she couldn't make it because she was in hospital after a mild heart attack. She sent a tape-recorded message.

Papa had bought us tickets for a cruise along the Volga to Astrakhan. He wanted me to show Vasu his and Aunty Olga's village. But because of Vasu's asthma, we didn't get further than Kazan. One evening as we were returning from a sketching trip he had a severe attack. I didn't know how to deal with it and the train trip back to Moscow was terrible, since he couldn't sleep or even lie down. He sat on his bunk the whole night, his body squeezed in, his shoulders bent forward, his breath coming in short hard bursts from his jammed lungs. Poor thing! He needed to learn to look after himself better, to avoid dust, perfume and sudden changes in temperature.

The day I returned from our shortened honeymoon I gathered all my perfume and fragrant ointments and creams and got rid of them. Now, I thought, he would have to learn to live with my natural smells, good or bad. That was it. His fault.

Vasu

I felt guilty and ashamed that I caused our honeymoon to end so miserably.

But I was relieved that the wedding was out of the way. It had been such a huge hassle. I hated all the paperwork and the humiliation of being interrogated and examined as if I were about to commit a crime. The worst obstacle was the cultural secretary at the Indian High Commission who invited me to dinner at his house.

He was a professional diplomat, a loyal government official of the Indian Foreign Service and reminded me that he was just doing his job, following orders and normal procedures. His main intention was, he said, to ascertain if I had thought carefully about the marriage and was aware of the consequences that might directly or indirectly result from it.

Over dinner we talked of everything but politics. His wife, he said, was a doctor and their two children, a boy and a girl, attended the International School but were learning Russian. The little girl wanted to be 'a Russian ballerina'.

His shelves were stacked with Tagore's books and there were records as well. I told them that on a trip to Tashkent, I had bumped into an old lady who had met our great Indian poet in Moscow and had the honour of presenting him with a bouquet. She had been just seven then but still remembered his long grey beard and saintly smile.

The formal part of the dinner-meeting took place in his well-furnished drawing room, where he sat at a desk with a Cuban cigar in his mouth. He offered me one and was strangely surprised that I didn't smoke. I told him about my asthma. Promptly he put his cigar out.

The major issue facing me, according to him, was that he knew from many previous cases that marriages like the one I was about to enter often went horribly wrong. Like the good lawyer he was, he listed possible problems, all of which were based on the undeniable fact that Anna was Russian. Did she speak Hindi or English? he asked me. When I shook my head, he looked serious. 'You see, this will be a great problem. It will make her life very, very difficult.' In addition, because she was a *komsomol,* a member of the Communist youth league, she would automatically become an object of interest for Indian authorities. 'The Soviets won't let her go without a written or unwritten guarantee that even if she won't spy for them, when required she will help them acquire what they term "useful information". You know that's how they work over here. We have to be vigilant. I hope you understand our situation.'

I told him that I understood the implications very well, and that my decision was final.

'No, no,' he insisted, 'please don't misunderstand me. As far as we're concerned you are of course absolutely and perfectly free to do whatever is in your own interests. My duty is to ensure that I've warned you. That's all.'

He gave me four weeks to think about his advice and if I hadn't changed my mind he would do everything in his power to, as he put it, conclude the matter successfully. He further advised me that although it wasn't an essential requirement, it would facilitate 'my case' if I were to obtain written approval from my father or someone else with authority in my family.

'So you still want to marry me?' Anna asked after hearing my account of the meeting.

'It's all so complicated.'

'So?'

'I have a month to consider.'

'After which you may change your mind?'

'You know I won't.'

'Why?'

'Because I love you, you idiot, that's why. Love you more than—'

'I know. I'm sorry.' She looked at me and grinned. 'Let's make a baby. They can't stop us marrying then.'

This was unexpected. I was stunned. 'Are you serious?' I stammered.

'Caught you, ha,' she said, and giggled. 'I was joking, stupid. It's too early to think about babies.'

Anna

I knew that he enjoyed touching me but looking at me,

he confided, gave him even more pleasure. Touching, he explained, brought everything too close, whereas looking restored the necessary distance. Looking and touching, he went on, were two different but complementary events of the same act of feeling the world. Take the opera glasses we hire in a theatre: through one end the world draws near and splits into minute details, while through the other it recedes and forms itself into one big whole.

It was true that he loved to theorise, but he loved even more to look at me, dressed or undressed. Like a child he adored my being with him and for him. I could feel how this pleasure lit him up from inside like a glow-worm. Then when I got into bed he would seem so warm, soft and cuddly that I'd feel like suckling him like a baby.

I loved his boyish face and found his attempts to disguise it with a beard and a pair of serious spectacles childish. I knew that his boyish look annoyed him but it wasn't in his nature to show anger or frustration. I had never seen him lose control. Only in bed did he appear vulnerable. Even when he was exhausted he would stay awake for me. I knew he couldn't go to sleep without me, but I wanted to be asked, implored: 'Can you please come to bed now?' But he just waited and waited, in silence. Patience, seemingly immeasurable, was his most definitive attribute.

He never missed a chance to watch me dress and undress, and if I felt like it, I would prolong these moments. I enjoyed seeing him in love with me and relished the intensity with which he desired me. But I realised that by being so open about his longing and his love, he had made himself especially vulnerable, and this realisation troubled me, because the power that I had inadvertently gained could have very easily emptied the noble feeling of love I harboured for him. I confess that at times I was tempted to exploit the precarious situation he had brought upon himself by letting his happiness be ruled by my often fickle moods and emotions.

When I shut the door to undress, he realised that something had gone wrong, that I was annoyed and was punishing him. When I came to bed fully covered he knew that I had made myself inaccessible, that on such nights I would judge his attempts to reach me as violations, that I wanted to be left alone. Strangely he never complained. Like a child, he had learnt to accept his fate. He felt miserable, I know, but understood that once punishment had been meted out and endured, life would once again return to normal.

But did life really regain its usual balance after going through these episodes of power-play and emotional torture? Didn't they corrode our trust in one another? It was as if we were unpicking one by one the seams which bound the fabric of our being in the world, because to be in this world is to be for and with someone.

Vasu

After the wedding we moved into the family *dacha*. Our life there was simple, straightforward and sensible. Most of the time we worked together. One big room was converted into a studio with a large drawing board and a tall table lamp not far from the window. Anna worked at a table in the corner editing my thesis and I helped her translate her book on Gelon. A celebrated English publisher was interested in it.

'You'll be famous,' I teased her, 'and further books and articles will be written about you and your book.'

'Don't be stupid,' she retorted. 'No one really cares. I'm writing this book because it's the best thing I can do.'

'What about your cello?'

'You know that I only like music because I've grown up with it.'

This sort of indifference disappointed me because I knew that she truly loved music and that archaeology too wasn't just her profession.

She sat and typed on a portable machine, asking questions whenever she was defeated by my awful handwriting or my cumbersome sentences. She forced me to break the really lengthy ones into several that were short and succinct. Convoluted ideas were reduced to coherent explanations neatly joined up with proper punctuation.

'Why don't you write the way you tell stories?' she complained. I would blame the strict conventions of scholarly work, the way it pretended to sound scientific, and the pompous authoritative third-person voice.

Anna listened impatiently. 'But your thesis is about people and places,' she said.

'So is your book,' I replied. This upset her even more.

But by and large she was happy with what I had written. Her main concern was that it didn't contain a single quote from Lenin. 'Without him, your thesis won't get through,' she nagged.

I also enjoyed translating her book, although it wasn't as easy as I had initially thought. I asked her questions, sought clarifications. That tested her patience even more.

'With translation you have to be careful,' I told her. 'It's like pouring water: the containers often differ in shape and size, so there are spills and awkward overflows—'

'I know that, thank you very much,' she interrupted, irritated by my patronising tone.

I was pleased that she had started taking English lessons. She had learned some German at school, where it was compulsory. She was finding English hard, the grammar and spelling in particular. But she was trying.

Anna

Vasu loved to talk about old and new cities. 'Tell me about Amsterdam,' I would ask him, for instance, and in a flash his whole appearance would change. He would become utterly glorious in this animated state. His voice trembled, his eyes sparkled, his head shook and his arms and hands wafted and waved. He would leap out of bed to get his sketch book, completely forgetting that he had nothing on and that the room was freezing cold.

He would jump back into bed and say 'Look!' and in less than a minute the shape of the city would appear on the page. He would draw and talk at the same time, words tumbling out as if he were scared that he wouldn't be able to tell me everything and that the moment would be lost forever.

'Amsterdam used to be a small fishing village near the mouth of the Amstel,' he told me, showing me the shoreline, the narrow delta and the meandering bend of the river. 'That's where it gets its name: the dammed Amstel.'

'First they built a sea-dyke to protect the village from the

tides, then they dammed the river and put a bridge across it.'
The dam and the bridge appeared on the page, followed by
a semicircular canal with a wall protecting the settlement on
three sides.

'In the seventeenth century, when a new plan for the city
was accepted, they constructed three canals following the shape
of the outer moat. They were joined by four others running
at right angles, creating a complex network more than eighty
kilometres long. Parallel to these ran the streets and the main
thoroughfares, criss-crossed by the famous bridges, steep,
arched and hump-backed. Along the streets they planted rows
of elm and lime trees and behind them stood the tall, gabled
red-brick houses of the rich burghers.'

He showed me his sketch. 'It's like a spider web, isn't it?' I
said.

'Yes it is,' he said, pulling up the bedclothes and continuing
the story.

'The Dutch mastered the design of water-cities. In the
Leninka I found an English translation of a pamphlet by Simon
Stevin, the Dutchman who refined the art of building such
cities. He was a genius. Soon other famous cities followed—'

'One of them our own St Petersburg,' I interrupted him.
'But of the others I have no clue.' He laughed at the phrase
'no clue', and I let him enjoy the moment, because it made
him very seductive.

'The other famous one was at the southern end of an
island, east of the Hudson River,' he said. 'It was called New
Amsterdam.'

'Which later became the famous New York,' I added.

I was amazed at the way he was able to remember the exact

shapes of so many cities. 'There's nothing particularly clever about it,' he said. 'All I need is one visual clue and the whole thing pours out by itself.' Brasilia reminded him of an eagle flying down from a hill, ready to land in the lake to take a dip. Venice, when he drew it, appeared like two hands clasped together.

He thought Alexandria the most beautiful city in the world. In his drawing it had the shape of an ibis lying on brown sand washed by the turquoise waters of a warm sea.

'Leningrad, if you could see it like a bird flying high in the sky, would appear as a triple-headed python.'

'And what about Moscow?'

'It's like you,' he said, smiling mischievously. He drew mounds, round and soft, intersected by streams and rivers. The best plan for a city in such undulating landscape, smoothed by glaciers, had to be a system of concentric rings.

This time I felt his hands and fingers tracing lines and shapes on my body, not his notebook.

One day he drew only a triangle, at the three corners of which he wrote: Topography, Technology and Translation. 'The shape of a city is defined by these three elements,' he lectured.

'Is it really so simple?' I teased him.

'Not at all,' he replied and added a fourth corner. This represented land and its ownership: its value, commercial and symbolic.

'I am looking for a word starting with T for it as well,' he continued, 'but I can't find it. So I call the system 3Ts and an L.'

I found it amusing, this drive of his to transform ideas into neat schemata with regular geometrical shapes, well-defined and properly labelled.

'What about Translation?' I asked.

'By that I mean communication, movement and flow,' he said. 'Communication brings people together and converts a town or city into what the Greeks used to call the *polis*. Plato said that an ideal city would be limited to the number of citizens who could hear a single voice.'

He sighed. 'Technology has changed everything. The polis has turned into megalopolis, a gargantuan agglomeration of space crowded with people. Communication so often fails in our modern cities.'

'If you're so attached to your T, why not call it Transport?' I asked.

'Translation is both exact and a metaphor. I love metaphors,' he confessed. He planned to write a thick book on the history of urban design using the 3Ts and an L as an organising principle. The largest section would be devoted to Translation because he was convinced that without communication, cities as living entities wither and die.

Once he got going, he was unstoppable. 'Cities need rivers, lakes, canals and fountains to relieve the unyielding built-up spaces. The flow and trickle of water adds a sense of time and, like a mirror, it produces reflections, fluid and flickering, for us to look at and ponder.'

'How will you ever finish such an ambitious book?' I teased. 'Why don't you work on something smaller, a bit more realistic?'

His face became sad. 'Yes, you're right. It *is* too ambitious. Just like your Papa's book on jazz.'

Vasu

We were sitting in the studio working when suddenly Anna looked at me and asked abruptly: 'Do you find me beautiful?'

It was so unexpected that I found myself unable to answer. I was scared my silence would be taken the wrong way.

'No need to hurry,' she finally said. 'Take your time – and when you've thought about it a bit more, please let me know.'

Then she rushed out the door.

It took me a full three days to come up with a proper answer.

'This is for you,' I said, handing her a sketch. In it she was standing holding the cello in her left hand. Her hair was gathered into a ponytail and her face, dominated by her big eyes, looked straight out. She was wearing a summer dress and her other arm was resting on the back of the chair. The window was open and a pigeon sat on the sill looking at her.

'So you *do* find me attractive?' she said. 'And don't say *of course.*'

I kept quiet and just as I was about to speak she came right up and kissed me. As she turned away I heard her sob.

'Sorry,' she said. She looked at the sketch and asked me if she could keep it.

I told her that of course she could and as she gazed at it again, a naughty smile appeared on her face. 'I like it – but I want to hear you actually utter the words as well. Tell me, *why* do you find me attractive?'

Then before I could say anything, she walked out of the studio.

Anna

I took a photo of Vasu sitting outside on the steps in his sky-blue shirt and denim jeans, his hair nicely washed and combed, his moustache and his pointed Lenin-beard in need of trimming. He looked so pensive and anxious. I could see it in the way his lips were tightened. When I touched him, he trembled.

I had been late home that night and he had been worried about me. I went inside, grabbed the camera and took the photo. He seemed on the verge of tears. I must confess that I wanted him to cry, to find out if he really could.

He didn't, but I kept the photo. 'This is for me,' I told him, 'and for our daughter to see and remember. This image will stay in the filing cabinet of my memory. Isn't that the way it works? Traces forever etched into our minds?'

I wanted to provoke him into saying something about memory in his own special style. He took the bait and began to tell me about the magical power of visual images and the way they inhabit the memory. Then he quoted his favourite Bergson and went into a long explanation of the relation between mind, matter and memory.

'The mind is not a receptacle, my dear Anna, where words and images find a place to nest or where, like bees, we deposit nectar. It's not the brain either, a mushy mix of grey and white matter. Memory doesn't live inside or outside our mind or body. It doesn't live at all, because its lifespan in the world is infinitesimally brief. Like a match which produces fire when rubbed against the rough surface of a box, so memory is produced each time we try to remember. We recreate it each time we recall.'

I felt terrible the way I laid such traps for him. The poor soul fell into them every time.

Vasu

There was no television in the *dacha* at Prudkino and we rarely bothered with the newspapers. 'In *Pravda*,' we would say, 'there is no *pravda* (truth) and *Izvestia* is without any *izvestii* (news).'

Our radio played only music. But rumours were everywhere. Often they would walk in with our visitors. When Aunty Olga came to stay overnight, she brought with her fresh stories of scandals and intrigues.

Soon I stopped reading Russian newspapers altogether but kept my ears open for anecdotes, jokes and stories. Whenever I had a few spare minutes I would note them down in my diary in Hindi, not because I wished to hide them from Anna but because I didn't want to forget my own language.

Leonid Mikhailovich seemed to ignore them both: the news and the gossip. He was too busy with his work. One evening he invited us to a ballet at the Bolshoi. He had told us that he would meet us near the main entrance but we didn't find him there and had to wait. When he finally arrived in a taxi – unusual for him – he found us both huddled miserably under a big umbrella. He hurried towards us, slipped, and dropped his bag.

We rushed to help him up. 'Are you all right, Papa?' Anna asked anxiously.

'Of course,' he replied.

By the time we entered the hall we found the artistic

director onstage introducing Plisetskaya's *Anna Karenina*. The director was short and round and spoke with a pronounced lisp. Luckily his speech didn't last long. As he left the stage he stumbled, looked out at the audience and laughed. People clapped and giggled.

The conductor arrived in the pit, the lights dimmed and the curtain opened onto a railway platform, much simpler than most Bolshoi sets. There were just a few props and a brass band on the right-hand side of the stage. The musical opening was brief. We heard the whistle of a steam engine and the rattle of wheels, followed by screeching brakes. Then the music became softer and we heard the sound of footsteps. Someone shouted *ostorozhno* (beware) as the dancers appeared on the stage.

I found the beginning slow and flat but the solo mazurka danced by Plisetskaya's Anna in the third scene made my heart leap. The moves lacked the natural elegance of a mazurka; her steps were clipped and the curves angular, her body awkward, nervy, perhaps a pointer to the tragedy that would soon unfold. The dissonant chords of the music accentuated the flow of the dance. The effect was intense. I turned to look at Anna and she caught my glance. She slid her hand into mine and squeezed it.

'Karenin,' she whispered and handed me the opera glasses to observe the unfortunate Aleksei Karenin. His dancing was more like a laboured choreographed walk. He seemed weighed down by fate and his own inability to forgive. He was dancing with a limp, I thought, and for a moment the limp with which Leonid Mikhailovich walked flashed into my mind.

Afterwards, over dinner at his favourite restaurant he told

us about an explosion of methane gas at one of the huge coalmines which had killed at least twenty miners. He was nervous because he had been asked to chair an inquiry, and wasn't sure how his recommendations would be received by the Party.

We didn't return to the *dacha* that night but stayed at the apartment. In the middle of the night Aunty Olga called. She was fretting about one of her Ukrainian friends who had married an American professor she had met at an economics conference in Paris. Although she had completed all the necessary paperwork and got the relevant approvals, she had still not been allowed to join her husband in New York.

'So what do you think she did?' she said after a pause. 'She went to the American Embassy and chained herself to the fence near the entrance.'

'That's it,' Aunty Olga concluded. 'No America for her.'

'Don't worry about us,' said Anna. 'Vasu isn't American. We'll be fine.'

'I hope so,' she said.

Anna

Vasu found an epigraph for his thesis, a quotation from Marx: 'Man lives by nature. This means nature is his body, with which he must constantly remain in tune if he is not to die. That man's physical and spiritual life is tied to nature means no more than that nature is tied to itself, for man is part of nature.'

I liked the quotation, which pleased him. 'Where did you find it?' I asked. He showed me a chapter called *Alienated*

Labour in the collected works of Marx and Engels. Marx borrowed the idea of alienation from Hegel and reinterpreted it to fit his own theories, he told me.

I wanted to say that the alienation we felt in this great socialist society of ours was as profound as that in any bourgeois one. But I didn't want to upset him either. Perhaps that's why I asked him instead about his fascination with Marxism.

I know that his integrity is unimpeachable. To please others for short-term gain is against his nature. But it often disheartened me that a man of his intellect could be so naïve and gullible.

He struggled to formulate his answer, and this amused me. I had never seen him like this before. If he has doubts, I said to myself, he can be saved. *From what?* I asked and scolded myself for being presumptuous and arrogant. What right had I to think that he needed to be saved and that only I could save him?

He became a Marxist because of Uncle Triple K, he finally said. He had inherited it from him, not only his Marxism but his whole way of being. The world he saw around him in India and the way he perceived it reinforced his belief. The books he read gave him confidence. He knew he wasn't the only one. There were others like him, with similar dreams and aspirations, and perhaps that was why books still remained the primary source of his inspiration.

But, he continued, he didn't believe in either Socialism or Communism. I wanted to object: Marxism without Communism is unthinkable. But one look at his face told me that he wouldn't be able to handle further interrogation. I gave up, knowing that now he would sulk for days.

The blame, I was convinced, lay with Uncle Triple K. Vasu should free himself. What good could come from living his life in the shadow of a mighty oak? To liberate others you need to liberate yourself first.

Why did I have to be so hard on Vasu? Did I really love him? Perhaps he should have freed himself from me, too. Perhaps he should stop believing that I was the sole source of his happiness, his sky-blue *dupatta*. But I also suspected that if I told him to go, he would depart without a word and never return. He would feel miserable but it wouldn't take him long to get used to my absence.

Vasu

Last Sunday Anna and her friend Vika gave a performance at the Chekhov House at Melikhovo. To celebrate the great short story writer's birthday, they had been invited to play a few short pieces. We took the train from Kursky Station and travelled to the small town of Chekhovo where, outside the station, we caught an old wartime bus driven by a young woman sporting a bright red parka. She greeted us enthusiastically, obviously impressed by Anna's cello case.

On the bus were an old couple, a few skiers and a teenager with a little dog in her lap. By the time we arrived at Melikhovo, the clouds had dispersed, promising a bright winter afternoon with clear skies and no wind. This was surprising because the winter had been terribly cold and windy. On New Year's Eve the temperature had dropped to thirty-eight degrees below zero and we had been forced to take refuge in bed.

The house was hidden in a thicket of leafless birches, limes and cherry trees. It was autumn when, with Natasha, I had last visited Melikhovo. 'To paint the autumn colours,' she had explained. She had completed two aquarelles but I couldn't bring myself to produce anything, overwhelmed, I think, by the dazzle of colours softened only slightly by the damp smokiness of the autumn air.

Now everything was covered in snow: the lawn, the flower-beds and the path around the pond. The trees were dusted with snow and their craggy branches dotted with hundreds of empty nests, shaking in the wind. In the field beyond the lawn deep footmarks led to a haystack covered in melting snow. Amid this bright whiteness stood the house with its dark walls, large white-framed windows and malachite-green roof.

The curator, Maria Andreevna, met us at the door. She clearly didn't know what to make of me. Her unease remained even after Anna had introduced us. I felt uncomfortable too. For a few minutes no one knew what to say. Luckily a young man appeared to ask her something about the heating, after which Maria Andreevna offered to show us round.

As we walked she told us that the performance would start at two o'clock and that there would be fifteen to twenty people in the audience, mostly local villagers but also a few visitors from Moscow. She showed us the lounge with its piano, cushions on the floor and chairs lined up along the walls. The French doors leading to Chekhov's study were open, and light from a large Italian window patterned the floor. The windows along the corridor wall were set with diamond-shaped stained glass. On the side wall, not far from a cuckoo clock, hung a portrait of Pushkin.

While Anna and Vika set themselves up in the lounge for their performance, I went outside with my sketchbook.

When the performance began there were only three men in an audience of women, mostly pensioners. Vika introduced Beethoven's Sonata in D Major, Op. 102 No. 2. The opening movement was brisk, she said, and although it contained some short lyrical motifs, the overall mood was sombre. The slow second movement, the longest of the three, would sound like a sorrowful song, but we should be ready for the final movement which was a fast-paced, playful, almost coquettish dialogue between the piano and the cello. She said that the sonata was perhaps a little too sad for a birthday celebration but that they had chosen the piece because they wanted to honour the melancholia of Chekhov's short life.

Vika and Anna began slowly and a bit uncertainly but soon relaxed, looked at one another, smiled and let the music flow. Anna had already alerted me to the final *fugato* movement. Unlike Vika, who preferred the slow second movement, Anna was enthralled by the *fugato*, because in it the cello took the lead. The cello, she had explained to me, would initiate the two subject-themes, to which the piano would reply.

When Anna began the third movement, she glanced in Vika's direction. She responded and soon they took off together, bouncing the *allegro* along with relish. The audience noticed the ensuing dialogue; several heads swayed and bodies swung. The applause that followed the climactic trill was genuine.

During the third movement I found myself wishing that Anna would turn just for a second and look in my direction. But she didn't. I felt miserable, like a child excluded from the joy she and Vika must have felt, transported into a world of their own by the music they were making together. Did I feel abandoned? No, just lonely, and not only because I had been left out but also because of the music itself, with its eerie, sad, yet oddly warm cadences.

I knew that both Anna and Vika had been anxious about selecting one of the most difficult of Beethoven's sonatas. At the rehearsals they had listened to Richter's and Rostropovich's interpretations and initially tried to imitate them. But soon they realised that they would have to find their own way, following the emotions the music evoked in them.

Their performance that afternoon showed that they had been right. Perfect it might not have been, but emotionally beautiful it surely was. If they were pleased with how they had played, they didn't show it. They merely looked exhausted. We didn't speak much on the way back to Moscow.

That night before we went to bed Anna observed that I hadn't touched or kissed her the whole day. 'Does watching me play in public intimidate you?' she asked.

I told her that it was hard to find the exact words to describe my feelings.

'Why don't you try?' she challenged.

I did try, but I failed. That night both of us found sleep hard. Lying awake and keeping quiet was even harder.

'Tell me a story,' she finally said. For some reason I began to tell her about Ariadne and 'the poor Minotaur'.

'Why "poor Minotaur"?' she wanted to know. Before I could say anything, she turned her face to me and said: 'You're scared that I'll leave you, aren't you?'

I nodded.

'Don't be silly,' she said. She kissed me, turned on her other side and fell asleep.

Next morning, as we lay in bed still half-asleep, she told me that she wanted me to come with her to Tatyur, the remote Siberian village. 'To see Papa's Lena and to sit in the shadow of Annushka, the Siberian birch,' she said.

Anna

From Garcia Marquez' *One Hundred Years of Solitude* I read Vasu a passage about Macondo, the village built by Jose Arcadio Buendia. Vasu calls its design 'perfect' and I know he likes it because it is near water, beside a river. The houses in Macondo are positioned with such precision that reaching the river and drawing water is just as easy from one as from another. Each house is so well-placed that it is completely shielded from the summer sun.

Vasu drew me a map of Macondo: the mountain ranges to the east, the swamps to the south and west. What lay to the north we are not told. We found Colombia on a map in our atlas and looked for Macondo, soon discovering that although the village in the novel is fictional, the countryside around it is real.

Shurik and Tamrico, who came to visit us last weekend, were also reading the book. Shurik had brought the English translation for Vasu and I was pleased to see how happy it had made him.

Vladimir, Katya and her little Yasya suddenly appeared at the gate. They apologised for coming unannounced but I suspect that Tamrico and Katya must have planned this so-called surprise. They were both very fond of Vasu. With me they were civil but the warmth they displayed for Vasu didn't extend to me.

I needed to relax with them and forget that if in the past they had found me snobbish, arrogant and unsuitable for their 'lovely boy', it was because they cared for him so much.

Of the four I liked Shurik best. His constant suppressed anger intrigued me, but I suspect it was just a mask. The pain and grief he hid inside must have been unbearable.

Shurik didn't find *One Hundred Years of Solitude* amusing. Sad and distressing, he called it. We shouted him down: 'You're wrong!' But everyone agreed that the plague which allowed no one to sleep was one of the best ideas in the novel. The people of Macondo can't fall asleep or even become tired. Then they lose their memory and have to label everything.

Shurik said he liked the memory machine invented by Jose Arcadio Buendia. It was a spinning dictionary mounted on a wheel operated by someone seated at its central shaft.

Shurik believed that in the Soviet Union we also suffered from a plague of insomnia. The tragedy was that no one here had the courage to invent a proper memory machine. In fact, the only machine in operation was designed to induce profound amnesia.

'We are doomed,' he repeated endlessly. Vasu had told me that Shurik had become more and more restless, as if despair were eating him from the inside. He looked pale and ill and seemed to have stopped smiling.

'We're all sick but have stopped caring about it,' he proclaimed. 'In fact it appears we enjoy our affliction, as if we deserve nothing better.'

He told us to read a book he had recently received from a Russian friend in Holland. The book's Orwellian title, *Will the Soviet Union Survive Until 1984?* intrigued me.

'Why don't you leave?' Vladimir asked him. Shurik didn't reply, but we knew that he would never go, because leaving would mean slow and painful decay in an alien land. I sensed that he still harboured some tiny hope that an enlightened tyrant would suddenly appear to announce that our system was in need of drastic surgery, that after all the masses not only craved bread and circuses but also wanted freedom to think and converse without fear or compulsion.

'You're mad, Shurik,' Tamrico laughed. 'A tyrant, enlightened or not, will always be a tyrant and fear will always walk beside him like a faithful dog.'

Vasu had told me that Tamrico wanted to get pregnant but was unable to convince Shurik. 'I don't wish to father a slave,' was his comment.

Vladimir and Katya looked happy, although it wasn't always easy to ascertain if people were really happy or just pretending. Katya was pregnant, and confident that this time she was going to make a girl. She had stopped smoking and wanted me to give up too. I was trying, but it wasn't easy.

Vladimir was slowly learning to enjoy the little fame that had come to him at last. Katya said that the day wasn't far off when he would be allowed to tour abroad. To Europe first and America soon after.

'We're very happy,' she parroted non-stop. I hoped it was true.

Vasu

Anna was crying, lying curled up in bed sobbing, with her face turned to the wall. I tried to touch her but she pulled away, got up and left the room. I found her sitting on the steps outside, smoking. I brought her shawl, which she took from me and put round her shoulders.

She moved to let me sit beside her. 'What's wrong?' I asked. It was past midnight and the night was dark and silent like the inside of a deep well.

'Nothing and everything,' she replied. She was no longer crying but I knew she hadn't calmed down. She allowed me to hold her hand and I felt her whole body quivering. A pine cone dropped off the nearby tree with a sharp plop, followed by another, and I saw two bright eyes peering out at us. I pressed Anna's hand and as we both looked up the long hoot of an owl broke the silence. It flew off into the dark leaving behind a heavy flutter in the dense cold air.

'What's wrong?' I asked again.

'Let's go inside,' she said. 'I'm cold.' She got up, waited for me, and we went back in together. She slept quietly for the rest of the night. I found it hard to drop off and wanted to get up and read. But she wouldn't let me, clinging to me like a frightened child.

When I woke next morning she was ready with her bag, waiting for me. She asked me to hurry and finish breakfast, then come with her. She gave me my own bag and after we had locked the door, we sat on the steps again for a few minutes.

It was raining when later we emerged from the Arbatskaya Metro station.

'The clinic isn't far,' she told me. She waited for me to offer her my arm and we walked without speaking. The guard outside the clinic looked at me suspiciously but let me in. The receptionist told us that we were early and would have to wait. Quite a few forms had to be filled in and signed.

At around two in the afternoon, the doctor called us to explain the procedure. I was asked to donate blood. It wasn't compulsory, I was told, but simply a request to compensate a little for the blood Anna might need. 'Of course,' I replied. But I wasn't allowed to go in with her. I had to wait at reception.

'Why don't you go for a walk?' suggested the woman behind the desk. 'It's not raining any more. A walk will cheer you up.'

I left the clinic wondering whether I should go and see Katya and Vladimir, who lived just a few blocks away. But as I stepped outside, a strange sense of loneliness descended on me. I looked around and felt utterly lost. The crowded street, the buses, trams and trolleys, the tall glass buildings with their shops and offices, and most of all the sun sheepishly peeping through the clouds, suddenly seemed to have turned into the weird silent landscape of a sci-fi movie.

For a few minutes I walked almost blindly, then looked up and found myself in front of a cinema. The show had just started and the place was nearly full, so the usher led me to a seat in the back row. After the film had ended, she woke me. I left remembering nothing of the movie and the time I had spent in the cinema.

A few weeks after the abortion Anna and I were invited to a special screening of Tarkovsky's *Solaris*. There is a sequence in the film where Hari, the duplicate wife of the scientist Kris

173

Kelvin, a woman created by the alien nebula, is injured, and he tries desperately to stop her bleeding. Then, to his great astonishment, he notices that the wound has begun to heal itself and the bleeding has ceased. The wound disappears and her unblemished skin is restored as if nothing had ever happened.

As the sequence unfolded on the screen, I suddenly realised that the film I had seen in the cinema near the clinic had been *Solaris*. So I *had* watched it. Like an after-image it had entered my memory and lodged quietly, sedated, as if by the sadness of that cold, wet afternoon.

That sadness soon turned to despair, compounded by Anna's resolute silence. I wanted to tell her that I was convinced I had lost her forever and that by losing her I had also lost any hope of being happy in this life. But no, I didn't say anything.

On my return to the clinic that dreadful evening I had found Anna lying on her side, looking away from the window, avoiding the sight of some plastic flowers poking out of an ugly vase perched on a wobbly bedside table. The white paint on the metal top had peeled off, exposing rusty scabs.

She must have heard me come in, but she didn't turn. I sat on the edge of the bed peering at the flowers, soiled, clammy and superfluous. The clock in the corridor outside ticked and ticked. Then she turned and allowed me to hold her hand.

'Where were you?' she asked, but didn't wait to hear my reply. She told me to go home and get some sleep, and come for her tomorrow. She tried to smile but failed and turned her face away again.

I left the ward without saying a word. I should have said something, I know. I don't know why I often fail to find the right words when they are needed most. It isn't because I am shy or clumsy. I think I am selfish. I truly am.

The return trip in the train that night was terrible. The carriage was almost empty and there was enough room to lie down on the seat. But I couldn't sleep. Outside the window the snow glowed in the moonlight. Whenever I leaned my head against the cold window and shut my eyes I was woken by the same vision. I am not sure if it was a dream because it felt as if I were awake. I saw water in my cupped hands and in the water there was Anna's moon-like face trickling through my fingers.

I knew it wouldn't be easy to exorcise what had happened. And any hope of redemption would have to be indefinitely postponed.

Anna

Should I have told Vasu I was pregnant? Yes – he deserved to know. After all, she was his baby too. Why do I say 'she'? I always felt that my first baby would be a girl. Not telling Vasu was selfish and cruel. But I didn't want to have babies, at least not then, and I knew he loved them. He would have argued for keeping our child as he often does: never raising his voice, listening carefully to whatever you say and responding. I didn't tell him because I was afraid he would persuade me to change my mind. And I didn't want to because I knew what was good for me. I was sure about that, dead sure. Of course a baby would have given me more power over deciding our future together. Sounds manipulative. Perhaps it was and perhaps that's why I didn't tell him anything until the last possible moment.

I did what I felt was right then. There is no need to feel guilty about it.

Why couldn't he understand the sheer hopelessness of our life then? Hadn't he learnt anything from Shurik? There was room for love but none at all for dreams.

'We are dying slowly,' I tried to tell him, and I knew that this disturbed him because it meant the slow death of his own dream for his people. 'People', what does he mean by 'people'? How does he know if 'people' want his help or that he can help them? For God's sake, who gave him the right?

He would often tell me that I was too cynical, that I had lost faith in the idea of progress, that I didn't want to think about the masses living in abject poverty for whom freedom was nothing but a hollow word. If I talked about freedom or the lack of it, it was only because the state that I criticised so vehemently had been instrumental in creating the conditions for people like me to worry about freedom. I hated this Marxist mumbo-jumbo but I did like watching him upset and animated. I never missed a chance to stir him up. 'So you agree,' I needled him, 'that my reluctance to demand freedom means that the great experiment of social engineering has failed and that there isn't anything wrong if people like me ask for more freedom?'

'QED,' I would yell, pleased that he had realised he had fallen into another of the traps I had so deliberately set for him.

He would look at me bemused and I would want to kiss him. But I knew he wouldn't let me.

It sounds like a harmless game, but harmless it wasn't. It did make him unhappy, and even though I didn't want to hurt him in any way, I also wanted him to stop being so naïve. I feared for him because I loved him. His only defence was to return to his shell. He sulked and brooded, wrote long letters to Uncle Triple K and went back to his books: Marx and Engels, Plekhanov and Lenin, Morris, Lucas and Sartre, reading them over and over. I felt sorry for him. His books seemed to reinforce his beliefs, purge his doubts and restore his confidence.

Aunty Olga suggested we go to Yalta for a few weeks, to enjoy the sea and the sunshine and drink Crimean wine. The travel and the sea air would 'heal your wounds', she said. Papa arranged a place for us in the Academy of Sciences rest-house. I decided to take my Bach with me and rehearse his cello suites.

Vasu

I was miserable that Anna hadn't told me she was pregnant. I despaired that she didn't ask me if I wanted her to keep the baby. Was she afraid that I would argue with her and force her to change her mind? Of course I would have argued. I would have pleaded, but in the end I would have left the decision to her.

Perhaps she no longer believed that I loved her.

That something was troubling her had been obvious. I should have asked her. She had been suffering and yet I had said nothing.

Did I really love her?

Vika had asked me the same question. I had phoned her to find out if she knew what was wrong with Anna. She told me she was behaving oddly at rehearsals: edgy, lost and at times teary.

'I bet she's pregnant,' Vika had announced, unable to hide her excitement. 'Talk to her, you idiot.' But I didn't. I was stupid and now I would definitely suffer.

I knew very well that Anna didn't want to have a baby – at least then. She wanted to travel, see the world and do exciting things. It would have been impossible to make her change her mind, even though she believed that I could have. Perhaps that was why she didn't tell me anything.

A few weeks after our trip to Yalta I received a letter from Jijee-ma. Anna saw the letter and wanted me to read it to her.

'For several months after your departure from Delhi,' I read, *'everyone was very upset with you, but now we have come to accept your decision. Many thanks for sending us her photos. Anna (is that her name?) looks so pretty and has such a nice, kind face. I would love to meet her and tell her everything about you and the family. Radha Bua (I hope you haven't forgotten Aunty Radha) is very pleased. "Your grandkids will be fair and white like the moonlight with eyes bluer than the sky," she teases me. She is mad. "What's wrong with the colour of our skin?" I tell her. "Not too dark and not too white. Wheatish, that's what we call it, tanned gently and lovingly by the sun." Radha Bua always wanted to marry a gentleman from England, and did you know that when she was sent to London to study business management, she got engaged to a black man from Jamaica? Our dear father was distraught. But your Uncle Triple K is very proud of Radha Bua, although this hasn't stopped him from calling her a greedy capitalist.*

'When are you coming back to India? I hope it happens soon.

We are planning a big wedding, with two brass bands, fireworks and a huge feast. I hope Anna doesn't mind going through the ceremony again. I also hope she isn't intimidated by us. We can be overbearing at times, but she should know that a marriage over here means marrying the whole family. Tell her that we'll love her more than anyone else and that we'll do our best to make her feel at home and happy. Please explain to her that she'll be very dear to me. I hope her father and her aunty can come to the wedding too. It would be a novel experience for them and I am sure they will enjoy the ceremony.

'I can understand her misgivings. I'd be frightened myself. Be kind to her, my son. Let her come here, stay for a while and if she doesn't like it, you can both go back. I won't mind. No one will mind. The main thing for me is to see you happy together. Please make this absolutely clear to her.'

'You really want to go back to India, don't you?' Anna asked.

I wanted to say 'Of course', but settled for 'I suppose so.'

'What do you mean?' she asked, and I felt sorry for lying. The reason was simple. Anna, I know, was frightened of going to India and I didn't want to upset her. Not then.

'I mean that I don't know,' I replied. 'I would like you to come, but—'

'But you aren't sure,' she said.

Anna

Vasu received a letter from a reputable university in India specialising in engineering, offering him a job. He was thrilled. It was one of the most venerable institutions of its kind in the country, he told me, more than a hundred years old. The hill station of Mussoorie and its nearby snowfields were only a few hours away. We could ski in the winter and there was even a skating-rink in the town.

I understood why he was so keen to tell me about the snow. He was silly, trying his best to please me.

'We can buy a house or some land in Mussoorie and build our own cottage,' he said. Then I asked him if they taught archaeology or history at this university. Of course they didn't. His smile disappeared.

'But they teach Russian,' he added after a pause to think. Instantly he realised the stupidity of this remark. I was annoyed. I wouldn't really miss archaeology, but having a job of some sort was important. To turn into a full-time housewife was beyond me.

Perhaps I could give music lessons. But who would be interested in Western classical music, let alone the cello, in a small Indian university town?

We knew Vasu could easily get a job in Delhi, Bombay or Calcutta, but he feared that I wouldn't enjoy living in any of these big cities. Delhi was too large and chaotic and next to unbearable during the hot dusty summers with their lengthy power cuts, he said. Bombay was even larger and had a humid climate with rains which could go on forever. The washing never dried, the walls were damp and swarms of mosquitoes hovered around, he told me.

Calcutta was better, less chaotic and more Western, but was one of the most humid places in the world, where you sweated all the time. A cold shower provided some relief but as soon as you dried yourself the sweat reappeared.

'And there are snakes, lizards, flies, rats, cows and monkeys,' I teased him. 'They'll bite me and gradually eat me alive.'

'And then there's the noise,' he went on, 'relentlessly following you everywhere, and an awful smell of piss, shit and dung that lodges in your clothes, gets under your skin and never leaves you.'

But most tiring of all, he explained, were people continually present around you, their sweaty bodies pressed against you, trying to touch and feel you.

I looked at him unable to see if he really hated India or was just trying to wind me up. I was sure it couldn't be as bad as all that.

'In India,' he said, 'you have to be very rich to live a comfortable life. On the salary of a junior academic we'll only be able to afford a few basic necessities.'

I soon realised that he was testing me, hoping to hear the words he so desired. 'I'll come with you,' he wanted me to say, 'and live with you forever.'

But I didn't say anything.

Like me, he understood that although we had committed ourselves to living with each other, this often extracted a heavy toll, eroding our own sense of being in the world. To be happy or to make those we love happy, it is sometimes prudent, and perhaps kind, to let them go.

'We'll try and see if it works,' I said. That didn't satisfy him, although he didn't say anything. Doubt; the inherent frailty of our plans and wishes; the transience of our desires, affections and commitments, were all hidden behind the words 'we'll try'. This was evident to both of us, and whereas for me doubt and uncertainty were part of life, to him they were nothing more than minor obstacles, easily overcome.

What really troubled him was the thought that I didn't love him as dearly as he loved me.

'I know you wouldn't mind settling down in Moscow,' I told him, 'but you need to understand that this place has lost meaning for me. It's my home, I agree. But I want to run away. Perhaps not forever. You believe that with time the system will change, grant us more freedom and allow us to exercise it without fear or force. But I'm not so sure. Perhaps you're right. Perhaps one day everything will suddenly become better and people will treat one another well. But I don't have time to wait. The only way I can drag myself out of my inertia is to leave – and as soon as possible.' She paused. 'I know it sounds awful but I don't want to lie to you. You know I love you. And you love me even more. So let's be completely honest with one another.'

Two months after the letter from Jijee-ma, Vasu received a letter from Uncle Triple K which carried dreadful news. I saw him reading and re-reading it and asked him if he were all right. He said no – and showed me the letter.

The news was so bad that I realised no words from me would comfort him.

'*Your Jijee-ma has been diagnosed with cervical cancer and the prognosis isn't good. She asked me not to tell you but I know she wants you to know. But don't drop everything and rush back. She wants you to finish your studies and to pray for her. "Don't worry about me", she says. "When the time comes, I'll be at the airport to greet Anna and Vasu."*'

I suggested he should go home to be with her. The thesis and the book could wait. I said that I would come with him. He looked at me surprised and I realised that this wasn't the right thing to say. That I had lied, both of us understood at once. What he had really wanted to do was finish the thesis and the book as soon as possible and take me back to India with him to stay. He feared that if I went for a week or a fortnight and took a dislike to the place, the doors would swing shut.

I knew how much he loved Jijee-ma. The idea of her being in pain was intolerable to him. But I didn't know how to comfort him. That night I pulled him close, but he resisted, asked me not to worry about him and went straight to sleep.

I lay awake listening to the wind and trying to order the scattered thoughts wandering through my mind. Suddenly a strange and rather wicked idea floated in. I was aghast that I was capable of entertaining such a dreadful possibility. I got up to go to the bathroom, turned on the light and looked in the mirror, feeling ashamed of myself.

The next morning Vasu appeared calm and composed. This irritated me but I needed to confess what I had thought. He laughed guiltily after I had finished, which infuriated me even more.

'Annushka, my dear,' he said, 'such thoughts have also crossed my mind. They make me feel bad and incredibly selfish too. But of course you're right. Once Jijee-ma is dead, I am free of her— and of India.'

I was shocked. 'What about Uncle Triple K?' I asked. He just smiled sadly. 'He'll understand. He'll feel bad – perhaps let down – but he'll understand.'

Vasu

Yes, Uncle Triple K would have understood my predicament. But to forgive me would have been hard. He was, I am sure, very disappointed in me and although I had tried a few times to explain my situation to him, his brief 'I know' and 'It doesn't matter' had left me feeling more disgusted with myself than ever.

The fact that I had now decided to go somewhere quite different, not return to India, would upset him even more.

A year earlier a professor at the School of Architecture in Venice had come to Moscow to attend a conference. He didn't know Russian but spoke English and I was asked to be his interpreter. I was surprised that he had read my paper on *Vastushastra* in an obscure German journal. Perhaps that is why he then asked me to work with him on a collection of essays on the role of emotion in designing urban spaces.

He had wanted me to show him 'my Moscow', which wasn't easy. I had no idea where to start. I had to ask Anna for help and she readily agreed to accompany us. She also invited the professor to a concert at the conservatorium where she and Vika were playing Shostakovich. After the concert we took him home to meet Leonid Mikhailovich and be shown his jazz collection.

'He likes you,' Anna had said after we had seen the professor off at the airport.

It took more than eight months for the invitation to work in a temporary position at the university in Venice to arrive.

'You deserve it,' Anna said after reading the letter. 'I hope you are going to accept it,' she added.

'I'm not sure,' I replied.

We didn't talk about the letter for a week. Then one evening walking home from the station Anna said that she wanted me to call Shurik and talk to him about the offer from Venice.

'Why Shurik? Have you told him?'

'I have.'

'And?'

'And he wants us to go.'

'Are you sure? Because he said something very different to me.'

'What did he say to you?'

'Don't ever go there.'

'Why?'

'He said: *It will ruin you both.*'

'Did he say that? Really? I don't believe you.'

I didn't tell Anna that Shurik was convinced that Russians such as he and Anna had lost the habit of freedom. Its sudden appearance would hurt and impair us both.

Instead I lied: 'Yes, he wants us to go.'

'You aren't lying?'

'No,' I lied again.

'Then why do you look so sad?' she demanded.

'I don't know.'

'You're worried about Jijee-ma. Aren't you?

'Yes – but not as much as I was. The chemotherapy is working. She's feeling much better.'

'That's great, isn't it?'

'It is. But—'

'But you're scared.'

'Yes. Of the new city. New language. New people.'

'But you love Venice. It's one of your lovely water cities.'

'Yes, but—'

'And I'll be with you. Me and my cello. You love us both and we love you.'

That evening we stayed outside and sat quietly near the little creek that ran close to our *dacha*. It was a warm summer evening lit dimly by a reluctant moon. In the dense silence we heard the water whisper. Suddenly a pair of yellow wagtails appeared. They hopped around for a few moments and then flew off to land again on the rotting trunk of a tree lying in the creek.

'Don't be so sad,' Anna said. She got up and walked towards the creek.

'Aren't you coming?' I heard her call.

She took off her clothes, tossed them in my direction and stepped into the water.

I couldn't move. I sat motionless as if tied to the yellow trail left in the air by the little wagtails. I saw Anna bend, kneel and lie down in the knee-deep water. And then she began to sing.

Please stop, I wanted to say, but couldn't open my mouth, choked as if by the immaculate beauty of the moment.

'I'm doomed,' I thought then. 'Doomed because I love her.'

Venice

Anna

'You either come here to die or to kill someone,' the man told me. He was drunk and as he spoke his body swayed. I was sure that he would slip off his chair and fall into the water. I had stopped for coffee at a bistro near a Venetian canal, after my morning walk.

'You'll love it, I promise,' Vika had remarked in Moscow. But after the excitement of the first few weeks I had become almost indifferent to this beautiful city. Every now and then a strange feeling of panic would grip me, as if something untoward were just about to happen. I should just have ignored the drunken man. He wanted me to stay and talk, and I would have because he looked so forlorn. But I was frightened by his bloodshot eyes and the uncontrollable shaking of his hands.

I didn't tell Vasu of this encounter, wary that he would refer me to *Death in Venice*. I didn't want to read anything for a while. In fact I didn't want to do anything except walk, look and feel.

I enjoyed the pure idleness of my days. I knew that it would have to stop soon, that I too would have to find a job. Vasu hadn't rushed me. He had willingly adopted the role of responsible husband.

We had arrived in Venice by the back door, as they say. The railway station was surprisingly dull and dirty and the hotel we stayed in during our first week was shabby too, except for the white façade with patches of peeled-off plaster, and bright red tiles on the roof. The window of our room opened on to a large and ugly square, the Piazzale Roma, the city's main road terminal, filled with cars and buses and smelling of diesel. The view from the windows of the dining room was just as uninspiring: a bridge and two flyovers. One brought the traffic from the mainland to the city and the other directed it to some warehouses. The bell tower of the little church next door to the hotel was the only beautiful thing and it brought us some joy.

Soon we found a place of our own in a block overlooking a park in the Campo San Giacomo dell'Orio. The architecture department of the university where Vasu was working was close by and so were the Rialto markets. For the first few weeks I went there every day, just to look at all the wonderful Italian fruits and vegetables: the shallots and onions, beans and aubergines and broccoli, bulbous pumpkins, chillies, grapes, fresh and dried figs, shapely pears, peaches, plums and most amazing of all, the fat orange mangoes.

The fish market too overflowed with plenty: *branzoni*, squid, red mullet, silver anchovies, eels, flatfish and crabs. Barges were loaded with lettuces, tomatoes and big bunches of bananas. One barge was piloted by a large woman always accompanied by a huge beast of a dog. But my favourite was the one moored under the San Barnaba Bridge. Because it was small, the fruit was piled right up to the roof of the stall.

A blind man would sit on a stool nearby and play his accordion. After a while I decided to bring my cello and play some tunes with him. 'Bravo,' he said after we had finished the first. He wanted more. I played some Russian songs and he responded with a version of *Kalinka*. That evening I earned my first Italian *lire* and an invitation to return whenever I liked.

I got to know Bella, the blind accordionist's daughter. She managed the barge and the shop with her husband, a huge man of enormous strength who could pull the half-loaded vessel along the canal all on his own, like a horse. He had tattoos on his back, shoulders and arms and used to be a sailor on a merchant ship.

They were amused that I didn't speak Italian and took it upon themselves to teach me the Venetian dialect. I didn't know the difference until Sophia demonstrated to me the pronounced softness with which the Venetians spoke.

I met Sophia Serino through Vasu, who had seen her in the studio of a well-known Venetian architect. He noticed her violin and told her about me and my cello. She also found me a part-time, three-day-a-week job in a music shop on Riva degli Schiavoni, not far form La Pieta, the church where Vivaldi played music as a concertmaster.

I first met Marco at the shop where he had come looking for some music by Monteverdi. Like me he spoke a mixture of Italian and English. We started talking and he told me that he had to come to Venice to work on improving his harpsichord technique at the music school. His home was in Sydney.

He said that he often played at a bistro and invited me to join him. Soon the idea emerged of a trio with Sophia on the violin and we began rehearsing and playing together, both for fun and money.

I had never wanted to be a professional musician because I lack the necessary discipline. But I needed the money and I enjoyed playing. Besides, Vasu was more and more preoccupied with his job at the university.

Marco was a handsome man and, what's more important, joyful. His happiness was infectious, his optimism glorious and his laughter warm and inviting. He wasn't very tall but his long arms and hands were always ready to hug and touch, and he wasn't shy about kissing or being kissed.

He was one of those men who when they take you out to dinner you know will choose the best wine and suggest the most delicious dish on the menu. But he wasn't a very good musician. He played rather mechanically and lacked the confidence to improvise and invent.

Sophia and I agreed, however, that he was charming. In many ways he was the opposite of Vasu who, according to Sophia, carried the weight of the world on his shoulders. 'Marco is a flirt,' she told me. 'You have to be careful with such men. They mess with your mind and heart and then leave you marooned.'

Of course Marco reminded me of Tonya's Paolo. That I had suddenly started thinking about the son of the locksmith from the village near Turin troubled me. I was worried that one day I would wake up and rush down to the railway station to buy a ticket for Turin. Sophia told me it was very close to Venice.

'I'll come with you,' she even said, although of course she didn't know why I wanted to go there. I knew I wouldn't do it, but the fact that I had to force myself to give up the idea of going to Turin surprised me.

Vasu

A few months after our arrival in Venice, Antonio, a fellow-researcher at the university, asked me to join him on a trip with his students to Pienza. For the first few days I couldn't keep my eyes off the buildings. But I soon became bored by Alberti's precise symmetry of shapes, colours and patterns.

In Venice I was confronted with the same tyranny of symmetry, accentuated by the presence of water everywhere, the upside-down images mimicking every structure. But the water also brought rhythm and smells and loaded the air with tiny globules of moisture creating colours. The city turned lilac in the winter mornings and rose and crimson when the sun went down.

The window of my office opened on to an expansive view of the Palazzo Vendramin-Calergi on the northern bank of the Canal Grande. A classical cornice sits atop three Corinthian columns delicately fluted on the *piano nobile*. The arches of its large biforate windows are topped by oculi which gaze at you inviting you to look back. It's the windows which make it appear unnaturally weightless, so light that I often felt it would rise on marble wings and float in the light air warmed by the soft moist *sirocco*. Then it would land with such immaculate precision that people would fail to notice that anything magical had happened.

My university class was small, with only five students, three young men and two slightly older women. It was touching for me that they were interested in my short course on *Vastushastra*, the ancient Hindu practices of architecture and urban planning. Simone, a woman from Nice, spoke Bengali. When she was young she had spent time with her parents in Auroville, the mission city established by Aurobindo Ghose in Pondicherry. She was disappointed that she couldn't practise her Bengali with me, since I don't speak it. There was also a couple from Sweden learning Sanskrit because they wanted to read the major text on *Vastushastra* in the original.

I would begin tutorials with a short introduction to a topic, then distribute the material and let them work on their own assignments. The room we used was big and dark and my favourite spot was a window leading to a tiny balcony.

One day I was standing near the window when I noticed how dark it was becoming outside. Just as I went to switch on the lights, there was a huge flash of lightning. Another ripped the sky in half. A crash of thunder followed. It rolled over the buildings, bringing a massive downpour. Drops as big as marbles rattled the roofs and hit the dense heavy surface of the canal water with such power that it seemed to warp. All water traffic stopped except for two motorboats speeding in opposite directions.

People ran inside. Only the foolhardy tried to brave it out in *vaporetti* and water-taxis. Suddenly lights in the windows of buildings across the canal began to splutter like splinters from sparklers. My heart trembled as I felt the tremors of still more rolling waves of thunder. The building literally shook, shuddering from right to left.

The storm was over in ten minutes. But overawed by its furious beauty we decided to end the class. 'Let's go to a café,' suggested Simone. We found a table, removed the empty cups and plates and sat down to listen to a young woman singing Duke Ellington.

That evening I hurried home to see if Anna had been out in the storm. I wanted to share my experiences with her. But she wasn't there. I found her note on our bed. 'I'm with Sophia, rehearsing. Call if you need me. I may spend the night at her place. See you in the morning. Love you.'

I phoned and Sophia told me that she had just gone out with Marco and Isabella to get ice-creams.

I liked Isabella, Sophia's six-year-old daughter. She was unusually perceptive for her age. I would look after her when Sophia and Anna were rehearsing or performing.

Sophia told me that Isabella liked my stories and the sketches I drew to illustrate them. Her favourite was about Misha, the clever monkey, and Gena, the stupid crocodile. She and I made drawings together as I spoke. Some of her drawings were fresh and creative and I encouraged her to work with different materials: pencils, crayons and even watercolours. Natasha would have been proud of what we produced.

Isabella and I fastened the drawings together to make a little booklet. There was Misha on a mango tree, Gena the crocodile in a lake, Misha riding on Gena's back as he swam in the lake. The most beautiful drawing of all was a mango tree loaded with fruit.

'It looks more like a Christmas tree to me,' I told her.

'It really does, Zio Vasu,' she agreed, and laughed.

The faces of her monkeys resembled my face.

'Why?' I asked her.

'Because I like you,' she said.

'And who is the crocodile?' I asked.

'Probably my Papa,' she replied.

Sophia was impressed by Isabella's booklet and agreed that she showed enough talent to enrol her for special art classes.

Anna

Isabella had grown very fond of Vasu and he adored her. Towards me she was either indifferent or formal. I didn't mind, because, to be honest, I don't know how to handle children. Vasu was a natural. All children loved him. And when he was with them all his inhibitions disappeared.

We went to the Lido to swim and Marco and Isabella came with us. The summer bathing season had almost ended so it wasn't very crowded, although it was still hard to hire a bathing hut for the day. We had a long lunch at a beachside café, but Vasu didn't have much time for us. Isabella had brought her Chinese kite and the two of them ran along the beach to test it. Then they sat on the beach drawing figures in the sand, chased one another and kicked and threw a soccer ball.

Only when Isabella was tired did Vasu find time to sit with us. Marco tried to engage him in conversation, but he didn't respond. Even Sophia couldn't persuade him to talk. As for me, I was used to these unexplained periods of silence. To change him would be impossible. Often the idea that I had to live with this for the whole of my life filled me with dread and even loathing.

'You don't like Marco, do you?' I asked him that evening.

'He's very nice and handsome.'

'But you don't like him?'

'I do. I just don't know how to relate to him. He's always so happy, so keen, so chatty.'

'Is that bad?'

'I just can't keep up with him. He's so quick at everything he does. Confident and arrogant. A go-getter.'

'So you don't like him. Does he intimidate you?' He didn't respond. I waited and asked him: 'Do you want me to stop seeing him? I can, if that's what you want.'

That was a tricky question for him. To say either 'yes' or 'no' would have been hard. Saying 'no' would have meant that he was lying and 'yes' would have proved that he was jealous, which was demeaning to him and to me.

So of course he didn't say anything. I stopped probing. That evening we cooked a meal together. Nothing special: just nice pasta with a sauce that I had learnt from Sophia. We hadn't done this for a very long time. He kindly let me do the cooking and helped to chop and slice the vegetables.

I opened the bottle of wine which the manager of the bistro had given me when we performed there. Vasu and I made love afterwards and we realised that we hadn't done that for a very long time. 'Just too busy, I suppose,' I said, I with my music and wanderings about the city and he with his work.

Afterwards, around midnight, I went out on the balcony to smoke and he followed to sit with me. He shouldn't have. Smoke is bad for his asthma. I was dreading that he would ask me to play. Luckily he didn't and we returned to bed.

'Did you notice that we've stopped sleeping naked?' he

asked. Of course I'd noticed, but this time I didn't reply. Then after a few moments he opened up. He told me that he was worried about me and Marco. Rehearsing and playing music together would eventually draw us closer. He had, he said, observed something similar watching me and Vika play.

'One day you'll find that I'm superfluous and discard me,' he said.

'But I love you,' I wanted to say. I didn't. I knew what he would have answered: 'So what? Love comes and goes.'

'What about our marriage?' I could have asked him. 'Doesn't that count any more?

'Maybe it has turned into a piece of paper signed in a registry office,' he could have replied.

Soon he was asleep, as always with his arm around me, holding me tight.

But he was right that I had been spending more and more time with Marco, not only at rehearsals with Sophia. Often we weren't rehearsing, just flirting and daring each other to go a bit further. Some of my notes to Vasu about being with Sophia were lies.

With Marco I felt at ease, happy and adventurous.

The first big row between Vasu and me was not long in coming. I was expecting it, because a week before we had got into an argument about a university function he wanted me to attend. I told him that I was busy and could not cancel a performance. He reminded me that it wouldn't look good if he went alone to a ceremony chaired by one of his professors. They were unveiling a significant monument created by Arbit Blatas, the well-known Lithuanian sculptor who had lost his mother in the Holocaust. He had installed seven bas-reliefs on the wall of the Jewish Ghetto in the Campo del Ghetto Nuovo. Only a few days earlier I had walked past the wall not far from Ponte dei Tre Archi and seen them being installed.

Vasu was visibly upset, rare for him. He reminded me of my Jewish grandfather, Tonya's father. He told me that I had a moral obligation to attend. I was enraged and told him not to bully me by dragging my grandfather into the argument. I didn't care if I was Jewish or not. The monument would still be there when I had time to go and see it. It was mean and unreasonable of him to force me to do something I didn't want to do.

I stormed out and didn't come home that night. I phoned to say that I was with Sophia. Luckily he didn't come to check, because of course I wasn't.

I blame Marco for the big row which followed that first argument. One evening Vasu had come back from work a little earlier than usual and I was sitting on the balcony smoking cigarette after cigarette. I knew that this was stupid, but only cigarettes helped alleviate the terrible bouts of weeping which occasionally overpowered me. Otherwise I would just cry and cry.

Vasu saw me on the balcony and said: 'I hate your smoking.'

'I don't care. Just leave me alone.'

He came out on to the balcony and sat with me.

'What's wrong?' he asked.

'Nothing and everything.'

'Please tell me.'

I told him that I had called Aunty Olga and that she hadn't been in. I had so wanted to talk to her. I didn't tell him that I had also tried Vika's and even Sergei's numbers.

He understood that there was something wrong but that

by asking again and again he wouldn't get anything out of me. So he finally left me sitting there, still smoking, and went back to the kitchen to cook.

After he had prepared the meal he came out again, and that's when I told him that I had lost $2000 at the casino on the evening he had asked me to accompany him to the unveiling ceremony.

'Which casino? You mean the one in the Palazzo Vendramin-Calergi?' he asked.

I nodded.

'So what!' he unexpectedly laughed. 'There's no harm in losing money in a building with such heavenly windows.'

He was certainly trying to calm me by making light of my serious error of judgement, but it somehow sounded very different. I felt my hand suddenly move to grab a piece of broken brick lying in the balcony floor.

He saw my hand move and looked into my face, stunned. Then he got up, took his coat and walked out the door.

He didn't return home that night.

I went to his office the next morning. He told me that he had slept on the floor in his sleeping bag. I apologised. He kissed me and told me that I shouldn't worry about money because the advance he had received for his book would more than cover my losses. But he would have to work even harder to meet his publisher's deadline.

We had breakfast in a café and he told me all about the storm he had witnessed standing at the window in his office.

'Peace,' I said, as I was leaving.

'Of course,' he replied. He kissed me and returned to work.

Vasu

Peace. We both knew that peace would never come to us again. We had failed each other, miserably.

We both needed some time apart to sort out the mess

Perhaps that is why at first I wasn't surprised by her absence. I had gone to Milan to attend a conference and on my return, she wasn't at home. I assumed that she was at the music shop, went to the office and tried to call her several times. The shop's phone was constantly engaged.

Late that afternoon I called into the shop to surprise her with the little present I had bought for her in Milan. The woman there told me that she hadn't seen Anna for more than a week and was wondering if she was all right. On the way back home I phoned Sophia and was told that she had last seen Anna on Monday, a week ago, and although she had appeared a little out of sorts, she had been friendly and chatty. She would phone Marco, she told me, and find out if he knew where Anna was. Then she would call me back.

I was tired from the travel and the hectic work of the conference. I took a few pills, turned on some music and went to bed. The following day I kept myself busy at work, taking my class on an excursion around Venetian gardens. I returned to the apartment quite late in the evening.

When I opened the bedroom door I saw on the floor, near the bed on Anna's side, a photo. I picked it up.

It was the only picture I had taken of her in Venice. Anna and Sophia were sitting on the Lido beach quite early in the morning before the sun had properly risen. Little Isabella was still asleep, stretched out between them, her head in her mother's lap and her legs resting on Anna's right thigh. Sophia was staring at the camera but Anna's head was turned a little to the left. On the sand in front of them lay her glass bangles: red, yellow, blue and green. Just near Anna's kicked-off sandal were her feet in their full magnificence, dusted with moist brownish sand speckled with mica flakes.

I put the photo back on the bedside table between two heavy books to flatten its folded corner. I noticed Anna's slippers poking from under the bed. She had gone but she was still there: her hair on the pillow, her smell in the sheets, her toothbrush in the glass and near it the tube of paste, squeezed as always from the middle.

I looked into the mirror above the washbasin and saw her face. 'What should I do?' I asked her. Her face in the mirror told me to go for a walk.

And so I did, to walk her presence away.

That first night I found myself on the island of Torcello. I don't remember anything about my walk except that I returned the next morning and slept again in my office. On the second night I walked again. I walked through the alleys and up and down the bridges, many times finding the dead-ends forcing me to turn back. Soon I was lost and had to sit down and lean against damp walls waiting for the map in my mind to tell me where to go. I walked and walked and found myself in the Ghetto. I noticed it only when I discovered that I was going round and round in circles.

It reminded me of the narrow alleys of Chandni Chowk in Old Delhi, with their tall three-, four- and even seven-storey buildings, simple and shabby with their peeling plaster, cracked red bricks, broken windowpanes and white sheets hanging on washing lines even at night. I bumped into boats and sat for a while in one of them, waiting for the moon to slide across the alley.

In one narrow street near a bridge a dog barked, got up and followed me. I didn't run away but stopped and let her catch up. She was friendly and stopped a few steps away, looked at me in a confused way and then wagged her tail. I searched my pockets and found a piece of dry bread which I offered to her. She smelt it, didn't like it, and turned away.

I left the bridge and saw that the lights on the third floor of a nearby house had come on. A window opened and a young woman looked out. She waved and before I could respond a sickly-looking old man thrust his head out and shouted at me to *fuck off*. He called me insane and I did feel like a madman, walking aimlessly simply to forget the unforgettable.

I must have wandered for another hour before I suddenly found myself in front of Café Iguana. It was past midnight but the place was open and still busy serving food and music: guitar, violin and bongos. I noticed behind the window glass a photo of Anna with Sophia and Marco. It showed what must have been their first performance together.

Suddenly a young man ran out of the café, followed by a woman. The two of them ran over a bridge, stopped, and leaning against the railing started kissing. I was scared that one of them would slip and fall. They continued to kiss and as I turned to walk away, I heard the woman shout 'You idiot!', as one by one yellow beads from her broken necklace fell into the water.

On the third night I drifted unknowingly into Dorsoduro. I knew the streets and canals well and yet on that night they seemed strange and unsettling. It was foggy and the waxy moon, sickly and sleepy, was shrouded in a rainbow-like halo. The streets were busy, which annoyed me at first, but then I got used to the crush. Some of the streets seemed familiar from my daily walk to and from the university, but yet no one stopped to talk and I ignored those I recognised.

I sat for a while on the bench near the fountain in Campo Santa Margherita. I had been there with Isabella and helped her sketch. Suddenly I felt the urge to see the golden globe that topped the Customs House, supported by two tired-looking figures of Atlas. I had never warmed to the Goddess of Fortune perched on the globe. She seemed so arrogant even though she was nothing but a weather-vane.

I turned and walked along the Zattere, stopping for a few minutes outside a café where a band was playing jazz. Then I turned right onto Squero di San Trovaso and saw that one of the gondolas near the workshops was turned on its side, exposing a big crack in the hull. In another a couple of pigeons slept soundly. An old man who was painting a new boat to turn it into a charming gondola offered me a cigarette. I declined but accepted his invitation to join him. He soon discovered that my Italian was basic, but that didn't stop him talking to me. I suppose he, like me, just needed someone with whom to share a few moments.

'India,' he said, looking at me. I nodded.

'Ravishankar,' he continued. I nodded again, and he got up, went to his work table and pulled out a photo. 'Roberta,' he said, pointing at the young woman in the photo with a *sitar*. His daughter was in India learning to play it. 'In Benaras,' he said. 'The holy city.' Raising his hands he brought the two palms together and said '*Namaste.*'

'*Namaste,*' I replied, looked at his daughter's picture. Soon I left him to continue my walk. I must have walked for fifteen minutes when I had the feeling that someone was following me. I looked round to see a tall young man wearing a red scarf and a white baseball cap. He came right up to me and shouted 'Money!'

I gave him my wallet. He opened it and found some notes, counted them, exclaimed in disgust and threw the wallet back at me. As I kneeled to pick it up, he kicked me hard, then picked me up and punched me in the face. I fell down and must have hit something sharp. As I tried to get up, he kicked me again, this time in the stomach.

'No money!' he shouted. 'Fucking foreigners, go home.'

It started raining again and the moon too vanished completely. I got up in some pain, left the narrow alley and discovered that I was not far from Sophia's house. My eye was swollen and I slipped several times as I climbed her stairs. Maybe I had sprained my ankle.

I reached the door and knocked. As I waited, suddenly my legs gave way and I fell, my head hitting the door.

It opened and from the floor I saw Sophia and, standing behind her, Isabella.

'It's Zio Vasu, mamma,' I heard Isabella whisper. 'He needs help, mamma.' I was covered in mud and bleeding from my nose and a cut under my right eye. They helped me get up and stagger inside. I sat on the floor struggling to take my shoes off. Sophia helped me remove my coat. As I lay on the sofa she examined my injuries. They were minor except for the cut under the eye.

'It will need stitches,' she told me. 'We'll go to the doctor in the morning,' she reassured Isabella.

I had sprained my ankle. Isabella fetched the ice-tray from the fridge and her mother put the cubes in a pillowcase and wrapped it around the ankle. Next morning the doctor stitched my cut but warned that the scar would take some time to fade.

'What were you doing out on the streets so late?' Sophia asked me as we returned from the surgery.

'I was walking,' I said.

'The whole night?'

'Three whole nights.'

'Why?'

'Because I couldn't sleep in that room without her. It was too hard.'

'I know.'

'No, you don't. You can't imagine. You really can't.'

Six months after that night I received a postcard of the Sydney Harbour Bridge with a short note on the back:

Privet. I am in Sydney. The weather is fine, blue skies and bright sunshine, and I am fine too. Don't wait for me, please, and don't worry. *Ya pridu; Yesli smogu; Yesli zakhochu. AHHA* xx

In a note that was mostly in English, only the greeting and the last three phrases: *I'll come; If I can; If I want*, were in Russian. She had signed her name in Russian, followed by the two kisses.

The date on the stamp was smudged. It took me a few

minutes to work out that it had been posted quite a while ago.

In the lunch break I phoned Sophia to tell her about the postcard from Sydney.

'What are you going to do?' she asked.

'I don't know,' I replied. 'It's too late now. And Sydney is so far away.'

She asked me to read out the card to her, which I did, translating the Russian.

'I can't come over now,' she said. 'Isabella is sick so I can't bring her with me. But why don't you come round this evening and help me cook a vegetarian meal? Then we can have a long chat. Isabella loves seeing you. You know that, don't you?'

Before I went out that evening I took Anna's things from our cupboards and put them into a suitcase which I dragged to Sophia's apartment. As I approached it I saw Isabella at the window. She spotted me and waved.

I saw her waiting for me at the door, smiling.

'Zio Vasu, Zio Vasu, I have some news for you,' she announced.

'Let him in, you naughty girl.' I heard Sophia coming. 'And get back to bed. You'll make him sick too.'

Sophia kissed me on the lips, drew back, examined me and said: 'You look fine. I'm glad to see you.'

I went in. I left the suitcase near the door of the sitting room.

'What's that, Zio Vasu?' Isabella asked.

'A suitcase with presents,' I replied.

Sophia recognised Anna's suitcase but said nothing.

Isabella was excited. 'Let's open it and see what's in there for me.'

'No, not now,' Sophia intervened. 'It's bedtime for you.'

Isabella looked at me, then at Sophia, then back in my direction, pleading.

'She can stay up with us, can't she?' I asked.

Sophia gave in, and Isabella brought in her doona, her pillow and her hot-water bottle and arranged herself on the sofa.

'So what's your news?' I asked her.

She looked at her mother, trying to guess if it would be all right to talk about happy things. She waited and after receiving a nod from her mamma proudly announced:

'I've won a prize.'

'Is that right?' I smiled.

'In the art competition. First Prize, Zio Vasu.'

'And what did you draw?'

'It's in the exhibition. You'll have to go and see it.'

'What's it about?'

'I don't know, but there's a boat in it.'

'And?'

'And there's a bridge—'

'And?'

'And on the bridge there's a little girl with a kite.'

'What sort of kite?'

'Looks like a Chinese lantern.'

I remembered the Chinese kite she had bought to the Lido and how we had tried very hard to make it fly – but it wouldn't.

I saw Isabella looking at the suitcase and I opened it. She jumped out of her makeshift bed and claimed every piece of Anna's jewellery for herself: the Indian bangles, the necklaces, bracelets and earrings and even a silver nose-bud that Jijee-ma had sent as a gift.

Sophia said she would go through the dresses and other clothes, keep whatever she fancied and take the rest to a charity shop.

'You really want to give everything away?' Sophia asked.

'Almost everything,' I said. I had decided on two keepsakes: Jijee-ma's nose-bud and the Budapest scarf.

Next morning Isabella returned everything except six bangles.

That night, by the time the meal was cooked, she was already asleep. I helped Sophia carry her to the bedroom. Back in the kitchen, Sophia looked at the postcard, read the message and put it down on the table.

We talked about work, her music, the launch of my book, Isabella's flu and the tides which, according to the forecast, were going to be particularly bad that winter.

'I'm sick of this city,' Sophia said. 'Sick of the water and the wretched smells.'

Like many Venetians she was fed up with the overcrowding and had been waiting for years for a chance to leave. She told me that her family came from Palmanova, a little town to the north-east. She had been born and brought up there and had come to Venice to study. Soon she had found a job, fallen in love, married and settled down.

'Isabella's Papa was a master glass-blower, like his father and grandfather. He was doing well: had an established clientele, reliable contacts with galleries, showrooms and tour operators, and was a good salesman. He knew how to make potential customers feel comfortable and important. He didn't cheat anyone. He just talked and talked, very fluently and easily convincing you of the extraordinary beauty of this or that piece of glass, praising its design, shape and colour. He was young and energetic and wanted to conquer the world.' She paused, and her face changed. 'Stupid he was, really stupid.'

'What's his name?' I asked.

'Patricio,' Sophia said. She continued with her story.

'Then one day he met a tall blonde American from San Francisco. She was older than me, yet still looked young and fresh. And the way she walked! You had to move aside to make way for her. She had power. No wonder Patricio lost his mind and his will to resist and couldn't sleep. He packed his bags and flew away with her. No sorry, no goodbye. Just left. Isabella was still tiny, just three months old. I felt so tired, so miserable and useless. Isabella cried non-stop and because I couldn't cope, I cried too. My breasts and feet hurt and I felt utterly useless.'

She paused again. 'You know what? The most awful moment is when you start hating yourself, blaming yourself for everything. Thank God Gloria, my younger sister, was there to rescue me from this mess. She lives in Milano, running her little boutique and designing her own material. Haven't you met her? She was in love with Marco too, head over heels, as they say. Who wasn't? He's such a charmer.'

'So Patricio knows about Isabella?' I asked.

'Of course he does. But she doesn't know him. I've only told her his name. It's easier that way.'

'Does Patricio write or call?' I asked.

'No, never.'

'Have you tried to look for him?'

'Have you tried to look for Anna?' she shot back. Then she looked at me and said softly: 'I'm sorry. I shouldn't have said that.'

'No need to be sorry.' It had been rude of me to ask. 'No, I haven't looked for him. It's his loss, not mine,' she said.

'But wouldn't one day Isabella want to know, find out and—'

'You want to know if she'll blame me. Of course she will. But she'll understand eventually. At least I hope she does. I also hope that she'll be kind to both me and her Papa.'

Kind. Who knows? Perhaps with time; perhaps after she has faced the consequences of her own decisions. But how often do we learn from the mistakes of our parents? Not very often. In fact we often commit similar mistakes, as if to fail is the natural attribute of our life. However hard we try, the time comes when the obverse of our goodness reveals itself, not as an aberration but a necessity, not as a brief moment of madness but a prolonged, incurable affliction of the body and mind.

For a few moments we were silent together. Then Sophia got up to make us fresh coffee. When she came back she sat next to me on the sofa, took my hand in hers, kissed it and said:

'You'll get over it. We all do. We have to, don't we?'

'Of course,' I replied.

'And don't worry about Anna. She'll be fine and you'll be fine and happiness will surely return.'

I spent the night on her sofa searching for one peaceful thought that could lead to sleep. But I tossed and turned. The window was open and the wind, moist and cold, flirted with the curtain. I heard the water slapping the boats; someone walked across the bridge; a bird fluttered, followed by another. Then there was a prolonged silence broken suddenly by a song, faint and hazy, as if heard in a dream.

Was it a dream or merely its shadow?

A week after the night in Sophia's apartment, we decided to go to Palmanova. Sophia wanted to see her parents and I wanted to explore the city.

Her father owned a small pottery shop in the main market and we spent the first day helping him out. In the evening they invited me to a simple family dinner to which Sophia's aunt, her father's sister, and her husband also came.

After dinner I moved to a corner of the room and began sketching.

I spent the following day walking through the city on my own. I climbed the tower in the centre to enjoy the best view of this seventeenth-century town built in the shape of a nine-sided polygon with radiating streets and a moat along the fortress wall. A tower stood at the centre of a hexagonal piazza connected by gates to the roads. If it had been attacked it would have been easy to shut the gates and seal off the city. Palmanova had been designed as a fort with a series of protective walls ringing it, but had seen only one battle. I made a few quick sketches, climbed down the tower and strolled to the nearby parade ground and arms depot.

Before I said goodbye, I gave Sophia's parents the three sketches I had done after their dinner. They liked them and wanted to give me something in return. Sophia's father asked her to take me to his shop to select a piece. I chose a long thin vase suitable for a single flower.

Sophia's mother didn't like it. 'Only one flower? Not lucky,' she said.

The boat trip back to Venice was tedious. It rained the whole way, cold and windy, forcing us to stay under cover. Isabella played with my camera and asked me to show her how to take photos. I did, and set them up. Each time she pressed the shutter she echoed its sound.

She wanted to take a photo of her mother and me standing near a railing with the sea in the background. She focused the camera, pressed the shutter and then became so excited that she dropped the lens cover she was holding in her other hand. Sophia tried to catch it but she was too late. It slipped from her hands and disappeared into the water.

Isabella was upset. All the rest of the trip she kept bewailing the lost cover.

As we approached Venice's Lagoon the rain suddenly stopped but the sky was still full of clouds, lit here and there with slivers of fading daylight. The boat moved slowly towards the mouth of the Canal Grande and just at that moment the lights came on. On the left was San Giorgio Maggiore with its white Palladian façade and its helmet-like dome and tall red-brick bell tower. The portico of the Doge's Palace appeared. I counted its seventeen doors topped with thirty-four arches on the balcony of the *piano nobile*. As I admired its lightness and airiness, I understood why this smelly city of water, stones and boats seduced everyone.

But once again the city failed to win my heart. It was too enchanting for its own good, I thought, too loud and bold, too ruthless and cold.

I was already yearning to go home, to India.

As it turned out, I didn't have to wait long. Just two weeks after the trip to Palmanova, a telegram from Uncle Triple K arrived. He told me to return at once: 'Jijee-ma is very ill.' I said goodbye to Sophia and Isabella by phone, telling them that I would leave two boxes of my watercolours, pencils and crayons for Isabella, with my neighbour. I said that I would miss them more than Venice, and that I would remember the city only because of them. Surely I would come to see them again, perhaps to celebrate Isabella's wedding.

The night before I left, it snowed. I went into the Piazza San Marco to have one last look at the domes of the Basilica under their white shroud. I spent the evening in a bar.

On my last morning I took some photos of the square, the bell tower and the Basilica.

Jijee-ma died just as I was taking the pictures. It was seven-thirty in the morning in Gurgaon.

A large print of my photo of the Basilica hangs in my office. It reminds me of the passing of Jijee-ma and the disappearance of Anna from my life.

Part Three

Wer jetzt allein ist, wird es lange bleiben

(Whoever is alone will stay alone)

Rainer Maria Rilke, *Autumn Day*

Moscow, August 1991

Vasu

'*Vladimir is dying,*' Katya wrote. '*He is sinking minute by minute and soon the doctors will stop feeding him altogether. He wants to see you. Come and help him walk the last few steps to the other side of life. Come, before he forgets that you came.*'

I was in Berlin at a conference. I read the letter during a session I was chairing. Soon I lost track of the proceedings, got up, excused myself and left the room.

The next day I caught the first train to Moscow.

During the long trip I tried to keep myself busy with an essay I was writing on emotions and their relationship with modern urban spaces. But I couldn't find the right voice and soon gave up. This was foolish because in no time at all my mind began to play tricks with my memory.

Although I had made myself stop remembering Jijee-ma soon after her death, I still felt her presence continually around me. Every time her daughter phoned I heard Jijee-ma in her voice, and that brought both joy and consolation. I was relieved that no special effort was required on my part to remember her.

With Anna it was different. I wanted to forget her – move on, as they say – but she stubbornly resisted all my attempts. In the end I decided that I would stop trying. That's when, out of pity or some other cunning intent, she relented and disappeared from my life. But I knew that she was still alive somewhere within me, ready to show herself, staring as if from the cracked mirror we had once upon a time refused to throw away.

'That mirror will bring you bad luck,' Aunty Olga had warned us.

'*Chepukha* (nonsense),' we had said, ignoring her warning.

Now in the train rapidly approaching Moscow, the city of my youth, I was beginning to wonder about my decision. I wanted to see Vladimir and Katya, no doubt about it, but I was also frightened that I wouldn't be able to resist the temptation to visit Leonid Mikhailovich and Aunty Olga. I could already picture it: there I was, standing at the door ready to ring the bell and it was Anna who opened it. She looked at me and I had no idea what to say or do. Even if she asked me to come in, my feet would fail to obey.

I used to carry a little photo of Anna in my wallet, but the day I left Venice I took it out and put it away. Soon all the photos of her vanished and her presence in my everyday life was reduced to a handful of after-images: the starry night at Gelon; the bed in the abortion hospital; the reading table near the window in Leninka; her bare feet poking out from under the quilt; and her cello standing quietly in the corner of the room.

Five years before in London someone had showed me a concert programme for the Sydney Symphony Orchestra and an unknown voice had begun to whisper to me. I tried my best to ignore it, but failed. The concert was wonderful and I was relieved that I couldn't find Anna listed among the players. A year before that, watching the telecast of a one-day cricket match from Sydney, I started searching for her in the crowd. It was silly to expect to see her at a cricket match but it didn't stop me from looking.

The proof that she had finally set me free came a few years ago when I tried to remember her face. I realised that I couldn't recall anything except the tiny mole just above the left corner of her upper lip. Nothing more than a mole. 'What a disgrace!' I thought then, strangely angered by my inability to remember her whole face.

Now I wondered in a panic if I had completely forgotten Vladimir as well. He had been a good Moscow friend, but in the last ten years I had only been in contact with him and Katya through occasional letters, New Year and birthday greetings and rare phone calls. In them, the bond of friendship remained strong. Katya's little boy, Yasya, must have grown into a handsome young man. The daughter which she had so desperately wanted to have with Vladimir had, never arrived. 'Complications,' I remembered Katya mentioning in one of her letters that also contained photos of the three of them in Prague on a tour. Now I tried to recall their faces and those photos, but failed.

But my effort wasn't wasted; it did retrieve a few memories of our times together. There I am, sitting with Vladimir in a train returning from his *dacha*. We have spent the day walking in the forest hunting for mushrooms. The sun shines for a while and disappears between the showers. He tells me about growing up in a small village in the Urals. His father was a master watchmaker who could take anything apart and then, without a manual, put it back together again, polished and good as new.

Vladimir had an older sister, Anyuta, who used to carry him on her back when he was little. One day she climbed a tree to rescue the newborn chick of a bee-eater abandoned in a nest. Vladimir stood under the tree watching. Suddenly she fell, the chick in her hand, broke her knee and punctured a lung.

But worse was to come. After three days, she died. His mother weathered the tragedy but his father couldn't bear the loss. He put away his tools and became a bee-keeper.

Scene number two: It's Anna's birthday. We are in a restaurant. Dessert is about to be served. Vladimir gets up from his chair, walks up to the little orchestra and whispers something to the bass-player. As he comes back to our table they begin to play a waltz. He kneels down on one knee in front of Anna. At first she looks uneasy, but then pushes her napkin aside, gets up and dances the waltz with Vladimir.

Here is another scene, shorter but more intense. I am in a park with a dozen other people on a warm summer night. The sun has long disappeared but it isn't dark. The air is soft and light and the sky clear, waiting for the stars to come out. A little book is lying on the floor near Vladimir's chair. He picks it up, opens it, looks in the direction of the others sitting on the grass, shuts the book and walks right up to the edge of the stage.

Then he begins to read: 'По.. слу.....шайте!' (Li....sten!). He waits for a few seconds for the audience to stop talking and pay attention to him, then continues:

Послушайте!
Ведь, если звезды зажигают —
Значит — это, кому-небудь нужно?
Значит — кто-то хочет, чтобы они были?
Значит — кто-то называет эти плевочки жемчужиной?

(Listen!
If the stars light up
It means that someone needs them?
It means that someone wants them to be there?
It means that someone dares to call these spit-lets pearly?)

This was my favourite Mayakovsky poem. Although I hadn't read anything in Russian for over a year, the words came to me effortlessly. I repeated them and a feeling of incredible lightness enveloped me. I looked out the window. Just above the horizon in the pitch darkness I saw a large star, its pale yellow light reflected on the rails running parallel to our train's. I wished the train would stop so that I could open the door, step into the darkness and vanish without a trace.

The spell was broken by a knock. When I opened the door the conductor brought me down to earth. She had come to tell me that the dining car was about to shut and that if I wanted anything to eat I should hurry. Otherwise nothing would be left but tea and soggy biscuits.

I wasn't hungry and asked her for tea. She returned with a

pot, some biscuits and chocolate wafers. She left the tray on the table near the window and glanced in my direction to see if I wanted anything else. I thanked her and gave her a few German coins as a tip.

She wanted to stay and talk. The train was passing over a bridge and I looked for the name of the river.

'That was Rudka,' she said and smiled. She told me that in less than an hour we would cross the Polish border and stop at Brest. There the wheels would be changed and guards would come to inspect my documents and luggage.

Since I had been in Moscow, everything in the political landscape of Eastern Europe had changed. The Berlin Wall had fallen; Poland was ruled by Solidarity; Vaclav Havel was President in Prague; in Romania Ceausescu had been deposed, captured and executed; and even in Bulgaria, the Communists had fallen. In the Soviet Union itself both *glasnost* and *perestroika* had fractured the hitherto monolithic structure of the state and the Party, which was rapidly losing ground. People like Shurik were beginning to question its hegemony. Strangely Vladimir seemed to have remained untouched by the events. His silence intrigued me. I remembered the little postcard he had sent me in Canada, on which he had scribbled a few lines from Pushkin's *Boris Godunov*. '*Smutnoe vremya* (the time of troubles) have arrived,' he had noted.

The casual way in which my documents were checked surprised me. My luggage wasn't examined at all, and my passport and visa generated only a friendly discussion.

'An Indian living in Canada, is that so?' they asked.

'I teach a semester in Canada each year.' They weren't interested in my teaching job or qualifications but one of them noticed that I was carrying some ice-hockey magazines and posters, which I had brought for Yasya. The young man was a keen player himself and a big fan of Maltsev, the striker of the Dynamo Moscow team. I gave him a poster.

The train arrived at Belorussky Station around nine in the morning. I gathered my bags, stepped down and automatically looked over at the opposite platform. That was where the bench had been where, when Aunty Olga, Katya and Tamrico had come to see us off at the station, Aunty Olga had sat because she had not been feeling well.

I took a few steps towards the bench that no longer existed, then stopped. I didn't want the absent bench to resurrect the face I had so desperately tried to remember and then forget a few hours before. There was no need, I reminded myself.

As I left the station I turned back to look at the big clock hanging on the wall above the main portico. Unlike the day of our departure, it was ticking.

'Quarter past nine,' I murmured and looked at my watch, which was still showing Berlin time.

It took me a while to find a cab. I was surprised that the square in front of the station, which used to be so busy, was almost empty.

When I finally did find a cab, I started chatting with the driver, who was from Georgia. Then as we turned into Gorky Street we were suddenly among a column of tanks and armed personnel carriers loaded with soldiers.

'What's happening?' I asked the driver.

'A military coup,' he said.

When Katya opened the door and saw me outside, her face expressed no surprise. Just a faint smile followed by a soft *hello* and a kiss.

'Welcome,' she said. 'You can't imagine how glad I am to see you. Vladimir is waiting for you.' She tried to smile again but gave up and then exhausted by the effort to control her emotions, she slumped on the stool near the door and began to sob.

'I am sorry,' she said after a few minutes.

'He is in the library. Please take off your coat, get rid of those awful shoes and let me see if I can find you a pair of warm slippers.'

Once they were found, I was ushered into the kitchen. Soon the kettle was boiled, a fresh pot of tea brewed, and a bowl filled with chocolates and lollies. I took a sip and thanked her for the lovely hot tea.

She swept breadcrumbs off the tablecloth, straightened it and said: 'I didn't know if my letter would reach you in time. I'm so glad that you've come. You must be tired and hungry. Let me do you a quick omelette.'

I reassured her that I wasn't at all hungry.

'You haven't changed much. The same delightful face and the same hesitant smile,' she said.

'You haven't changed much either,' I wanted to say, but couldn't because she had in fact changed quite a lot: grown old, put on weight. Most painful of all was the change in the colour of her skin. I recalled the wonderful smoothness of what Tamrico often used to call her *luminous skin*. Now she looked tired and the blankness in her eyes was frightening.

She noticed my silence. 'Don't tell me that I look fine

too,' she said. Not waiting for my response, she continued: 'Because I don't.'

She glanced out the window and then turned back to me.

'You know, the most painful thing in life is the feeling that you can't ever experience the pain suffered by those you love, as they themselves experience it. Any pain you endure is principally your own, and try as you may, the thought always plagues you that your pain is not enough, just not of the same measure. And that's when you begin to question your integrity, your honesty and most of all your love.'

She held her mug of tea in both hands, warming them without drinking. After a short pause, she went on: 'I told you he's in the library, behind the closed door. I'll take you in, but I want to be sure that you're ready for him. Do you still remember his face? It's completely changed.'

'I'm not sure if I do remember,' I wanted to say. Instead I took from my bag the sketch I had made of Vladimir in the train. I repeated for her Mayakovsky's little poem about the pearly spit-lets in the sky and how much I admired the way Vladimir used to read it aloud.

'I can still remember the words,' I said. 'And now I know why.' She took my sketch, looked intently at it, smiled wanly and then turned away.

Slowly she rose and fetched from the bedroom an album containing photos of Vladimir, one for each month of the preceding three years. I was stunned by the indifference with which each picture recorded his rapid decline.

Five years before, she told me, he had been diagnosed HIV-positive. This had gradually developed into full-blown AIDS. She had been unable to organise proper medicines or treatment and no doctor or nurse had been willing to look after him. He had rapidly lost weight, and when the previous year he had caught pneumonia, he had deteriorated even faster. A few months ago he had completely lost his voice. Now he communicated in indecipherable whispers, croaks and desperate cries.

'He's going down rapidly,' Katya said. 'Soon he'll be gone. We don't want ever to leave him alone so we take turns sitting with him, beside his bed. Tamrico is there now. But if you want to you can go in and see him.'

Tamrico already knew I had arrived. She greeted me with a silent hug and then left the room.

On the bed, white as any stretch of fresh snow, was Vladimir. His head, bald and small, resting on two pillows, seemed tiny as a little boy's. His eyes were shut and his arms lay at his side, hands and fingers absolutely still, legs straight and in the place of feet just a small hump. Only his head and the shape of his feet showed that there was indeed someone lying under the sheet. Without them there were only folds.

'He's ready to dissolve into thin light air,' I thought. The only movement was the occasional quiver of his body. The only sound was a slow and steady drip into his arm.

The bed was almost in the middle of the room. Beside it stood a chair and a little table. There was a tall lamp in the corner illuminating half the room. On one wall hung a framed copy of Kiprenksy's portrait of Pushkin, and on the other, a large framed poster of Chagall's *White Crucifixion*.

As I sat with him, I found that Vladimir slept most of the time, only occasionally interrupted by the few words Katya whispered in his ear. During the day sunlight flooded the room from the window near Pushkin's portrait, and in the evening the soft light of dusk entered from a smaller window in the opposite wall. Even at night the curtains were never drawn.

'He likes natural light and fresh air,' Katya explained.

Now Katya went up to Vladimir, leaned down and murmured something in his ear. After a few seconds his eyes opened, his face turned in my direction and he smiled, and for a tiny moment I caught a glimpse of the face I had dreamed in the train.

I sat down, pulling the chair close to the bed, taking his hand and pressing it gently. There was little response. As I was about to withdraw it I felt a slight tightening of his grip and left it there. After a while his grip relaxed, reassured that my touch was real and that I wouldn't desert him. Thought, I felt, was still living in his body and the disposition to feel joy and pleasure, and to give and receive them, hadn't departed. I felt his grip tightening again and his arm moved slightly. I gazed into his face and found his eyes open, trying to reach me, and his lips quivering. Katya had crept in again and was indicating that Vladimir was trying to say something to me.

I leaned forward and heard the words: 'Berlin ... Rosa Luxemburg Platz Station ...'

Vladimir was trying hard to speak but couldn't get out any more words.

'Why Berlin?' I wanted to ask. But Katya had turned away, distressed by his desperate attempts to speak. I patted his hand, letting him know that I had heard him.

'This coup won't succeed.' Shurik was certain of it.

'Who knows?' Tamrico wasn't so sure.

'The army can be so ruthless.' Katya was frightened.

'But most of them are conscripts: young, fresh and apprehensive. They won't open fire on unarmed people.'

Shurik was adamant. 'Civil war scares everyone.'

'It didn't eighty years ago,' I said.

'Then it was different. It was class war,' he said. 'Brother attacked brother. Now there are no classes, just poor and not-so-poor people.'

In the sitting room the television was left turned on at a low, hardly audible volume. Normal programmes had been suspended, replaced by ballets, operas and concerts.

At the end of the corridor, Yasya's room was a mess. 'Young boys and girls keep coming and going, excited about what's going on in the streets,' Katya told me. The kitchen was by far the noisiest room, with the radio on constantly. Every snippet of information was carefully analysed.

Yasya and his friends went out to the barricades near the White House, the Parliament building. They kept us informed about the events by calling us from a nearby hotel where one of Yasya's friend worked as an accountant.

Shurik began to look worried. He had been to the White House several times, inspected the scene around Manezhnaya Square and talked to the soldiers in the tanks lined up ominously along Kalininsky Prospect. He had contacts in the KGB who could give him news from inside. What gave him confidence about the resistance was that the security forces, the army and the KGB were divided. Most soldiers hated the KGB, and it contained warring factions.

The most dangerous threat, he said, came from the Alpha Group of the KGB, a special unit of crack commandos. They had been involved in the January 1991 assault on a Lithuanian television station in Vilnius, resulting in at least fourteen civilians being killed. He had a friend who knew one of these commandos and who was desperately trying to reach him to discover their intentions.

Yasya told us that President Yeltsin had finally emerged from the White House, mounted a tank and given a rousing speech. He was accompanied by a retired colonel, which would have unsettled some of the soldiers. Yeltsin shook hands with one of them and joked: 'I hope you aren't going to shoot your President, young man.'

Yasya had been standing right next to the tank and had heard everything perfectly. 'Yeltsin is brave, isn't he?' a woman in the crowd had said to her companion. 'He's brave because he's drunk,' her companion had laughed, 'but only he, the *Sibiryak* (Siberian), can save us.'

'He comes from Sverdlovsk,' shouted someone else. 'But does it matter?'

Yasya told them that he had pulled out a packet of gum from his pocket and offered it to a young soldier. 'Not allowed,' the soldier had told him, angrily. An old man standing nearby encouraged the soldier, but he wouldn't yield, even though he was obviously hungry. Then a woman offered chocolate bars to other soldiers. One of them took a couple and hid them in his pocket.

'Take this apple, please. It's better than chocolates,' a young woman with a red scarf said. She produced a couple of large and tempting apples, which also soon disappeared.

A soldier murmured to Yasya that they had been warned not to accept food from the huge crowd in front of the White House. Chocolates or biscuits could be poisoned, they were told.

'These are fine, son,' a man who could have been a retired soldier tried to reassure them.

'That's what they told us when we marched into Prague.'

'But this is Moscow. Here we're all are Russians, aren't we?'

'He won't shoot me,' a *babushka* standing under an umbrella said. 'I'm a grandmother, just like his.'

'Yes, she looks like you,' the young soldier replied.

Every time Yasya phoned, Katya warned him to take care. 'Keep yourself out of trouble, do you hear, away from trouble?' she cautioned him. 'Don't bait the soldiers. They're young and inexperienced and tense. Don't irritate them. I want you back home safe and sound.'

'Safe and sound,' Yasya repeated each time.

The following evening I would meet Yasya and Lena, Shurik's daughter, in front of the White House and stay there all night. Katya was in the kitchen. 'The *Vremya* is on,' I heard her calling. 'Come and see what they're showing.' It was a short news report, but quite daring for the main news programme of the national channel. Yeltsin read a statement criticising the putsch. The camera moved away from him, showing the barricades near the White House. Commentary continued, interrupted by Yeltsin's loud voice. Most intriguing were pictures from Leningrad, where a similar protest against the coup had begun.

'Our darling Seriozha Medvedev will be in trouble,' Tamrico said about a well-known newsreader.

'And not only him,' replied Katya. 'What about the

producer and the crew?' She had worked for a few months with the producer's wife.

'Aren't they brave to report? Now people at the barricades know that they're not alone, that others care about them and will join them, tanks or no tanks.'

I wasn't so sure. In Tiananmen Square in Beijing, not long ago, the world had watched as an unarmed young man had dared to confront a column of tanks. He had walked right up to the leading tank and, ignoring the huge gun pointed at him, begun talking to the soldiers.

He had escaped unharmed, but hundreds of other protestors had been crushed under the tanks or shot on that June night in 1989. Had they seen that on Russian television?

'No – and perhaps it's just as well,' Tamrico replied. 'Imagine how that would have frightened people! But we all watched the attack on the television station in Vilnius. It was really scary.'

'Yes, that was terrible,' said Katya, 'but Shurik thinks it shows how brutal power can be resisted. The best way to resist, he says, is to remain peaceful—'

'Shurik sounds more and more like Gandhi these days,' said Tamrico. 'I'm not convinced. Fear can force people to do silly things. But Shurik believes that Russians are different, not as cruel and despotic as Asians. When I tell him that Gandhi was an Asian and that there is a bit of Asian in every Russian, and furthermore that his comments are racist, he just smiles. He won't change his mind.'

I said nothing. What could I say? I was only too aware of the misery, deprivation and cruelty of India, not all of which could be attributed to poverty and colonial oppression. But

I wasn't about to agree that Asians were somehow naturally flawed. So I didn't say a word.

My mind was troubled by two events unfolding simultaneously. On the streets a couple of kilometres from our house, a tense spectacle of life and death was playing itself out. Then in a tiny closed room nearby, one of my dearest friends was waiting to die.

'What should I do?' I thought. 'Should I join Shurik, Yasya, Lena and the others at the barricades or should I go to the library and sit beside Vladimir? Should I grieve for my friend or go and witness history? What will happen? Will it end in bloodshed or will people at last show some real courage, step back and find a peaceful way to resolve the crisis?'

I spent most of the next night in the library with Vladimir. The doctor came and told us that the end was near.

'We can stop the drip now,' he said. 'He has gone beyond pain and suffering. Morphine is useless now.'

'Are you sure, Ivan Vasillivich?' Katya said. 'I can hear him moaning.'

'That will soon stop,' the doctor replied. 'He's now too weak to make a sound. I'll come again in the morning. But don't hesitate to call if you need me.'

When the drip was removed, all signs of movement disappeared and calmness descended on the room. The scene was set for Vladimir's final exit. I found it hard to sit there. The room seemed to have transformed itself into a flat painting, expunged of time and place.

'Have I stopped living too?' I wondered.

Vladimir was clinging to life and when I looked carefully at him, I saw him move slightly. At the windows the curtains blew and we heard drops of rain against the window. Tiny puddles of water appeared on the floor. I got up to close the window and heard faint sounds of heavy trucks, the rumble of moving tanks and the muffled voices of the crowd outside.

Then I was alone in the room. I felt anxious. I had seen dead people before but had never experienced the exact moment of dying. 'Does the last gasp of air empty the lungs and they collapse?' I asked myself. 'Is there a sound, a snort perhaps or a cry or just a soft noise like a damp firecracker unwilling to go bang? What sound does the spirit make when it escapes the body?' For Hindus, it's the *prana,* the breath, born from the mouth of Adipurusha, the primeval being. But is the *prana* the last breath? Does it leave the body to travel with the wind in search of some greater being? Earth to earth, as they say, ashes to ashes, dust to dust and nothing afterwards but endless wandering through the memories of those who have been left behind, until they themselves vanish.

I was glad that Katya didn't leave me alone for long. Soon she came to sit with us and we waited in silence for death to leave the windowsill, step gently across the floor to Vladimir and, without waking him, take him away.

We both dozed. At around five o'clock next morning I woke to see Katya standing near the bed, speaking to Vladimir.

'I had a dream,' I said, 'and I saw you with Yasya.'

'I know. I heard you mumble in your sleep. But I too had a dream of Yasya and you.'

'How strange,' I said and began to describe my dream.

231

'I saw Christ on the cross. His face was pale, paler than anything I have ever seen. His arms hung uselessly and in the middle of the palms of his hands were red spots of blood. His head was bound with a white scarf and around his hips was a white cloth with black stripes. It was so small, so inadequate, that I wanted to remove my shirt to cover his bruised legs. The wind ruffled his cloth very slightly and blew my hair which, to my great surprise, was long and red.

'I was standing on the side of a hill and could see men and women sitting in a boat rowing with their bare hands. Behind them was a village on fire. Flames, bright red and yellow, reached the sky, mixed with clouds of smoke from burnt-out huts. I heard shouts, the footsteps of soldiers, then gunshots. I saw you walk past, your head covered in a blue scarf with silver spots, holding Yasya in your arms. His little head was resting on your shoulder. You looked at me as if I were a stranger and said: "Run away, my boy. The soldiers are coming." But I didn't run and you disappeared, walking slowly along the dirt track cutting across the slope.

'No sooner had you gone than I heard Vladimir's voice. I looked for him but couldn't see him, even though his voice was all around me. I tried to listen carefully. "Minutes pass while I, Matthew the Levite, sit here on Mount Golgotha. And still he isn't dead!" Then again: "The sun is setting and death hasn't yet come." Then there was a long pause, after which the voice came so close to me that I felt as if it were my own. "God! Why are you so angry with him? Ask death to come and take him away."

'The voice was lost in the wind, leaving me alone. Still I didn't run. I waited and waited, confident that someone would come to tell me what I needed to know. He finally appeared. I recognised him immediately. He wore a green gown and cap and carried a sack on his right shoulder. "Get up and walk," he said. "The Messiah has gone and the Cross has vanished. It's time for you to get up and go too."

'I looked round and found that on the hill there was no one to be seen. Nothing but stones and dust and above them a completely empty sky. I felt sudden heartbreaking loneliness.'

'But he is still here,' said Katya.

We both approached the bed and listened. Vladimir was still breathing.

It took several days for me to make sense of the dream. After Vladimir's funeral, when the room had been emptied and turned back into a studio, I got the chance to look properly at Chagall's *White Crucifixion*. There I saw the pale figure on the cross, the people in the boat and the village on fire. I also saw the person in the green gown. Chagall described him as Ahasverus, the Wandering Jew. In the foreground of the painting was a woman in a scarf carrying a child in her arms. 'I must have been looking at the painting just before I was overcome by sleep,' I thought. Vladimir's voice I could explain, but the words he had spoken mystified me.

Shurik told me: 'Go and look at Chapter 16 of Book One of *The Master and Margarita*.' I found the words in Bulgakov's novel. They were the words of Matthew, the Levite.

The following evening I went outside to join the crowds at the White House.

I walked along Arbat Street, reached Smolensk Embankment and turned right to see the flimsy and hastily erected barricades which looked quite incapable of stopping tanks. At Smolensk Square, both on Kalininsky Prospect to my right and on Kutuzov Street to my left, I saw a long column of tanks surrounded by people holding umbrellas. If they were ordered to attack, I thought, and if they followed those orders, there would be utter chaos.

The square and streets close to the White House were lined with barricades. The material from nearby construction sites had been easy to pile up, but everyone knew that wire-mesh fencing, metal rods, wooden planks, tyres and blocks of concrete would at best only hinder tanks and would merely delay the final assault.

But resistance on the streets was spontaneous and carried its own simple logic: people would do what they could with bare hands and bodies, but would not attack first. Should the tanks advance, they would move aside. Their main aim was to shame the soldiers.

I decided to walk along Kalininsky Prospect looking for the clinic where twelve years before Anna and I had lost our baby. On the way I saw the cinema where I watched *Solaris*. I reached the cinema theatre and realised that I didn't have the courage to go further. I turned back. Not far away was the wreckage of a trolleybus run over by a tank. Some young people were taking pieces of the wrecked bus and piling them in front of the barricades. Two girls of nine or ten stood on another tank and waved to the crowd. A boy with a lollipop protruding from his mouth slid up and down the barrel of its gun. Young men stood on other tanks holding up placards and posters.

Some tanks were draped in the Russian tricolour flag from pre-Soviet times. This juxtaposition of tanks, trucks and unarmed people swarming around them trying to domesticate them, to make them look friendly and less threatening, seemed bizarre.

A young soldier appeared out of a tank and began talking to a *babushka* who wanted to feed him *pirozhki*. People were loaded with bags containing whatever food they had found at home. Everyone felt that the soldiers had been on duty for hours without anything to eat or drink.

'Keep them fed and entertained and they won't shoot,' said a woman near me. Others in the crowd said she was right.

At around seven that evening, I heard a huge roar from the edge of the crowd and saw people running in the direction of the Kalinin Bridge. The tanks also seemed to be moving.

'They're coming,' someone shouted. All the soldiers disappeared inside their tanks. As they too began to roll, the crowd retreated.

'It's going to start,' a man with a loudspeaker announced. I made my way towards the White House. I was delighted when I saw Shurik, Yasya and ten-year old Lena under a flimsy, plastic shelter.

'Did you hear that the tanks are coming?' I asked Shurik.

'Yes, but it's a false alarm. They're not going to attack, at least not now,' he said, with great certainty.

'I saw a girl like you on top of a tank,' I told Lena.

'I was up on one yesterday,' she said proudly. 'Have you seen Mama?'

I told her that Tamrico was with Katya and that she was fine, but that they were worried about her and Yasya.

Lena told me about the ice-skating school she was attending.

'One day I want to compete in the Olympics,' she said.

'That's wonderful,' I told her. 'If I'd known, I would have brought you a pair of ice-skates from Canada.'

But she was preoccupied. 'Do you really think they'll attack us?' she asked nervously. Everyone was turned towards the square where some movement in the tank columns was clearly taking place.

'Hard to know,' I said.

'Can we stop them?'

'Of course we can. Haven't we already done that?'

I told her that the best thing was that people in the crowd were friendly and carried no weapons. The soldiers could see they weren't threatening them.

'Fear and panic lead to disaster,' I said. 'It's good that no one is trying to whip up fear now.'

'But what about the soldiers and militiamen who have come over to our side? If they attack, the army is bound to retaliate,' Yasya said.

'Our soldiers won't attack,' said Shurik. 'They've been ordered to stay calm. What's more, they know they can't match the army.'

Out of the uneasy movement in front of the White House, slowly a chain of command was beginning to emerge. The people inside had realised it would be dangerous to let the protestors react spontaneously to events, according to Shurik. The protestors were tense, tired and visibly scared. They needed guidance. Every so often one of the members of Yeltsin's government would come out of the White House, mount a tank or stand up on a table, and make a short speech. The loudspeakers from inside also kept us up to date about what was going on.

On portable radios the news came from everywhere: the BBC, Radio Free Europe and Moscow Radio. Someone had even managed to plug in a television set. To add to the cacophony there were guitars, accordions, violins and balalaikas. Earlier in the day the great cellist Rostropovich had entered the White House and waved to the crowd from a window. And other performers had also joined the protestors. The folksongs and ballads of the bards Vysotsky and Okudzhava were continually being sung. Then someone else would play the humorous skits of satirist Arkadii Raikin. Lena told me that an hour before she had seen the stand-up comedian Genady Khazanov in the crowd, cracking jokes. 'He's so funny, isn't he?'

Rumours spread like grass fires. One said that soon a curfew would be declared, probably between 11pm and 5am. Another said that the trains in the Metro would be stopped. As soon as the crowd had been ordered to disperse, an attack would begin, said a third. Shurik said that he had seen soldiers preparing to take their positions in and around the White House. They had removed their uniforms and, armed with Kalashnikov rifles, were ready to defend the President.

At 9.30pm *Vremya* announced the curfew. News came through the crowd from Manezh Square near the Kremlin that tanks were beginning to move in the direction of the White House. By this time Lena was tired and ready to sleep. Shurik and Yasya left her with me in the shelter and went off to find out what was happening. The news they brought back was sobering.

Those guarding the White House were ordered to be ready at midnight, we heard. Some bulldozers and tractors were brought in from nearby construction sites and positioned in Tchaikovsky Street, where the attack by the commando group was expected to start. Half an hour later there was shooting from the direction of Smolensk Square. The news was that soldiers in armoured cars were trying to break through the barricades. We saw people running and calling for help, then running back towards the square. We heard gunfire coming from the White House. It was a short exchange lasting just a few minutes.

Shurik had disappeared again. As soon as the firing started, Lena woke with a start. I had no idea what to do with her. 'Should I take her inside?' I wondered. It had begun to rain lightly and a woman sitting nearby took off her jacket and wrapped it around the little girl, asking her to be calm and brave.

'It's no use going inside,' said the woman to me. 'We're much safer here. They want to attack the White House and kill Yeltsin.'

Fortunately there was no further shooting, just a tense calm. The rain stopped and the sky cleared. Soon a half-moon appeared, followed by a sky full of stars. We could see the bright lights on the Kalinin Bridge. The mood of the crowd lifted.

We saw people standing at the windows of the Hotel Ukraine, waving and signalling with torches. 'What's happening there?' Lena asked, pointing.

In the morning we would discover that a twenty-two-year-old veteran of the Afghan War had tried to stop one of the armed vehicles attempting to break through the barricades. He had climbed over the tank and attempted to cover the front with a tarpaulin sheet, but slipped and been dragged alongside it and crushed. Two friends who had rushed to help him were shot dead by the soldiers.

At two o'clock in the morning, out of a drowsy silence we heard loud cheers. We saw Eduard Shevardnadze, the foreign minister, walk into the White House. On the way he stopped, shook hands with some of the protestors and thanked them for their support. As he was entering the building twenty or so motorcyclists arrived from Kutuzovsky Prospect. The cheers erupted again. One of the riders took a loudspeaker, stood on a table and made a short speech, ending with the good news that the soldiers had started leaving Kutuzovsky Prospect.

'They're pulling out!' he shouted. 'We've done it.'

Then we heard the blare of horns from ferries on the river. They had assembled near the bank and blew and blew, their way of announcing that they would stay there to support the protestors.

The next cheer came when someone turned on the radio and the voice of the newsreader at Moscow Echo was heard. '*Tovarishi,* we're back,' he announced, 'and the news is good. No attack!'

'Didn't I tell you?' Shurik was thrilled. He had reappeared. 'But do you know why?' He lowered his voice. 'My friends tell me that the Alpha Group chickened out. The plan was to bomb the first and the second floors of the White House, storm the office of the President and, if he resisted, kill him there and then. But an hour before they were due to attack they were told that there were five hundred heavily-armed soldiers inside the White House and that there could be a bloodbath. Do you know what they did next? Something most unusual for a KGB unit. They summoned the entire force and asked each of the commandos to vote. The decision was unanimous: they would disobey any order to attack. Amazing! Even the KGB has gone soft.' He looked pleased. 'So now we can go home and relax.'

'Let's go now,' said Lena.

'Yes,' Yasya agreed. 'I want to sleep for a week.'

I took both of them home. Shurik wanted to stay on at the White House for a while. As we passed the wreckage of the trolleybus Yasya picked up a piece of metal sheeting with the route number 49A painted on it.

'A souvenir for Papa,' he said, smiling.

Yasya didn't get to show the souvenir to Vladimir. He passed away at three o'clock in the morning, unaware of the loud horns of the ferries that had gathered at Krasnopresnenskaya Embankment. Ivan Vasillivich, the doctor, arrived, did a final examination and signed the necessary papers. The undertaker was informed and soon the body was ready: washed, dressed and laid in the coffin. The wreaths were placed and friends and relatives would soon start coming.

I didn't stay in the room for much longer but found a chair in the kitchen and waited for the first rays of sunlight. I was tired, but sleep would have to wait. Katya appeared busy, although there wasn't much to do; everything had been organised. Soon the funeral would be over too.

At around five o'clock an old man with a long grey beard came and told Katya that he was ready. He looked like a priest, but Katya said that Aleksei Nikolaevich was a sculptor who had come to prepare a death mask of Vladimir's face.

'Do you want to help?' she asked.

Aleksei Nikolaevich was an expert and needed very little help. He washed Vladimir's face to remove any grease and dust, and then coated it with plaster of Paris. I fetched hot water from the kitchen to mix the powder. It took fifteen to twenty minutes for the mask to set. Once it had hardened, Aleksei Nikolaevich asked me to help him remove it. We peeled it off and placed it near the window to dry. A cast of Vladimir's right hand was also prepared. The face and the hand were carefully washed and dried.

The funeral took place on the following day, 23 August 1991. It was a Friday and quite sunny for an autumn afternoon. The ceremony was simple. Yasya made a short speech. He didn't cry, not once. An actor friend from the theatre read a poem and Vladimir's body was cremated. I was told that Katya and Yasya would take the ashes to Sverdlovsk and release them into the waters of a river. I was given a handful in a bottle and asked to take them to Berlin to empty into the River Spree. Katya wanted them near Vladimir's father and mother who had died in Berlin during the War and been buried somewhere in the nearby battlefields.

Shurik would later tell me something else about Berlin. During one of his visits to the city, Vladimir had shared a needle with a stranger, in a park outside the Rosa-Luxemburg-Plaz Station as he waited for Katya. She had been held up answering an urgent call at the hotel.

❄ ❄ ❄

The day after Vladimir's funeral I visited Aunty Olga.

I had spent most of the day in the Lenin Library, looking for material for my essay. In spite of the turbulent events in the streets, the reading room was full. I ordered my material and while I was waiting for it to be brought down, went to the café. It looked different, smaller and overcrowded. The old relaxed atmosphere had disappeared and the women serving the food were deliberately slow and unfriendly. In the reading room there was dust on the floor and the lights on several of the tables were broken.

I tried not to head for my old table but as soon as I entered I couldn't stop myself. I found it easily, but it was occupied. An old woman in a nurse's uniform adorned with a row of medals was taking notes. I walked on and saw that the glass in the window near Anna's favourite table was cracked. The seat was empty. I pulled out her chair but couldn't bring myself to sit down. I went into an adjoining room and worked there.

On the way to the library I had called in to the Moscow Art Theatre to buy a ticket for a new production of *Uncle Vanya*. A young woman holding a baby in her arms had approached me. She said she was an actress who had lost her job a few months before and now needed help. I didn't let her finish her story. I gave her a ten-dollar note and walked on.

Beggars were now everywhere in Moscow. They were on the streets, in the Metro and outside shops and hotels. In the Soviet days I had occasionally met beggars, but then they were usually alcoholics wanting money for their next drink. Even more surprising were the number of people buying and selling little things: tomatoes, shoes, batteries. I saw young men and women carting boxes on trolleys, setting them up wherever there was space and selling music cassettes, records, chocolate bars, T-shirts, soap and washing powder, condoms, chewing gum, calculators, books, magazines and pornography.

There were *babushkas* outside the Metro standing behind little tables. One of them was selling a few carrots, two cabbage leaves and some misshapen sweet potatoes. The woman next to her offered two tubes of German toothpaste, an ancient hairdryer and two plastic aprons. An old man in an army uniform sat on his stool, his medals set out on the ground, waiting for a buyer. A retired nurse, his wife perhaps, held out an album of wartime photos. A blind man played his accordion and sang out-of-tune songs. A young man with a Lenin-beard stood on a wobbly table and declaimed poetry. A woman nearby was dressed as a clown, juggling with five knives while holding a wooden spoon with an egg on it in her mouth.

Shurik was right: *perestroika* had turned the whole city into a marketplace.

The stately Metro, jewel of the capital, was shabby. The escalators were dirty and the air heavy with moisture and dust. Shurik had warned me about what it was like. 'The ventilation doesn't work properly and no one replaces the lights. It isn't safe down there any more.'

I got into a carriage, found a seat and opened a book. But I couldn't concentrate. I was having second thoughts about visiting Aunty Olga and Leonid Mikhailovich. It didn't seem right. I got out of the train at the next station, walked up the steps and found an empty bench on the street.

A teenager with dark hair and bright red lips came and sat beside me. 'I am Lolita,' she said, 'and you are a foreigner with dollars. Do you have dollars?' I didn't answer but thought of the three boxes of Belgian chocolates I had bought in Berlin for Aunty Olga. I opened my bag, gave one box to the girl and walked away.

The bag also contained two Dizzy Gillespie cassettes for Leonid Mikhailovich. 'It would be silly not to deliver them,' I thought. 'And they would be offended if they found out that I had been in Moscow and didn't visit them. They can ask me whatever they want. Who cares? It doesn't matter now. I should meet them, Anna or no Anna. Now it's just between them and me.'

I was certain they had always liked me. At least Leonid Mikhailovich had. Aunty Olga? I wasn't so sure. According to her, I had never been the right man for Anna. I was too reserved, too serious and too full of myself. But once Anna had made up her mind, the matter had been settled. Aunty Olga had had no choice but to accept her decision.

'Perhaps I'm wrong,' I thought. 'But so what?' I knew that if I wanted to leave Moscow feeling I had done everything I needed to do, I would have to get rid of my terrible angst about the past.

I didn't want to go inside the Metro station. I soon found the right bus and reached the block of apartments without much trouble. I pressed the button for the lift and only then read the handwritten note: *Out of order* followed by *most of the time* and *forever* in different hands. I started to walk up the stairs. I finally reached the third floor, located the door and rang the bell. I heard it echo inside and waited. When nobody came I pressed it again, but still the door didn't open.

I had turned and started to walk downstairs when I heard a door open. A middle-aged woman from the neighbouring apartment called me back.

'I'm looking for Leonid Mikhailovich and Olga Mikhailovna,' I said. 'They used to live here.'

'Yes, they used to. When did you last see them? You're a foreigner, aren't you? You must be one of his students.'

'Ten years ago I was a student – but not one of his. I knew Anna quite well.' I was embarrassed. Maybe she knew the truth.

'Please wait. I'll get my husband,' said the woman. She called to him to come out and talk to the foreigner from India. 'A good friend of Anna's,' she shouted.

The husband came out, shook my hand, glanced at his wife and turned to face me.

'I'm afraid Leonid Mikhailovich is dead. He passed away two years ago.'

I was stunned. 'And Aunty Olga?'

'She's well. A few health problems – nothing major, just old age,' the woman replied. 'She must have gone to the shops. She should be back soon. You're welcome to come in and wait.'

I thanked them for their information but didn't go in. I knew where the shops were but decided to wait for Aunty Olga in the park.

It was cold and windy. I recalled the family's frequent complaints about the location of the apartment block. I also remembered how Anna used to enjoy walking in the forest, especially in winter.

'The smell,' she used to whisper, 'the beautiful smell. I'd love to turn into a squirrel and scurry up the trees to talk to all the handsome owls sitting there looking at me with their glassy eyes, and hooting. And you know what? Each owl would have your face.'

As it got later and later I had almost decided to leave. Then I saw an old woman walking bent over on a stick, moving slowly and holding a shopping bag in her left hand. It was Aunty Olga. I stood up as she approached the bench. She seemed to recognise me at once, which was good, since I didn't want to frighten her.

'*Zdravstvuite,* Olga Mikhailovna,' I said. 'It's me, Vasu.'

'*O bozhe* (Oh God)!' She nearly lost her stick. She tried to retrieve it but then dropped her bag and the milk bottle inside shattered. There was a sharp crack and milk started leaking out. I picked up her stick and escorted her to the bench. Then I went to rescue the bag. I removed the broken bottle, shook off the spilt milk and shoved the loaf of bread and packet of cheese back in.

I must have cut my finger on the broken glass, because there were drops of blood on the ground.

'Blood,' she said. 'Have you cut yourself?'

'Yes, but don't worry.' I took out my handkerchief and wrapped it around my finger.

'Where's your hat?' she went on. 'You'll catch cold.'

'I'll be fine. It isn't too cold. Let me go to the shops and get you milk.'

'I don't need it. I still have half a bottle in the fridge and a few cans of condensed. I don't need much.'

We sat silently together on the bench, wondering what

topics we should avoid. The neighbour came out of the building with her dog. Aunty Olga was by then ready to move. 'Let's go up. I feel cold. I'm not young any more and the autumn this year hasn't been kind.'

We walked together, Aunty Olga doing her best to avoid talking with the neighbour.

'She's very nosy,' she grumbled, 'and gossips shamelessly.'

The climb up the stairs to the third floor was hard for her. We had to stop every few minutes. 'My knees hurt,' she said, 'and there's something wrong with my hip. I'm falling apart. Just like everything in this country. Luckily, the kids from the primary school sometimes come and help me.'

Very little had changed inside the apartment although it seemed run-down. The wallpaper was peeling, the taps dripped and the enamel on the bathtub was coming off. Aunty Olga still lived in the same room but the other two were shut up. The piano still stood in the library but the mahogany table had been cleared of its books and papers. The bookshelves were neatly ordered, each volume in the company of other books of the same size and shape.

In the kitchen, Aunty Olga asked me to help her boil the kettle. The tea she brewed was strong and black, and I was told to take out a bottle of fresh blackcurrant conserve from the cupboard. She also opened a packet of gingerbread.

As we were about to sit down to eat and drink, I opened my bag and took out the chocolates and the cassettes.

'These are for you, Olga Mikhailovna.'

'Call me Aunty Olga, as you used to. No need to be formal.' She looked at the cassettes. 'You know about Leynya, don't you?'

'Yes, the husband of the woman with the dog told me.'

'Cancer, may God bless his soul. He just wouldn't stop smoking those awful cigarettes of his. Died before finishing the proofs of his jazz book. I had to do it for him. I didn't mind. Anna helped as well. She came for the funeral. She brought Maya with her. Leynya didn't see her before he went. He died here, at home, in his room. Didn't want to go into hospital.'

She took a sip of tea. 'Anna must have been at the airport when Leynya died. We took the ashes to Tatyur, found the wooden cabin and the birch tree and scattered the ashes around it. I have a photo of the tree.'

'Who is Maya?' I wanted to ask, but Aunty Olga ordered me to go to her room and fetch a photo album from a drawer in the bedside table. As I walked in I saw that, amazingly, it hadn't changed at all. The bookshelf looked a little fuller but the icon of *Bogomateri* was still squashed in between the books.

I stood for a few moments waiting for the door to open and Anna to walk in, take off her nightshirt and—

'Have you found the album?' I heard Aunty Olga call. 'It's in the top drawer.' Then after a pause: 'You men are all the same. Can't ever find anything.'

I found the album and made myself leave the room. Aunty Olga opened it and showed me some photos. In them I could see no one but Maya. The rest of the world seemed to melt away.

Who is Maya? The question appeared out of place. I knew who Maya was. I knew it as soon as I had heard the name, from the very sound of it.

Aunty Olga watched me looking at the photo. 'She's gorgeous, isn't she?' she said, and then after a pause added, 'She's yours, you know.'

I know, I wanted to say. But I couldn't utter a word.

I felt completely lost. As I tried to recover, I suddenly found myself stranded in an unknown street of my childhood. I was returning from school and my right hip and thigh hurt as the heavy canvas schoolbag rubbed against them. I had scraped skin off my thigh and there was blood, enough to stain my shorts. I was weeping loudly, taking no notice of the people around me. Huge tears rolled down my cheeks and my nose was running so that snot was everywhere, down the front of my shirt and the sleeve. I would run for a few metres, then walk, then run again.

I rushed into the house, threw my bag on the floor and burst into Jijee-ma's room. She had been sitting on the bed talking to a seamstress. I didn't care. I ran to her, buried my head in her lap and cried and cried. After a few minutes in Jijee-ma's lap I calmed down. 'Govind pushed me and hit me,' I told her. My cuts were swabbed and I was given a glass of sweetened lemon cordial. 'He wanted to see my new pencil-box and I didn't want to show him, because he's a thief. He snatched it from my hand and it fell on the ground, and as I went to pick it up he pushed me hard and kicked me. Govind is bigger than me but no one came to help me. They just stood and watched. Some even giggled.'

What I didn't tell Jijee-ma that day was that the big new hand-lens which Uncle Triple K had given me had been broken in the scuffle. It had been this that had made me cry and run. The cuts, blood and pain were not important. The lens had been more important than anything else in the world.

But that had happened many years ago, in that other world called childhood.

'Yes, Maya is gorgeous,' I said, still in shock and confused. 'Please tell me more about her.'

'So you don't know anything?'

'No.'

'You didn't try to find out?'

'No.'

'You didn't suspect?'

'I did, but—'

'Didn't know what to do? You just let Anna go. And that was it.'

'Yes, I suppose I did.'

'Why, for God's sake, why?'

I was finding it hard to answer. 'Perhaps I was selfish; perhaps I was too proud. I felt betrayed. I felt abandoned and hurt. I felt like a victim. Yes that's the right word: victim.'

Neither of us said anything for a few minutes. Then she got up and walked out of the kitchen. I heard the toilet flush. She called me to help her back. We sat down and she picked up a photo. Then she returned it to the album and started talking.

She told me that Maya would be eleven in September; that she was a bright child, naturally gifted; that she was kind and sincere; that she spoke three languages, Russian, French and English; that she played the guitar and composed her own songs; that she wanted to be a journalist or a writer; that she came to Moscow every other year; that she hated boys and would never marry or have her own children, but would adopt a couple from Vietnam or Angola; that she didn't like the beaches and surf for which Australia is so famous; that on her sixteenth birthday she would go with one of her friends, a dancer, to the very centre of the country to spend a year with a community of what she called 'real Australians'; that she hated her mother for being so selfish and self-centred and for deciding not to do anything worthwhile with her life; that she despised her mother's awful choice of lovers, who always turned out to be mean and arrogant; that she wanted her *babulya*-aunt to keep her grandpa's books and papers safe, because when she was twenty she would write a book about him and his agitprop wife; that she would read every single book of Marx, Engels and Lenin to understand what was wrong with the system that gave birth to a monster like Stalin; that she despised the multinational corporations which ruthlessly exploit the poor in Third World countries; that when she was eighteen she would release her first record of revolutionary love songs—

'I like her,' said Aunty Olga, 'Doesn't she sound like you?'

'Just a little,' I wanted to say. 'At eleven I didn't know much about the world.'

I left Moscow in early September and spent some time in Leningrad, Kiev and Odessa. I even risked visiting Yakutsk, and was surprised that no one harassed me for travelling without a proper visa. A student at the Institute who remembered Leonid Mikhailovich took me to Tatyur. I managed to locate the birch tree with the bench beside it and sat there for a few minutes.

The student told me that Maria had been killed in a boating accident, and that the cabin now belonged to a local club of nature-lovers who used it as a meeting room.

I wanted to catch a boat up the River Lena, but the student warned me that the water was beginning to freeze and I would be marooned.

I returned to Berlin in the last week of December. One bright sunny day I went to the River Spree and scattered Vladimir's ashes which I had carried with me in an urn.

The following day, as children were opening their Christmas presents, Mikhail Gorbachev signed some papers in the Kremlin and the Soviet Union vanished forever from the face of the world.

For some a dream was over. For others, a nightmare had reached its end.

I left Moscow promising never to return. But I did return, not once but many times, each time taking away with me a fragment of the city attached to something given to me by a friend or acquired in a shop, theatre or forest.

After Vladimir's funeral Katya had asked me if I wanted to keep something of his and I chose the book from which he always used to read. It was signed by his mother and had been given to him on his fourteenth birthday.

From Shurik I received two small photos, one showing Lena standing on a tank. But the thing which would determine the future course of my life was a small photo of Maya with her guitar.

Maya meets her Papa

Anna

I hadn't expected a call so early in the morning, since Aunty Olga knew the time difference. I picked up the phone and the question came straight at me. No hello, no sorry, just: 'Has Vasu phoned?'

Of course he hadn't. But her question confirmed what I had seen on the telly. The man standing with Shurik and Yasya in front of the White House was definitely Vasu.

'He's in Moscow,' Aunty Olga said.

'I know. I saw him on the news. So he came to see you?'

'Yes.'

'And you told him about Papa?'

'No. The nosy neighbour told him.'

'Was he upset? Vasu was very fond of Papa.'

'Of course. But he was more upset about something else. He even cried. I'm sure you know why.'

'Yes, I suppose I know.'

'So why didn't you tell him about Maya? That's so terrible

Anna, so horrible.'

'I know. But I didn't. I don't know why. Perhaps I was selfish. Perhaps too proud. Perhaps I felt betrayed and hurt. I just don't know.'

'He said the same thing when I asked him why he didn't go looking for you. Even his words were the same,' said Aunty Olga. 'Stupid.'

'I know him. He's so correct, so self-righteous, so bloody decent.'

I was furious at myself for the anger I was showing.

She said: 'You're still angry at him, aren't you? But you were the one who left him. And you never even told him why.'

I didn't reply and for a while Aunty Olga was silent too.

Then she said: 'He asked for Maya's photo and I couldn't refuse him. I've given him your address and phone number too. He's sure to call you soon – or write.'

'Let him call.'

'But you should let Maya know. You don't want to hurt her, do you?'

'She'll be upset, but that's normal. I was upset too, don't you remember? Sooner or later she would have found out. I'm sure she already suspects something.'

There was silence between us for a few moments and then I asked something which surprised us both. 'How did he look? Was he all right?'

Aunty Olga told me that he had seemed more depressed than usual, probably because he had come to say goodbye to Vladimir. He had also been shocked by the coup and the rapid collapse of the Union.

'He looked old and tired and burnt out,' she said. She

described how he had spent a night in the apartment sleeping on the floor in the library; said that he had given her two packets of Belgian chocolates and hadn't known what to do with the jazz cassettes he had brought for Leynya; that in the morning as he was leaving she had gone to the window to see him walking away and that he had seemed desolate. She felt really sorry for him.

'Meeting Maya would make him happy,' she said. 'Do your best to make it happen.'

Maya

A couple of nights ago I heard Mama talk to someone on the phone. Must be Babushka Olga, I thought, because it was quite late at night and she was speaking Russian. I was already in bed and could only hear a few words.

Usually Mama tells me everything about her conversations with Babushka, but next morning she said nothing. I'm ready to wait. Let's see how long she can keep her secret from me.

My full name is Maya V. Eisner. Like all Russian names, the letter 'V' stands for my father's name.

I did ask Mama once about my father's name.

'Do you really want to know?' Mama had said. There was something strange about her tone, and not only her tone, but her whole face, particularly around the eyes. She looked hurt. It made me ask myself why I was putting her through this. But I needed to find out more. However this time, so as not to disturb her, I just said 'Not really' and pretended to forget our exchange.

But I didn't forget and I am sure she remembered it too.

One thing I know for certain: she wouldn't have told me the truth then. She's very clever, you know, good at spinning stories and all that bullshit. Sorry, I shouldn't have said that.

I know I could always phone Babushka Olga and she wouldn't hide anything from me, if I asked. So why haven't I? Am I crazy or what? No, it's because I'm in no hurry to meet my father. I'm fine here without him.

They say that he is alive and well and that one day he'll certainly come looking for me. I don't feel any strong urge to meet him. I don't need him at all. I'm quite happy without him.

Anna

We live in a small cottage attached to Milos' big house up in the Blue Mountains outside Sydney. Maya likes the cottage but for me it's nothing more than a place to stay, although I'm pleased that we don't have to move for a while. I'm happy living with Milos and he seems satisfied, at least for now. It's a simple arrangement that suits us well.

During the summer the cottage is rented to the tourists and Maya and I move into the main house and look after them. Maya knows the area well and often takes them on guided walks. I cook for them and in the evening if they are in the mood to be entertained we play for them.

Milos bought *Laura*, the house, from an architect who designed it for his wife. But she was killed in a car accident before she ever lived in it. The house has two storeys, the second up among the leafy canopy of grand old trees. Milos' studio is up there, surrounded on three sides by a deck. We can walk along the deck and touch the leaves.

The studio has a huge east-facing window that is much bigger than the ones on the other three sides. A fireplace sits in the centre. The dark parquet floor is covered with cheap rugs and carpets. The studio contains two chairs and a wooden divan stacked with cushions. It is unusually tidy and empty for a sculptor's studio. Milos has a workshop on the ground floor where he does the dirty work. In the studio he just waits for the muse that often arrives in the form of women of all shapes and sizes. Their faces, I've noticed, aren't pretty but their bodies exude pleasure.

Does their presence annoy me? Occasionally.

'Why don't you say something to him?' Maya scolds. But we both know we don't have a choice, at least for now.

'He gets his usual quota from them,' I could have told her. 'That means I'm spared.'

I consider myself the housekeeper. My job is to look after Milos as well as his house. Luckily there isn't much to take care of, which leaves lots of time for Maya and me to do what we want. I give music lessons and sometimes work in an antiques shop in Katoomba. Once a fortnight we visit an old Russian woman, Larissa Andreevna, who lives in a small dilapidated house down in Bondi. We help her with the chores around her house, fill the cupboard with groceries and ensure that her fridge has enough food for a fortnight. We read out her mail to her, deposit cheques and pay bills. Most importantly we talk to her in Russian.

'I miss being called Larissa Andreevna,' she tells us each time we visit her. Then she begins to mumble the same old story, which we all know is believable but not quite true.

In her story she is the 'real' Lara in Pasternak's *Doctor Zhivago*. Unlike the Lara of the book she accepted the offer of a rich merchant, a spy, and escaped to Shanghai. There he tried to pimp her in clubs and bars and for a short time she complied. 'To make a bit of money and buy some time,' she says now. She doesn't blame him for anything. 'Those were bad times.'

Larissa Andreevna came to Sydney just before World War II and opened a salon in Bondi where she became known for her 'secret' séances. Her knowledge of the tarot was phenomenal and so was her knack for reading bumps on heads, hairy or bald. She even tried her hand at acupuncture and enjoyed considerable success in the use of Chinese herbs, potions and other similar concoctions to 'cure' people.

'It was such fun,' she often laughs, 'and made me good money too. People are so stupid and gullible, I tell you.'

Maya

'I have something important to tell you,' Mama said. We were washing our hands after putting away some gardening tools in the shed. Saturday afternoons were for gardening and we both enjoyed pottering around together, gossiping and listening to music on the radio.

On this particular Saturday, she went quiet.

'Is it about Babushka's call?'

'So you listened in, did you?'

'Just a few words. I was sleeping you know. And then in the morning you didn't say anything so I knew you were hiding something. You're such a bad liar, Mama.'

'I was going to—'

'I know it's about my Papa. I did hear his name. It's Vasu, isn't it? I wrote it down as soon as I got up that morning.'

'What else did you hear?'

'Nothing much. Then I went to the library to look it up. An Indian woman at the reference desk told me that it was an Indian name and that all ancient Hindu architects were called Vasu. So is he an architect?'

'Not exactly. An urban designer.'

'And you met him in a library?'

She was amazed. 'How did you know that?'

'Where else would you two be? Not at dances, that's for sure.'

She pushed a large packet towards me. 'This is for you,' she said.

The Canadian stamps on it were really beautiful. Inside were two envelopes. One was open and addressed to Mama. I read that letter first, then opened the other that was addressed to me. After reading a few lines, I got up and moved to the other end of the garden and sat on a rock near the little pond to finish it.

I read the letter twice. My first reading was quick, just to check if it contained anything tragic or terrible. The second was slow and careful.

Then I folded the two A4-sized sheets and put them in my pocket. There were also three photos in the packet. One showed a small house and the other two a large lake, which Mama said was Lake Ontario. There was no photo of my father. Later I found his picture on the dining table where Mama had left it. It was a little black-and-white picture of a man sitting by himself on the steps of our family's *dacha* in Prudkino. On the back there was no name, just a date in Mama's writing.

We decided to go and spend the night in the open in our favourite spot, near Evans Lookout. We often go there to sleep in the company of stars. Mama pinches a bottle or two of wine from Milos' precious cellar, and I fill the thermos with strong coffee. We sit up singing and playing the guitar.

That night we sat for a while leaning against the metal fence and watching the darkness creep up on us. The night was raven black; the tiny sickle moon dim against the glorious stars. They were slow to appear but once they decided that it was their night, they flooded the sky with such abundance that my heart ached with joy.

Then I heard Mama crying, quietly as she always does. I didn't stop her. I wanted to hug her but I didn't. 'Let her cry,' I said to myself. 'She needs to let it all out. It will help her relax.' That sounds silly, doesn't it? But crying always seems to calm her down.

While I was waiting I started strumming on the guitar. Finally she looked up at me, smiling her lovely sad smile. I suddenly wanted to give her a big sloppy kiss. That was unexpected!

'In the photo he looks like a boy,' I said. 'Does he still look like that?'

'I bet he does,' Mama replied. Overhead we heard a possum moving in a tree. She picked up the guitar, strummed it, and began to sing. It was her favourite song, about her lovely Staryi Arbat, an old part of Moscow.

'She'll never give up these corny songs,' I thought to myself.

Soon, as usual, she asked me to join in.

'*Davai vmeste*,' she said and waited for me to begin. Suddenly I was overwhelmed by the stars, the melody and her beautiful voice. We sang together, in perfect harmony.

'Feels good, doesn't it?' she said after we finished. I knew that my dear lovely Mama was pining for her Russian home.

Mama once showed me a photo of a little girl with a ponytail sitting on the back of a wooden bench, leaning against a woman. 'I was three then,' she said pointing at the girl, 'and that's Tonya, my mother.' Babushka Olga is touching Mama's tiny shoulder.

Grandpa Leynya must have taken the photo. I have another picture, also taken by Grandpa, of me when I was three. I'm sitting in a boat on the lake in Gorky Park. Babushka Olga is beside me, holding me tight with her arm. Mama sits opposite, oars raised to row. The colour in the photo is fainter than it must have been on that beautiful autumn day.

It's strange that I remember so little about my early childhood, spent shuttling between Moscow and Sydney. I do remember the stench of vomit on those long flights, all stuffy cabins and turbulence. I remember new schools and new friends and my vain attempts to create Rusinglish, a strange mixture of Russian and English words. I also remember Babushka Olga's sweet buttery *kasha* and Grandpa's night-time stories.

But most of all I remember how lonely I felt. I was always missing someone. Mama would bring me to Moscow and leave me with Babushka Olga, returning to Sydney after a week or ten days. A few months later she would reappear to take me back to Australia, forcing me to leave Babushka behind.

I miss Babushka, my Olga from the Volga. She should have come to Australia and lived with us. We aren't rich but we could have looked after her. It was hard for her to live in Moscow without Grandpa Leynya.

Mama laughs when she hears me pronounce the word 'Leynya'. She thinks I talk like Babushka Olga. Do I?

Babushka Olga died alone in the Yasenovo apartment with no one except her *Bogomateri* watching over her. By the time we arrived she was already in her coffin ready for the crematorium. That time we stayed in Moscow for ten days, sorting out her things and finding a lodger for the apartment. 'Who's this young man? I asked Mama as we sorted through Babushka Olga's things. She was looking hard at a small black-and-white photo of a spunky young man she had found in one of Babushka's many handbags.

'Misha Schubert, the violinist,' mama replied. 'He and Babushka went to the same music school and used to perform together. They were engaged to be married, but the War came and changed everything. Misha volunteered, was sent to fight at Stalingrad and was killed by a sniper and buried in a mass grave. That was it for Babushka Olga. She had some flings but never found another love. That's why she didn't marry. She committed her life to her little brother Leynya instead, and to me, his motherless child.'

'We are truly strange creatures.' These are Papa's words, not mine. I would have said that we're just human: sad and pathetic but often incredibly beautiful.

I met Papa for the first time at Babushka's funeral in Moscow. Mama hadn't known he was coming and didn't hide her disapproval. She hadn't realised that Babushka Olga had summoned him once she knew that she would soon die.

My fourteenth birthday was a week after the funeral. It was a very quiet day. In the evening we went to see Viktyuk's production of *Lolita* at the Mossovet Theatre. Papa came with us and didn't say much, but he had a happy smile on his face all through the performance.

'Papa is very quiet, isn't he?' I said to Mama. This was a big mistake. She kept going on about it. She really hates him.

When I am with him on my own I call him 'V' instead of Papa. The letter 'V' stands for my middle name. For an Indian it must be hard to be called 'V' and not Papa – but really, he isn't very Indian any more. He'll get used to it.

It's winter in Moscow now, dark and cold. The river will be frozen and the fish curled up in the water underneath. The humpy hills and the valleys in between will be covered in snow and horses will move gingerly, lingering to let out puddles of warm yellow piss that freezes straight away into knotty, beady strings. The cedar trees above have a strange oily, musky smell, and in dreams I sometimes imagine myself on a branch turned into a brown squirrel.

When I tell Mama about such dreams she laughs and says that in her dreams of being a squirrel she used to be on the look-out for handsome owls. How bizarre!

I found out about Vasu, my real Papa three years ago. Mama thought I'd be upset, even furious. But no. I didn't cry, not for a minute. For a few days I felt numb and sort of lost, a black feather floating in the cold misty air. Yes, that's right:

floating without purpose. But right after she told me I just gave her a kiss and a hug and went for a long walk with my Walkman.

'You are so much like your Papa,' she told me a few days later. The resentment in her voice was sharp. Is it really my fault if I've turned out to be like him?

A few years before I found out about Papa, Mama got herself Milos, whose house we've been living in for the last six years. I knew this would happen eventually. I was just surprised that it took so long. Mama refers to him as 'Milos, the wealthy Czech from Prague'. He's a sculptor and while he works, Mama plays for him on her cello. She used to model for him too. To keep him interested – or at least that's what she told me.

Milos wanted me to sit for him too – but nothing doing. I could see how desperate he was: the way he would look at me when Mama wasn't around, walking up and standing too close, as if trying to smell me. He was like a hungry horny beast.

Now he doesn't do that. Perhaps Mama has said something to him.

'He's a creep,' says my friend Mandy. Perhaps he tried it with her, too. She said she was going to ask her older brother to teach him a lesson. I had to ask her to stop coming to our house. She didn't, which was good. I don't know what I would do without her. She's my only real mate.

But now she's in Perth with her father, who like Grandpa is a geophysicist with a mining company. Mandy tells me that her father knows about Grandpa and his work and has read most of his books and papers. Amazing or what? Bloody marvellous!

'We need Milos,' Mama often tells me. Of course she wants to convince me that she isn't just interested in his money. I have decided that she probably isn't lying. But why does she allow Milos to be so rude and offensive? Yes, he does speak Russian and we like the sound of Russian around us, but surely this isn't enough to let him walk all over us. I wouldn't put up with it. No way!

And why can't Mama find herself a proper job? She's so clever with all her degrees and qualifications, and she plays the cello like a professional. I wish she would stop pretending to be weak.

I remember how we watched the crowds in the streets and the reports of the coup in Moscow on the telly. Mama was terrified.

'I'm worried about Babushka,' she finally said. 'I hope she hasn't gone out to the barricades.' We searched for her among the crowds. We couldn't see her, but Mama did recognise some others. 'Shurik,' she mumbled. 'I knew he'd be there.' Then she saw Yasya and someone else.

She tried to get a copy of the tape from SBS, where she works occasionally doing subtitling. She knows a lot of the weirdos there, people like us. But she couldn't get the tape. She even asked Milos to help, but for once he couldn't pull any strings.

When we phoned Babushka after the coup she sounded fine, just a bit cranky, most probably from the pain in her knees and in her crook hip.

'Why don't you come over here and stay with us?' I asked her.

'I can't,' she replied. 'I want to, but I can't. It's too far, my darling, too far.'

'*Slava Bogu* (Thank God), the coup failed,' she said on the phone. '*Slava Bogu*, the people walked away from the precipice and *Slava Bogu*, it ended without violence and bloodshed.'

Slava Bogu .... *Slava Bogu* .... I like the way these words sound.

❀ ❀ ❀

'*My dear Maia/Maya,*' my Papa starts his letter and then asks me which way I spell my name. '*If it is Maia I would assume that you are named after Maia Plisetskaya, the famous ballerina at the Bolshoi.*' He goes on to describe the ballet *Anna Karenina*, whose première he went to with Mama and Grandpa.

I'm planning to surprise him by letting him know that I have read the novel in Russian and that I didn't like it. I didn't like *War and Peace* either. Too many words. I like Chekhov more and enjoy Kuprin too, but my favourite is Leskov and his *Lady Macbeth of Mtzensk*. I doubt if he would agree with me, but I don't care. I don't have to please him. If he doesn't like me, too bad. He'll have to accept me as I am.

'*But if your name is spelt Maya, let me tell you that my mother's name, your other grandmother's, was Mayavati. It was often shortened to Maya.*' He writes that his mother died giving birth to him and that he was brought up by his older sister whom he used to call Jijee-ma. The word 'ma' means mother in Hindi, he says.

It was a fairly long letter and a bit all over the place, as if he were trying to defer the main point. Right at the end he made it.

'*I am thrilled to know about you, and I am so grateful to*

Aunty Olga for giving me your photo and address. Slava Bogu. May God bless her kind soul and may He bless your Mama and you.'

Slava Bogu. Those magical words.

A fortnight later came the phone call. I was expecting it. He had already warned me in the letter. He talked for a few minutes with Mama and then asked for me. For a man with such a boyish face he has a deep, throaty voice. I was amazed that I couldn't detect any tension or unease in it.

'That's what he's like,' Mama said afterwards. 'Always balanced and in control. It often scared me, that discipline of his.'

Papa and I talked mostly in English with only a few words and phrases in Russian. He apologised for his Russian being rusty. In Canada or India he rarely had the chance to talk to anyone in the language.

His first letter contained a bank draft for a thousand dollars, which was great. Mama and I had never had that much money at once. We were pleased but uneasy and didn't cash the draft for a few weeks. Slowly, however, we got used to the cheques arriving each month and I started believing that I deserved them, that I needed to be looked after.

From then on I received something from him every week: letters, photos, drawings, books, little gifts like cassettes and scarves, and bigger ones such as shoes and even an elaborately embroidered Indian dress. But in my letters to him he still remained 'Dear V'.

He called once a fortnight at the same time, often from different places. By then I knew that he travelled a lot. He once tried to phone me from Sydney Airport, but I was away on a school trip. During an Easter break he rang from Auckland. I would have loved to hop on a plane and meet him, but he didn't invite me.

'He would never ask,' Mama told me, 'not because he doesn't want you to come and stay. No, he just doesn't know how to say it. He's waiting for you to ask. It's not pride, not at all. He's always loved children and I know he's over the moon to have found you. He just doesn't want to show that he needs you. He's always been like that, keeping his feelings under lock and key. He'll never pressure you to accept him. He'll just go on waiting for you to ask and then do everything in his power to make you happy. He's a stoic, like Grandpa Leynya.'

After Babushka Olga's funeral he invited me to stay with him in Toronto. 'Not alone. Your Mama can come too. The house is big and for most of the time it's empty.'

Although I felt sorry for him, I said no. I didn't want to leave Mama alone and I was pretty sure that she wouldn't come.

'I need more time to think,' I told him.

'Don't you feel lonely?' I remember asking Mama once.

'Of course,' she replied. 'Who doesn't? Even when you're in love you can feel lonely, left out. To love someone isn't easy. Often you have to pay a price and it can be high. Then you start looking for an excuse, any excuse, to escape. But escaping doesn't set you free. You're trapped by your own failure. That's when you begin to appreciate the pleasure of being alone.

'There is a word *Toska* in Russian. I don't know the English translation but I remember one of Chekhov's stories called *Toska*. One dark wintry evening in St Petersburg a coachman tries to tell his passengers about the death of his young son. But no one gives a damn about his loss, he soon realises. He whispers instead to a tired horse happily munching rotten oats from a bag hung round his neck. Snow falls, the horses move wearily forward, bells ring, the footmen shout, and an old woman slips and collapses. No one comes to help her either. That's not in the story; I just imagined it.

'Loneliness is bliss when you want to be alone but a curse when it's thrust upon you. That's when you feel abandoned, like Chekhov's coachman.'

I wrote down this conversation with Mama in my diary. I miss her and although I'm in India with Papa, I feel lonely without her. I had asked Mandy and her boyfriend Patrick to come with me. We enjoy travelling together. Mandy is strong and very daring whereas Patrick makes us laugh, keeping our spirits up. They've gone to Bangalore and will spend a fortnight in South India. Then I'll catch up with them in Jaipur and we'll make a short trip across the desert, returning to Delhi to fly back home.

The long trek through Bhutan exhausted me. I'm still suffering from diarrhoea and a sore throat. A young girl called Malati, only a couple of years older than me, looks after me here in Delhi. She complains when I try to help her with the housework.

'Your job is to give orders, little *memsahib*,' she tells me, 'and mine to follow.' I enjoy being pampered but feel ashamed to be waited on by her all the time. She tells me that Papa usually lives by himself in this big house, calling on her only when he has guests. But she knows that I'm not a guest. She must realise that I'm his daughter. What puzzles her is my inability to speak Hindi. When I explain to her that I was born in Australia and that my mother comes from Russia, this confuses her even more. She laughs when I refuse to sit in a rickshaw and be pulled by old men, and disapproves when I give money to each and every beggar on the street.

'It's not right,' she scolds me. 'You're spoiling them.'

I've travelled with Papa and met some great people. We went across the Siwaliks to the Doon Valley and then up to Mussoorie in the mountains. We spent three days walking and trekking.

Papa took me to a village where he has started a new project. The idea is to build ecologically sustainable houses for sugarcane farmers. The two main problems are no cheap fuel and no water you can drink. If the fuel isn't cheap enough, they chop down trees. The alternative is to use dried cakes of cow dung. They're free, but the acrid smoke in the little huts with no windows causes problems. So Dr Sharma, one of Papa's colleagues at the University, has designed a new type of stove. It uses briquettes made of dried leaves. They burn really well and provide more heat.

'Local technology for local problems,' he said. He's right. He's also experimenting with a portable solar cooker which looks like an overhead projector and costs only a few hundred rupees.

At home Malati uses the same sort of cooker to make

boiled rice and kidney beans. It's dead simple. Two separate pots with rice and beans are placed in the cooker at around eight in the morning and by noon they are nicely cooked. Dr Sharma is convinced that cooking like this can reduce the use of electricity or gas by up to twenty-five percent.

He showed me some brochures. They're too simple to attract buyers outside India. Here the cookers will sell well. They would also be great in Australia where the summers are long and sunny. But can we Australians be bothered? We laze around and go to the beach, consume a lot and waste even more.

In India, according to Papa, the main problem is water. Most of the water the villagers use is straight out of the river. Even after boiling, it's not completely safe to drink. Sinking tube wells is the only solution. But the water from them is often contaminated with arsenic.

Papa has found a guitar for me in one of the shops in Mussoorie and I've written two new songs. One of them is about a little girl I often see in the park outside. She sits on the brick fence and watches kids her age play hopscotch. Her right leg is twisted from the polio she suffered as a child.

The other song is about Mama. Do I miss her? It seems I do. I used to think I could live happily without her around. Not true. My freedom from her lasted only five days. Of course I don't miss her whining and whingeing, her endless pestering me to do this or that, but I do like her being around. I miss her voice and the way she walks, swiftly and softly.

When I left home six weeks ago, Mama was rehearsing Gorecki's *Symphony of Sorrowful Songs* with the Symphony Orchestra. It's great that she is going back to music, and this time it looks long-term. She always took the lessons she gave very seriously, going out of her way to help her students. I used to sit through the lessons and listen because I love the way she talks about music.

'Why did you drop archaeology?' I asked her once.

'Because I don't feel at home anywhere,' she said, 'and not because I don't want to. When I left Russia I left my past tucked in those suitcases I abandoned – and I'm glad I did,' she said.

'What about doing archaeology in Australia?'

'Here it's even more difficult,' she said. 'I don't have any feeling for the land or the people or their histories. The land is beautiful, no doubt, and the people too are honest, fair-minded and proud. Yet I still feel uneasy. It's as if there is something immoral, inherently wrong, for Europeans like me to be living here. Even my cello seems out of place. Once I asked Milos to find me a didgeridoo player with whom I could improvise some Bach. He completely dismissed the idea. He called it not only stupid but ridiculous.'

She looked at me. 'Tell me, is it really so ridiculous?'

I didn't know what to say. I was confused myself. But for her to ask Milos was even more ridiculous. How would he know, the pompous old bastard? I don't like him at all. I know that without him our lives would be much harder. But he really is a dishonest prick.

'I don't feel at home anywhere.' Mama often says that. But what does it really mean? I don't understand her angst. Perhaps I'm too young. Perhaps I don't want to belong to a particular place or people. Just travel like a global citizen? But what about my Australian passport with my stamped photo? 'Tattooed forever,' as Mandy says.

Why is the world so complicated?

Before we left, Mandy came from Perth to stay with us. We went with Mama to the dentist to get a tooth that was giving her trouble treated. Mama riffled through an old *National Geographic* and I heard her ask the receptionist if she could borrow the magazine for a few days to photocopy an article.

At home she pulled out a typed manuscript which looked really old. It was an English translation of her thesis on the Scythian town of Gelon. The article she had found in *National Geographic* was about the gold dug from the Siberian kurgans; it also had an interview with one of the professors she had worked with.

Later that evening I saw her reading another manuscript, the book she had never finished. I found the manuscript in the garbage bin the next morning.

I took it out. The cover and the page listing the contents were ripped. I found sticky-tape to repair the damage and put the manuscript carefully away in a box.

In India I once went to Papa's lecture on the architecture of nomadic camps and settlements. The theatre was packed. His assistant told me later that his lectures were very popular and that students from all over the campus came to hear him.

'He's a bit of a celebrity you know, your father,' she said and smiled.

'Why didn't Mama finish her book?' I asked him afterwards. He looked at me in surprise. It was the first time I had called her 'Mama' to him. And until then, discussing her had remained out of bounds.

'I don't know. She should have. It's such a good book, you know. Have you read it?'

'Only the first few pages. Did you help her with the translation?'

'Yes of course. And she was kind enough to mention that I did. She shouldn't have. I didn't deserve it, not at all—'

'Are you sure?'

'Absolutely. She helped me too, with my work, far more than she realises.'

'How?'

He laughed. 'By keeping in check my infatuation with Marxism.'

'Is that over now? I mean, the infatuation?'

'The infatuation is, but not my faith in it or my hope that it could still succeed. Equality and freedom for all. Who can resist a dream like that?'

He paused and smiled. 'I still sound like a true believer, don't I?'

'Yes. But is there anything wrong in believing in something so splendid?'

'Splendid, where did that come from?' I thought.

Again he looked surprised. 'I remember saying something similar to your Mama once when she was helping me edit my thesis. I wanted to use a famous quotation from Marx. She read it and said: "Do your really believe in all this?"'

'Did you? And do you still believe it?' I asked.

'Yes to both. But I've also become more sceptical these days. I'm a rational believer and I've selected the ideas which fit in with what I want to do now. The romanticism has sadly gone. Like a vulture I've picked the juicy bits and left the rest to rot.'

'So you were a romantic revolutionary once?'

'Yes. Aren't you? All those songs about the little girl with polio, the sweat-shop kids and the famines in Africa. I got the bug from Uncle Triple K. Like every true Marxist he wanted to change the world. And of course I was trained as a scientist and Marxism seemed so neat and ordered. Its beauty lies in the very simplicity of its conceptual architecture: base, superstructure, dialectics, alienation. It seems engrained in the very nature of things to move towards a final resolution, a sort of nirvana.'

I wanted to change the subject before he got too carried away. 'Why do you call her "your Mama" and not "Anna"?' I challenged.

'Perhaps that's the only way I can think of her now. You're the bridge between whatever remains of us two.' He looked sad. 'But bridge isn't the right word. You're a semicolon perhaps, a sort of stop-start.' He smiled. 'I hope you don't mind being called a semicolon. It's just a metaphor—'

'A semicolon? I think that's funny. Do you still love her?'

'No.'

'Do you miss her?'

'Yes,' he said immediately. No pause, no hesitation.

'How do you miss her?' I was scared that I was going too far. He had every right to tell me to shut up. But he didn't.

'I miss her cello, the way she used to play, embracing it. I miss the songs she used to sing and the stories she told about the land and the cities buried underneath. I miss her passion. I miss the way she walked with her arm in my arm when we were in Venice, her laugh, her smell that always made me snuggle up to her—'

He paused for a moment and then said something terribly

sweet: 'And I miss the way she would let me cuddle up to her, with my arm around her belly and my finger in her belly—'

'—button.' Oh my God! How embarrassing! I too was fond of that comfy spot. I told him that Mama would try to remove my hand after I had fallen asleep but that it would always return to the lovely little knot.'

'Isn't it silly of us to talk like this?' he asked.

'Not at all. She's my Mama. I love her a lot and you loved her too, once upon a time. Isn't that so?'

'Yes, once upon a time.'

'But you never found anyone else. This house hasn't even the faintest smell of a woman. You've stayed lonely, unattached, unwanted—'

And that's where he stopped me. 'No more,' he said, and walked out of the room.

I sat quietly for a while until Malati came in to see if I wanted tea or coffee and to tell me that dinner would be ready soon.

I heard Papa working in his study. Then he put on some music: a Bach cello suite.

I got up and went into the kitchen to watch Malati roll *chapatis*. She asked if I wanted to help her. She showed me how to use the little towel to press them from one side so that they rise and grow fluffy, soft on one side and crunchy on the other.

That evening Papa showed me Irina's photo. Then on his computer we looked together at the aerial shots she had taken of Venice, Paris, Rome and Budapest.

'Are you lovers?' I wanted to ask. He looked happy when he talked about her, which I liked, but which also made me sad. Because of Mama? Perhaps.

She will certainly enjoy hearing me called a semicolon. Just imagine: I open the door, walk in, and she calls, 'Who's there?'

'A metaphor,' I reply.

I bet she'll complain that I'm becoming more and more like him. Am I?

❀ ❀ ❀

Yesterday I met Papa's Uncle Triple K and Mala Didi. Uncle looks so old and frail and doesn't talk much at all, just sits quietly and smiles, like Papa. Mala Didi (I think she's his wife) looks after him. She seems kind.

'What a lovely girl!' she said as soon as she saw me. She made me sit beside her and didn't let me move away, even for a minute. We spent most of the day with them and Mala Didi began to tell stories about Papa when he was a child. Only then did Uncle Triple K join the conversation. But I could see it wasn't easy for him.

Later that evening Papa told me about the attack in which Uncle Triple K had lost his left eye. His stutter didn't start immediately afterwards although there was some awkwardness in his speech. He and his doctors thought it would pass but it didn't. Mala Didi blamed herself. She had wanted him to go to London for treatment but was overruled each time she raised the subject. When his real stuttering began it was already too late. Gradually, Uncle Triple K had been forced to stop making speeches. As usual he tried to hide his despair by joking about it. But he didn't succeed.

'I don't need to speak any more,' he would say. 'The dream is over.'

His problem, Papa explained, was complicated. The attack on his head must either have damaged that part of the brain which controls the movement of the mouth or the part connected with understanding and expressing language. The excessive use of tranquilisers and painkillers could have accelerated his deterioration, Papa said.

Mala Didi said she didn't want me to leave 'empty-handed'. 'You're my grand-niece, you know,' she kept reminding me. I didn't know how to respond and of course Papa didn't say anything.

I love Mala Didi's present, a cotton sari printed with Madhubani designs. It's not too loud. I'll ask Malati to teach me to how to put it on. Now Mandy will want one too.

As well as the sari, she gave me a hundred rupee note. 'To buy yourself sweets,' she said. '*Jug Jug Jiyo* (live long) my darling,' she said, kissed both my eyes and asked me to visit her again.

Viola da Gamba

Anna

Something happened to me in the shower. At first I didn't take any notice, but once I stepped out and began to dry myself, I felt a piercing stab in my left breast. I looked at myself in the mirror and touched my breast. I examined it carefully as the medical brochures tell you and felt a lump the size of a small pea. I could feel it even more after my fingers explored the similar spot in my right breast.

'No need to panic,' I told myself. 'Wait until I show it to the doctor.'

My GP agreed that I should check out the lump with a mammogram. The news wasn't good, but even then I wasn't unduly alarmed. My panic started only after they said I would need a biopsy. I was told that I would have to undergo a small operation to find out exactly what the lump was doing in my breast. My GP suggested that it would be a good idea to ask someone to accompany me when I had it done.

Maya was away, backpacking through India. Milos was

travelling in Europe. I didn't want to call him because I was unsure if he would interrupt his tour and return. This wasn't included in our agreement. We were lovers, not friends, ready to share joy but not grief or pain, which were to be managed on our own. Sounds selfish, but that's how it is.

I needed someone close to be with me. In fact I needed Maya. I decided to phone Vasu to see if she was still with him. But she had left Delhi two days before I called.

'I can find her and ask her to contact you,' he said.

'Can you? That would be very kind of you,' I said, astounded by my formality. He noticed this at once.

'Thanks for looking after her so well,' I went on. 'She's really enjoying her trip.'

'I don't know. She looked happy when she left and seemed quite keen to get home.'

'Why? I thought she loved travelling. She told me she wants to spend a whole year with a group of Mongolian nomads and write a book based on her diary. She can be quite independent and adventurous, you know.'

'Of course.' And then Vasu told me about the rickshaws in which Maya refused to ride. He said that she had made quite a large donation to a local primary school to help it buy a water-cooler for the pupils. He said that she had bought herself a second-hand guitar and was writing songs. 'She's a good singer, your Maya.'

'I know she is. And I miss her.'

'She misses you too,' said Vasu. 'She's written a song just for you.'

We chatted like this for a while, jumping from topic to topic but keeping the conversation focused on Maya. It must have surprised both of us to find that we were talking in Russian, but even then we didn't dare stray from the immediate present. Our shared past remained out of bounds.

I mentioned the mammogram and told him a biopsy was scheduled in two weeks. Maybe he could explain the situation to Maya? It would be lovely if she could come home to be with me.

'But it's not an emergency,' I stressed. 'Don't alarm her.'

'I understand,' he replied, and I think he did. He asked how bad the doctors thought the cancer was.

'We all have to wait for the biopsy.'

'Please take care of yourself,' he said.

'I'll try,' I managed.

Vasu

After Anna's call I couldn't sit still. I cursed myself for being so formal.

'Please take care of yourself.' How useless. So stiff and uncaring. Why didn't I press her to tell me more? Why didn't I let her know how much her news worried me? Why hadn't I told her I would be thinking of her?

An hour later I phoned her again. The phone rang and rang. I tried again and then a fourth time. But I couldn't reach her.

A day and a half later Maya left India. I went to see her off at the airport. She didn't appear too anxious, but nor did she have much to say. I gave her a hug and said: 'Please look after yourself and your Mama,' and after a moment of silence between us: 'See you soon.'

Before walking through the departure gate she turned and waved. I waved back as she repeated my words: 'See you soon.'

It took me a week to arrange the visa. Three days before the biopsy I was knocking on the door of the cottage in the Blue Mountains. Maya opened it.

'I didn't mean *so* soon,' she said. 'But it's great that you've come.'

She turned and called: 'Papa is here.' Without waiting for Anna to answer, she continued: 'Come in. She's in the shower.'

Anna

I've been helping with the rehearsals of Gorecki's *Symphony of Sorrowful Songs*. I'm enjoying the work, although after chemo and radiation for my cancer, I often feel exhausted.

'Take it,' Maya insisted when I asked her if I should accept the offer. She's right. The work has kept me busy, leaving me little time to think about pain and death.

Maya has now taken off again, this time to Mongolia, as she planned. That's good. I don't want her to worry about me. She's young and strong and more than capable of looking after herself. I don't want her to postpone or change her plans for my sake. She calls once a week and sends letters and postcards every other day.

Vasu came to stay with her while I was in hospital. He was in Australia for more than a month. When I came home, he went back to India. Before he left we filed for divorce. The documents from the Family Court came through last week and I posted them on to him straight away.

Now our separation is official. He is free of me and I am

free of him, even if we both know that this isn't the freedom we were hoping for. He will be dismayed to actually receive the documents. Strangely I was too. But it had to happen, and *Slava Bogu*, it has happened now, while I am still alive. The doctors have given me five more years, and if I'm lucky and look after myself, another five after that. I'll be fifty-seven then. A bit young to die. Maya will be twenty-seven and I might get a chance to sing songs to my grandson. Who knows?

The other day I noticed that I am beginning to forget Papa's face. The effort it took to imagine it frightened and exhausted me. All those photos don't help much and their silence saddens me. In desperation I go back and play the tapes. He loved the piano but his singing wasn't good. However, as I hear his voice, his face in the photos comes alive and I begin to feel how intensely I miss him, especially now.

I have a few precious tapes where I accompany him on the cello. I used to enjoy improvising with him, especially after I returned from my self-imposed exile in Prudkino. Playing together healed the wound. I'm not sure if I forgave him his lies, but somehow music softened my anger.

'He was wronged,' I told myself, 'and he doesn't deserve that all over again.' I believed that he loved me more than he had ever loved Tonya, my unreliable mother.

The world often talks to us in whispers, Aunty Olga used to say, particularly when it wants to disclose its mysteries. She taught me the music that kept my ears and heart open. I can't say that I have learnt the trick fully, but I do remember moments of intense revelation. On such brief, rare occasions, I feel as if I am a little girl again, walking naked in a sunlit shower. The grass tickles my feet, the wind warms my skin and my ears are full of silence, fluid and sonorous.

It is music which has kept me sane. I hope it will help me now to face this ordeal with grace and humility.

It has taken me a while to bring myself to look in the mirror again. Each time I went to the shower I used to cover the mirror with a towel. I also moved all the other mirrors in the house out of sight and persuaded my hands against touching the ugly scar from my operation.

I knew I couldn't go on like that. Redemption finally arrived through Maya, who like a gentle, merciful angel stroked my wound and then took my hand and guided my fingers over its rough surface.

Since my illness, Maya has matured beyond her age. Our roles too seem to have reversed. Now she is the one who mothers me and I acquiesce, willingly following her appeals, demands and instructions. She calls my scar 'the wounded crescent' and assures me that one day she will write a song about it. She believes that through her songs she can tame the ugliest and nastiest threats. She's a dreamer, my Maya, and this scares me. You need to be practical to overcome the cruelties people inflict on you.

I hope Vasu can help her find the right balance. He knows the way, the so-called middle path. I am sure that's the reason he has survived the upheavals of our lives. Only music used to disturb him, especially when I played my cello. He would wait in silence, gazing intently at me and the cello and then walk right up to me and sit on the floor leaning against my chair, as if he had entered a state of perfect quiescence. But as soon as I touched him, his body would betray the tension secreted inside and he would suddenly appear incredibly fragile.

I have often wondered why music affects us so much. How does it manage so easily to alter the whole texture of our emotions? It either magnifies them out of all proportion or diffuses them so thinly that we are neither able to notice their presence nor define their immediate cause. When I am sad I hardly ever pick a joyful piece, but look for something sombre or outright sad, as if C Major chords would insult my grief. I allow the melancholy tones to linger, hoping to find the measure of my own sadness. Perhaps then it might release its grip. The tempo and movements which I crave are slow and languid; they don't completely overpower the grief but make it a little more congenial.

Vika often used to talk about music in terms of colours and shades. 'I paint with music,' she would say. Music for her was bright or dull, dark or light, smooth or jagged. Its effect on me in those years was much more nebulous; only rarely was I moved by it. Something has changed since then. When I think about music now, I feel as if I can touch the world and it touches me in return. The music purls through my body, soft and warm like a baby's feet.

I have begun to feel that music by its nature is engrained in our bodies. Like a voice it streams out of me. I read and learn the score and after it has been rehearsed, it becomes part of me. Something similar happens to those who hear it; my presence, real or imagined, is always conspicuous. The sorrow of the music is refracted through my sorrow. In the music itself, it may be diffuse, but when I play and people hear the music, my body playing, it thickens the sorrow, as drops of lemon juice curdle lukewarm milk.

I remember playing Debussy's *Beau Soir* with Vika, a short

piece, moody, lyrical and quite difficult. We played it late on a bright clear day with not a hint of cloud, and yet as the piece unfolded it seemed as if I were sitting outside beneath summer rain, soft and warm. The cello imitated the wind and the piano the drops of falling rain.

Vika was shocked afterwards when I told her I was wet.

'What do you mean, wet?' she asked.

'Physically wet,' I said and laughed.

'You're crazy,' she said, but I knew I wasn't. Music affects me physically. I don't know the reason, but it does and I'm sure I'm not alone in this. I remember a little girl I met in Yalta years ago. She would hear me play, come silently inside, stand near the window leaning against the wall and then slowly begin to move. Her dancing movements were slow, soft and fluent, but at times out of sync with the music. She had long arms and when she was tired she would sit on the floor near my chair, her arms folded round her knees with her face resting on them, looking at me so intently that I would often miss some notes.

She would notice my error and smile.

'Why do you dance?' I remember asking her. 'The music makes me feel sad, that's why,' she answered. 'Even this one?' I asked and played the Allemande of Bach's Suite No. 6, the one Pablo Casals calls joyous.

'Yes, even this one,' she said and smiled.

'But it shouldn't,' I challenged.

'It does because it's so beautiful,' she replied, and went quiet.

In Venice Sophia took me and Marco to a concert where I heard the viola da gamba played for the first time. I have always loved the cello, but for the first time I thought that perhaps the viola da gamba was the instrument to which I should have given my life. 'I hope you aren't angry with me,' Sophia said afterwards. 'Not angry but betrayed,' I wanted to say, 'and not by you but by my own desire.' I felt as if I were about to embark on a secret love affair.

Now I know who was playing that day. Sophia has recently sent me a recording of his Bach Suites. In that first performance he played three suites by a seventeenth-century French composer, Sainte-Colombe. The Gavotte in C Minor literally took my breath away. I wanted to run out of the hall, hail a boat and sail out into the open sea. 'Like that girl in Yalta,' I remember thinking then, 'I too have a natural disposition for sadness.'

Marco noticed my sadness. 'Come with me to Australia,' he had said a week after that concert. 'You'll be healed,' he promised. He was wrong. So was I. Vasu too knew the nature of my affliction, but he chose to keep quiet, hoping that it would pass. He was wrong as well.

'I'll find a gamba for you to play,' Marco kept telling me. Finally I gave in. I shouldn't have.

'He's a liar,' Sophia had warned me several times.

'I know he is,' I wanted to tell her. But I didn't.

The viola da gamba was just an excuse. The urge to run away from Russia, the cello and poor Vasu was much stronger.

In Gorecki's *Symphony of Sorrowful Songs*, the soprano voice carries the full weight of the grief. The accompanying music really just creates the atmosphere. Without the voice much of the pathos would be lost. Voice and words possess the power to drown us in a sea of sorrow. Gorecki opens the symphony with strings which seem to repeat the theme endlessly, creating the dark, dense surface of the sea on to which the keys of a piano drop notes one by one, like pebbles. As the surface of the water parts, the lamenting voice rises, just enough to be heard. Then it disappears and we wait for it to resurface. The music generates a sense of expectation and then forces us to wait for it to be realised. We wait and wait and when finally the moment of fulfilment arrives we feel ourselves free and blessed.

The string *fugato* is impressive, particularly when it reaches its climax, but it seems that the strings are called in merely to reiterate the sorrow which the voice so forcefully expresses. I wonder what a more alienated tonality would have done to the composition. I like tension in musical chords, harmony punctuated with brief moments of heightened dissonance, not a sustained assault of unpleasant sounds but just enough to make us long for a return to the harmonic line.

Gail, the conductor of the symphony orchestra, has noticed that although I like the Gorecki symphony I would personally have chosen something different. It's the ease with which it expresses sorrow that disturbs me. I value understatement more than wilful explicitness, a hesitant glance more than a sustained stare. I have heard Shostakovich's *Leningrad* only once and that was more than enough for me. His string quartets, by contrast, sound new each time I hear or play them.

Gail laughs at me. My preferences are out of line with her limited understanding of Soviet music, which she expects to be loud, bold and colourful. 'There is nothing unusual about me,' I tell her. The fake brilliance of Soviet public performances would force anyone to look for more subtle and ambiguous modes of expression.

Gail has asked me to suggest something for the orchestra to play next year. The name that came instantly to mind was Schnittke. I like his expressionistic style and his pessimism. Even his joy is tainted. Vika and I were lucky to hear his 1978 Sonata for Cello and Piano rehearsed in Moscow and at once wanted to try it ourselves. Once heard, who can forget the ten-minute-long third movement, a sustained alternation of lyrical and intensely melancholy themes fading into one of the most audible silences ever composed?

Aunty Olga knew Schnittke's mother. She used to teach German in Engels, the capital of the Volga Republic, and although she tried several times to introduce me to him, I always felt too shy and intimidated. The last ten years of his life were marred by illness following a massive stroke which led to a coma. Vika has recently sent me a recording of his 1986 Cello Concerto, which he composed a few months after miraculously regaining consciousness. For weeks he couldn't remember a word of Russian and spoke only German.

I don't think I'll suggest this concerto, since I know Gail wouldn't like it. The lament of a single cello, followed by wailing dissonance, may disturb her. You have to listen to it again and again to appreciate its musical structure and feel its emotional impact. I call it *To Silence* and often wonder if in his coma the music Schnittke heard sounded like this.

Vika has returned to Moscow. She often phones and talks for hours. 'Don't waste your money,' I tell her, but she doesn't listen. Her few letters paint a sorrowful picture. 'Home doesn't feel like home any more,' she complains. 'The whole city has been turned into a messy shopping complex ruled by the *mafiosi*. In this fiefdom of the oligarchs, corruption rules supreme. The Soviet *blat* (corruption) seems a minor aberration by comparison.'

'Why don't you go back to your lovely Switzerland?' I say.

'You must be joking,' she replies and tells me that although she has decided to keep her Swiss passport she is determined to settle down again in Moscow.

'Why don't you come home too?' she often asks me. 'Don't you think it would be fun to live together?'

'Perhaps,' I want to reply, but keep quiet. She knows that I am tempted.

She has inspected the Yasenovo apartment and assures me that it needs only minor renovations. 'I'll look after you,' she says, 'and when you begin to feel better, we'll start playing together again.' When I ask her about her physicist husband, she laughs loudly, saying that she could leave him tomorrow. 'He's so boring and uptight,' she adds, and giggles like a teenager.

'You've gone mad,' I tell her. 'Give me time to think.'

'We'll get you a gamba,' she says and from the silence that follows we both know that she has overstepped the mark.

'A gamba would be good,' I reply, to release the tension. Then she tells me about a workshop in Basel where her husband has a friend whose grandfather owns a partnership in a workshop reproducing antique musical instruments.

'You only have to say you'll come,' she announces, and waits. The final bait, I know, has been cast.

The year is about to end, I mumble to myself, and so is the millennium. Perhaps Vika is right. Perhaps the time has come for me to pack up and go home.

'No need to pack,' Maya would say. 'Just go and don't look back.'

She is wonderful, my Maya, so straight and determined. I hope she is all right. I hope she is happy.

❀ ❀ ❀

Vasu

It's a bright sunny day. The autumn has all but gone and the winter is nearly here. The sunshine has appeared as a blessing from the heavens to mark this special occasion. Maya and I are leaving the Metro station on our way to see Anna and Vika in their new apartment. Maya has a copy of her little book on Mongolia and can't wait to hug her Mama. I am not so keen. I would rather walk with Maya up to the door, then turn back and sit in the park before returning to the hotel and spending the evening reading and writing.

In the morning I'll catch a flight to Venice to meet Isabella. A week ago I received an email from her inviting me to attend the opening of an exhibition of her architectural drawings and photos. Attached was a flyer and a photo of Sophia. Isabella's reply to my answer: 'Congratulations, I'll try,' was brief but emphatic: 'No trying, Zio Vasu – just come. We'll wait for you. And yes please, bring Maya with you if she's free and wants to come.'

'Not a word about Anna,' I had said to myself, and although I wasn't sure if the omission was deliberate or just an oversight, it made me sad.

For a very brief moment I thought that I should ask Ira to come with me to Venice. I even phoned her but she was out and I didn't have the resolve to phone her again.

I had met Irina at a conference in Paris. Her Russian name drew me to her. 'Can I call you Ira?' I had asked her in Russian, trying to appear friendly. She could have asked why, but she didn't. She just smiled and said *konechno* (of course).

Ira works in a restaurant on rue del la Gaîté not far from the cemetery, and rents a small apartment on the fourth floor of a block overlooking it. She used to be photographer and took wonderful aerial shots of cities.

Whenever I am in Paris, once or twice a year, we spend a week or so together. We enjoy making love and although it happens only rarely, we have learnt to be patient. We aren't in love as we would have been many years ago when we were young, but we do love one another in our own uncomplicated way.

'A part of us dies each time we fall in love,' I remember Ira telling me once. 'You're wrong,' I could have argued. But I didn't. Ira is right. There is no need to complicate things. None at all.

Acknowledgements

I thank Roland Bleiker, Dominique Sweeney, Stephanie Anderson and many other friends who read different sections of the manuscript. I am grateful to David Pereira for checking that I haven't written anything silly about music. Diana Giese worked with me to give the manuscript a coherent narrative shape. I am indebted to her for her support and encouragement.

Subhash Jaireth was born in a small town in Punjab, Northern India. Between 1969 and 1978 he spent nine years in Moscow studying geology. He has published poems in Hindi, Russian and English. His book *To Silence: Three Autobiographies* was published by Puncher & Wattmann in March 2011 and has recently been performed as theatre piece. He lives in Canberra, Australia.